THE ZIGZAG ROAD TO HAPPY

Anita Heavens

Published 2016 by Terrapin Publishing
Copyright © Anita Heavens 2015

Terrapin Publishing Limited
60 Melfort Road,
Thornton Heath, Surrey CR7 7RL

ISBN: 978-0-9933178-4-2

With thanks to all who supported me in the process of completing this book, especially Miriam, Jane and Kieron for all their encouragement, help and thoughtful feedback.

BOOK CLUB DISCUSSION POINTS ARE INCLUDED AT THE END OF THE BOOK

I heard the slight creak of the bed and saw her moving shadow in the patch of faint light on the wall. I was really cold and wanted to rub the tightness in the small of my back, which ached from sitting cross-legged on the floor for so long. But I didn't want to draw her attention. Not just yet; a few more moments of peace.

Then I heard the early morning crunch of the apple she kept by her bed each night. The sharp click as her teeth met, the rustle of the polyester bedcover as she reached for a tissue to wipe her mouth, the anxious yet angry voice that whispered my name. All the usual signals that another day in my life had started.

"Morning, mummy," I whispered back, although there was no-one else to hear even if we shouted. That would usually come later.

"Well? Anything?" she asked in a hushed voice.

I wondered if she really believed there would be 'anything' when she'd woken me at two in the morning to tell me she thought there was someone in our flat. Did she really believe there was someone so scary beyond the bedroom door that we shouldn't go through to check, or to call the police? I could hear nothing, but suggested we could at least shout for help out of the bedroom window. Her response was to ask me scathingly if I wanted to cause a scene with the neighbours.

Instead she decided I should sit on the floor facing the door and watch the door handle.

"Wake me if you see it move," she ordered, climbing into bed and pulling the blanket up around her ears. Partly I thought the whole thing was ridiculous, yet I couldn't help wondering if she was right and there was someone on the other side of that door. I felt nervous and slightly sick as I sat shivering in my cotton nightie, scared to take my eyes off the shiny brass handle where flickers from the reflected light of the street lamp outside the window gave the impression of movement.

"No, nothing, mummy," I reassured her, kissing her cheek as I went across to the wardrobe to get my school uniform. Even so I felt edgy as I eased open the bedroom door and made my way to the bathroom, jumping as her voice suddenly pierced the hushed atmosphere.

"You're not going to school today, Nicola, are you? You can't just leave me here after a night like that!"

"There was no-one in the flat, mummy, nothing happened. I have to go to school, I have mocks today, they're important."

"More important than your own mother?"

There were lots of questions like that punctuating our relationship, questions that couldn't be, shouldn't be, answered if there was going to be any semblance of peace between us. Partly I knew she'd be fine while I was at school, better than I'd be after the sleeplessness of our night-time drama. Yet another part of me, always hovering ready to kick in, felt worried and guilty and unsure how I was supposed to deal with the situation.

I felt the familiar stinging in my eyes as I poured out some cereal. Not the stupid tears again, how pointless! Tears of frustration, sadness, anger. I quickly pressed the tea towel to my eyes as I heard mummy leave the bedroom. For goodness sake, I told myself, you're not a child, you're sixteen years old! I knew mummy didn't need to deal with my baggage: she had enough of her own. So I was smiling and putting cups out for the tea as she came into the kitchen.

As she started talking, the usual overpowering stream-of-consciousness talking, a little voice inside me was pleading, begging me to rescue her from all of this. A little voice I'd heard often. Lately it seemed quieter, weaker, more hopeless yet even more desperate. When the voice pleaded like this I so wanted it to stop, to go away, yet I knew deep down I was terrified that it would disappear and I would be left with just empty silence inside me forever.

1

"We need a month's rent in advance, dear," said the elderly nun, her half smile wavering and her plump hand outstretched towards me.

She sat primly on the other side of the large wooden desk while I perched on the edge of my chair, praying that my stomach wouldn't rumble out its hunger into the silence. My hand instinctively went to the pocket of my cotton skirt, even though I knew the few coins I had in there wouldn't go anywhere towards the rent. Calm, keep calm I told myself, summoning a smile from somewhere.

"I'm afraid I don't actually have it at the moment, Sister," I said in my sweetest voice. "I start my job tomorrow, so I can pay you at the end of the week," I added hastily, fearing the place she had offered me in this hostel was about to be snatched away, leaving me homeless on the streets of London.

"Oh dear, that puts me in a very difficult position, Miss Ellis," she muttered, sucking her breath in hard and tapping her pen briskly on the desk. Another agonising silence followed, during which I smoothed my long hair and tried to look confident and more mature than my sixteen years. Her grey eyes studied me and my own brown ones met hers briefly, noting that the smile had almost broken through and was hovering around her pursed lips. Suddenly her hand reached out and grasped mine.

"Do you know what, dear? I am going to take a risk on you, because you have the face of an angel."

I thanked her somewhat shyly, unsure whether to respond to the angel comment. I wasn't even sure how to look like an angel, but I was used to being what others wanted me to be. So I opened my eyes as wide as possible and smiled sweetly, hoping I could keep up the impression at least until I had the rent for her.

Once the necessary paperwork was completed and I had been given a list of the hostel rules, I followed another nun along some gloomy corridors and up a wide staircase, to a large impersonal dormitory on the first floor. It was lined with identical metal-framed beds along two walls, each with a white pillow and pale blue blanket. The nun waved her bat-like arm vaguely towards one by the window, before silently abandoning me to my new home.

Sitting on the chair at the side of my bed, head throbbing, I reflected on my incredible day. A day of leaving home, travelling to London, securing myself a job and, finally, managing to get this hostel place. I felt proud and excited but also somewhat fearful, especially as clouds dulled the light from the tall windows and the slightly musty air in the room became chilly. Too unsure of the rules to risk disturbing the blanket, I lay down on top of the bed. By snuggling into the soft pillow I was finally able to relax for the first time that day.

"Hey, you! What you doing on my bed?"

The harsh voice woke me from my doze, and I sat up to see a plump blonde girl in an orange mini dress standing over me and glaring angrily.

"Who do you think you are, bloody Goldilocks, trying out the beds?" she continued with a sneer.

No, I wanted to say, I'm Nicola Ellis and this is the first day of my new life. A life where I'm important and I don't have to always fit around others to keep them happy. A life where I can discover who I really am and fill my new world with people who will accept and appreciate me, perhaps even love me. A life where I am happy.

However, I was pretty sure she wouldn't be impressed by my speech, so what actually came out of my mouth as I jumped off the bed was a pitiful mumbled "Sorry."

Another girl came over and took hold of my arm. "Don't be so mean, Pat. It's just a mistake," she snapped at the blonde as she steered me to a bed by the door. "This is the free bed, kid, so if you're joining us this must be yours."

I smiled gratefully at her, warmed by the responsive twinkle in her green eyes.

"You are joining us I assume?" she asked, slightly impatiently.

"Oh, sorry, yes I am. I'm Nicola, I just arrived."

"Well I'm Kirsty," she said, tucking her long black hair behind her ears to reveal beautiful high cheekbones, "and I've been here for bloody ever."

Sitting shyly and self- consciously on my allocated bed, I watched the room gradually fill until I was surrounded by eleven other girls, presumably in a similar situation. Similar but not the same I realised when they brought out boxes full of magazines, snacks and chocolate. In the chaotic family life I had escaped from I was used to missed meals, but I had eaten nothing since the day before. My stomach rumbled like crazy as others untwisted the little blue bags and sprinkled salt on their crisps before munching them noisily. The girl in the next bed would probably never know how much it meant when she offered me one of her biscuits, and only my pride stopped me asking for a second one.

The hostel washroom was clean and bright with four sinks and the usual cubicles, but no soap, shampoo, toothpaste or towel. That first night I rinsed my face and private parts with warm water and swilled out my mouth with cold, before getting into the strange hard bed and using the corner of the sheet to dry myself. Lying there in the dark, watching mysterious shadows moving across the ceiling and listening to the gradually reducing chatter of the other girls, I had the first chance that day to reflect on the enormity of what I had done.

It had been building for months, my mother's mood swings and aggression increasing and my days becoming more and more controlled by her desperate and constant need to talk. She had been stressed and angry for a long time, but

3

when my father first left, over a year ago, we had become closer for a while. Without their rows gentleness settled over the home, and although I desperately missed daddy it seemed best he was gone if it meant she could be happy. I really did think she was happy for those first couple of months, before the dark days crept in. Dark days when she told me I didn't need to go to school and was angry when I did, seeing it as a rejection of the opportunity to spend time with her. Dark days when I would arrive at school late, because she wouldn't let me leave, homework not done because she had made me sit listening to her all night. Dark days when I innocently gave these true reasons to the teachers, and was accused of lying. Until I learnt to really lie by saying I missed the bus or just forgot to do the homework, and still got punished but was at least believed. It became harder and harder to come home on those days, never sure what I would find when she opened the door. It might be anger, sometimes directed at me or sometimes at others, with long involved stories of past injustices and arguments in which she was always the powerless victim. Other days it would be tears, seemingly endless tears, and stories of hurt, pain and abandonment she felt she had endured at the hands of strangers and of those I had thought I'd known as loving family members. Then there were the 'happy' days, when she'd dream up 'treats' such as spreading a tablecloth on the floor where we'd eat sandwiches and biscuits while she laughed a lot and coaxed me into joining in with her as she sang along to songs on the radio. In a way I preferred those evenings to the others because it felt she wasn't hurting. However, the tension at the picnics was enormous, knowing that at any moment the anger or the tears could take over, leading to another long sleepless night filled with words. Somehow I believed the words would eventually heal, if I listened long enough and found the right words to respond. Yet it was the endless words more than the rages that brought me to the point where I knew that if I were to survive

4

I had to abandon her. So that morning, after another angst-filled sleepless night, I had dressed in my summer school outfit and stolen from her purse enough money for my train fare to London. Suppressing tears, I promised the angry face of the mother I loved that I would see her later, before leaving my childhood behind forever.

I felt guilty at the stealing and lies, but perhaps the first sin really is the hardest because lying had certainly got easier as this day had gone on. So when I had responded to a job advert on the board in Victoria station that morning, and got an immediate interview, I was quite fluent in listing my 'A' levels and describing how well suited I was to work as a filing clerk in their insurance company. It would be a whole month later, at my probation review, that my manager would tell me in confidence that sixteen-year-olds like myself don't have A levels and that he'd offered me the job based on my initiative rather than my phoney qualifications.

Waking that first morning in the hostel brought home how young, ill-prepared and alone I was. Most of the girls were from Ireland or the West Indies and formed little groups as they prepared for their day, choosing outfits to wear, applying makeup, sharing jokes. They appeared so confident and mature, teasing each other and discussing plans for the evening, some of them occasionally glancing over at me with a brief smile or curious look. Although I wanted to make friends I didn't want anyone to notice I was washing without soap and getting dressed in the same school clothes I had taken off the night before, the green skirt and white blouse fortunately not looking too much like a uniform but also nothing like the smart clothes I saw them wearing. They looked like the trendy sixties fashion models I'd only really seen in magazines, whereas I looked like a throwback to the nineteen-fifties. One kind girl showed me the kitchen where I could cook my breakfast, unaware that I had no food or money to buy any. I made my excuses and hurried through the hall to the front door. The nun I'd been told to call Sister Agnes stopped me to check I had my key and to remind me that if I did not come in by eleven o'clock tonight the door would be bolted. Little did I know then how significant those words would become in shaping my future.

It was a long walk from the hostel to the insurance offices, especially on an empty stomach, and a few times as I made the twice daily trek over the next couple of weeks I found myself wondering why I hadn't stolen a bit more from my mother's purse. It turned out that my angelic face was slightly more trustworthy than my words; there had been nobody to tell me that in the real world of work you aren't paid at the end of the week, that they hold a week's wages in hand. The nun reluctantly accepted she would have to wait a bit longer for my rent, but at sixteen years old I was presented with a riddle; if you have no belongings, no money and no-one to ask for help how do you get through two weeks living in London and looking after yourself?

Each day became harder and I was glad my body had become used to ignoring hunger on my mother's bad days. I struggled through by stuffing myself with the free biscuits and tea that it was part of my job to put on a table in our office at break times. My work colleagues found it funny how many biscuits I could devour, and made jokes about the way I disappeared at lunchtimes to eat in a restaurant in style while they made do with the small staff canteen or their humble sandwiches. Of course I didn't eat in style but I didn't want them to know I couldn't even buy a sandwich, so there was more walking to find quiet park benches where no-one would spot me.

At the hostel the smell of the variety of food the girls cooked was nauseating because of my hunger. Some evenings I would stay out until they finished cooking then casually saunter into the kitchen, hoping desperately that someone had ignored the rule about washing up immediately so that I could find food left on dirty plates, even in saucepans. One evening I was slapped in the face by Pat, the fiery blonde girl whose bed I had taken, who had left her macaroni cheese in the pan while she answered the telephone and returned to find me devouring the last of it, having assumed it was leftovers. Other nights I would just get into bed early and hope to sleep despite the noisy activity going on around me. Those evenings served a double purpose; apart from attempted oblivion to the hunger cramps it also meant I could rinse my one outfit in the washroom, hanging it on the hot water pipes to dry as I wrapped myself in the bed sheet. The sheet would later serve as a sari while I ironed my clothes in the utility room, to wear yet again to work. There a few colleagues had started to make comments about my 'uniform' little knowing how right they were and I laughed along, claiming I didn't want to waste my good clothes on the workplace.

Actually, it was not the clothes but the shoes that really bothered me. My flat black leather school shoes made me feel childlike and dumpy, while the other girls each had several pairs of high heeled shoes which they would try on in the morning with different outfits before tottering out the door. It struck me as a waste that beautiful shoes would just sit under the beds all day while their owners were at work. So I started 'borrowing' shoes which I smuggled out in a paper bag, put on when some distance from the hostel and popped back in the bag before I arrived home, slipping them under the appropriate bed whilst their owner was out of the dormitory. The five and six inch heels made the long walk to work and back pretty painful, but was well worth it for the confidence I felt whilst wearing them and the way the young guys at work sneaked glances at my legs. Like any sixteen-year-old I enjoyed such attention, while it lasted. Which turned out to not be very long, as on the way home from work one evening I tripped and broke the heel of someone's beautiful cream suede shoe. Although I managed to get them back under her bed and no-one ever knew it was me that did the damage, the uproar that ensued when she discovered the broken heel made the idea of 'borrowing' any more shoes too terrifying to contemplate.

Gradually I started to feel a bit less alone, as different girls would make small talk with me in the dormitory or the crowded lounge downstairs. After her initial friendliness I had hoped to become closer to Kirsty but, although she would greet me in passing, she was good friends with a small curly-headed girl called Anne and they always seemed to be out or surrounded by other girls. So I was still very aware of being an outsider as I listened to the Irish girls who sat in the lounge, chatting of home and singing songs to cheer themselves up. One of their favourites, *Mountains of Mourne*, was a song my mother sang a lot when I was small, so I had mixed feelings about hearing it and remembering those happier times. The West Indian girls tended to stay more in the dormitory; often late at night they would turn off the lights, pass around salty pieces of fish and put saucers of rum in the middle of the floor, setting fire to them then laughing excitedly as they watched the flames dancing and lighting up each other's faces. Once they accepted me they would occasionally offer me small glasses of rum, but after discovering how sweet and strong it was and how it made my head throb the next morning I decided it was not for me.

Somehow I got through that first nightmare fortnight to payday, feeling my skirt becoming looser and looser and fighting the light-headedness and vague sense of unreality caused by the lack of food. Although I knew things were going to be really tough for a while, because of having to pay two lots of rent out of one pay packet, at least I could now eat basic foods each day and buy myself toiletries. I even managed to buy a cheap pale pink lipstick which did wonders for boosting my spirits. Finally it felt I might be in control of my future, and could start to live rather than just survive.

"Ok, you can look now," said Kirsty, placing a small mirror in my hand. I was both scared and excited as I looked up at her laughing face. Kirsty had the bed across from mine in the dormitory, recognisable by the multi-coloured spread she put over the regulation blue blanket each evening, and had been one of the first girls to show an interest in me. She was really popular in the hostel because of her enthusiastic and rather eccentric approach to life, rushing into new experiences without any apparent fear or self-doubt. Although she was only a year older than me, in a way she reminded me of the mother I remembered from when I was very young. I think she initially took me under her wing, after I'd been there a while, because she could see how little sense of identity I had, how easily I could be moulded. Gradually we did become real friends, in a way, although I couldn't understand what someone as beautiful and worldly wise as she was would get out of a friendship with old-fashioned mousey me. Yet somehow she really liked having me around, perhaps because I was her project and was becoming her creation. Today had been an enormous step in that process, as I had finally agreed to let Kirsty and her friend Anne give me a makeover. Even before I looked in the mirror I knew, from the smell of ammonia and the long strands of my brown hair lying on the washroom floor, that it would be a big change. Slowly I lifted the mirror.

"Oh wow, Kirsty, it's amazing," I shrieked, as I looked at the honey blonde beehive framing my face.

For a couple of years, I had asked my mother to let me get my hair cut and styled like the girls at school, but she just told me I should brush my waist-length brown hair a hundred times each night to make it shine.

"I'll show you how to brush it," said Kirsty, as if she'd read my thoughts. "The more you backcomb it the bigger it

9

looks." She attacked the new blonde style with extra vigour, brushing section by section and spraying each liberally with the sticky hairspray Anne passed to her.

"Now for the make-up," said Anne, producing a pan stick foundation from her own bag and drawing streaks across my forehead and down my nose and cheeks.

"I can rub it in myself, Anne," I laughed as she started to massage it into my skin.

"Secret is to rub it under your chin as well," said Kirsty. "You've got a brown face and white neck right now."

"And red cheeks," I said, looking at the rouge she'd smeared on.

"Don't worry, we know what we're doing. We don't get all the guys after us by looking natural, do we?" asked Kirsty.

It was true; they were really popular with the local boys. Many evenings I'd see them sitting on the wall outside the hostel while boys parked their motorbikes nearby and four or five hovered around, posing and vying for the girls' attention. So I relaxed and stopped trying to have any influence in their creation. I was therefore quite overwhelmed when I saw the finished product, my brown eyes seeming twice their size thanks to mauve eye shadow, black liner and thick mascara and my lips pale and matt under the heavy lipstick.

"Wow, I look like a model," I gasped almost involuntarily and immediately felt embarrassed that I could have been so arrogant. Kirsty and Anne simply laughed.

"Yep, just like us!" they chanted, almost in unison.

Sadly, the nuns weren't impressed by my new image and became increasingly unfriendly towards me, making it clear that they preferred the shy insecure child that had arrived such a short time ago to the slightly more confident young woman I was turning into. Whilst Sister Agnes had been quite reasonable when I'd explained that I couldn't keep the promise of paying the rent at the end of the first week, she seemed to then see this failure on my part as grounds for commenting on everything I did, especially how I dressed or if I talked to boys. She became quite haughty and dismissive whenever I spoke to her, perhaps because she had misidentified an angel or failed to save one from the sinful world she thought I was entering. Good qualities about me including the fact that I worked hard, never missing a day at the office or even being late for work were totally ignored.

Although on one memorable occasion I was very late due to my 'new' skirt. Feeling miserable about my lack of clothes one evening, I suddenly had the bright idea that I could make myself a mini skirt out of the cover of a cushion one of the girls had put in the bin, because the stuffing was falling out. It was dramatic black and white zebra print, and whilst not quite Mary Quant I thought it would look very fashionable. After borrowing a needle and black thread from Mary, a friendly Irish girl in my dorm, I stitched away enthusiastically and was very excited to put it on for work the next morning. Several girls commented on how good it looked with my white blouse and it was with a confident stride that I set off for the office, still walking it to save on fares. I guess that stride was probably to blame for my subsequent shame when, as I passed some wolf-whistling workmen digging up the road, the stitching down one side pulled apart and my beautiful skirt fell to the ground, tripping me up in the process. Amid yells, hoots and laughter I gathered the remains around me and beat a hasty retreat to the hostel to change, remembering how many years ago I had been told that pride comes before a fall. This didn't stop me improvising, once I got over the embarrassment and saw the funny side as it became a hostel anecdote; I just learned to secure my stitches a lot more strongly.

"Don't worry about them," said Kirsty when I was upset by a muttered comment from Sister Agnes implying that our morals left a lot to be desired. "They're just frustrated old witches!"

"You can't say that!" I giggled.

11

"She can, 'cause she's right," Anne joined in. "They were probably scared they wouldn't get a guy so didn't try." I felt a bit guilty as I laughed along with them, stopping suddenly as I heard Kirsty say,

"Bit like you, Nicky. Maybe you'll become a nun."

"I just haven't met anyone yet," I protested.

"Well you won't if you sit in here every evening," Kirsty responded, a sweep of her outstretched arm taking in the bleak hostel lounge. "You should come out and meet the gang." I couldn't believe she was actually inviting me to join them, to be one of the chosen few. It was with a mixture of fear and excitement that I accepted, surprised at how casual my voice sounded.

And so my social life started, despite the nun's disapproval of my transformation, as I joined my new friends on the wall.

During my first couple of months living in London I had got used to people at work starting to talk with me and apparently like me. A spotty guy from the life assurance department would even perch on the edge of my desk to chat occasionally. Yet sitting out there on a summer evening, as the young men in their leather jackets hung around, smoking their cigarettes and appearing to be fascinated by everything Kirsty said as she swung her nylon covered legs and twiddled the ends of her glossy black hair, was unlike anything I had ever imagined. Suddenly I felt attractive and interesting and...alive! It didn't matter that the boys were more interested in Kirsty and Anne than in me, I was used to that from school days, or that the boys themselves were a bit pimply with greasy hair and a strong smell of cigarette smoke. I was just unbelievably happy to be allowed to be there with this group, to listen to the banter and watch the flirting, to feel part of something for the first time in so, so long. As the dusk drew in the atmosphere would change, some of the guys would drift off and I would mumble an excuse that nobody listened to and go indoors. I knew that shortly my two confident beautiful friends would make their choice of guys for the evening, climb onto the back of their bikes and zoom off into the night. I was growing up fast but I wasn't yet ready for that, even if I'd been asked, so I settled for waiting until they returned, just before the door was locked, with exciting tales of dark fields, nibbled ears, sloppy kisses and second base gropes! My interaction with boys had been limited to kisses and cuddles during a shy and innocent short relationship, plus teasing banter on the school bus or in my local coffee bar. So I thought these stories of the motorbike trips were very brave and glamorous.

One evening there was a new guy I hadn't seen before. One of the regulars, Steve, introduced him as 'my weedy brother Tony' and everybody laughed. Steve was muscular and quite tall with thick black hair, and often took Kirsty off on his bike, but his brother wasn't much taller than me and fairly slight. His equally black hair was longer than Steve's, curling slightly on the collar of his leather jacket. To my surprise he sat near me on the wall, rather than looming over us girls as the others always did, and he didn't join in any of the chatter. Which made it all the more surprising when, after a while, he spoke directly to me.

"Sorry," I stammered, turning towards him. "What did you say?" He smiled a gentle but slightly mocking smile.

"I said you've got the best looks; pity you haven't got any personality."

I couldn't believe my ears. How on earth could he say that? Firstly, I knew I didn't look better than my friends and secondly, how could he know if I had any personality if I hadn't even spoken? I jumped off the wall and walked up to the front door of the hostel, planning to say I didn't feel well if anybody asked why I was going in so early, but of course nobody did ask or even notice. Once in the dormitory I got into bed without bothering to wash off the layers of make-up, and in my head had a furious argument with Tony about him having no right to judge me, and about me being a really interesting person if anyone bothered to find out. Eventually the anger abated and, as I sobbed into my pillow, I realised how lonely I felt, how much I wanted others to be interested in me beyond the painted face and how a brief excitement had flared when I realised Tony had actually spoken directly to me.

Although I acted very aloof when Tony sat near me the next evening it didn't stop him smiling at me every so often, asking my name and making small talk about films and his favourite bands. After a couple of nights, it felt petty and childish to keep ignoring him, and gradually we started talking to each other. I was surprised to hear he was still at school, studying for his A levels and that, like me, he enjoyed

Shakespeare and Tolstoy as well as the Rolling Stones and The Yardbirds. He was even more surprised than I was at how much we had in common, and eventually I got an explanation of his 'personality' remark that had upset me so much.

"I thought you were stuck up, because you look so good." I raised my eyebrows questioningly.

"You do." he said. "With that hairdo you look like Dusty Springfield. Did you know she was born in West Hampstead, near here?" he added as I started to laugh. "But I thought because you never said anything you were an airhead," he explained with an apologetic grin that made it hard to be angry with him.

"Some people don't bother to speak unless they actually have something to say," I snapped, half-jokingly, then shot a quick guilty glance at the other girls, praying they hadn't heard. They were too engaged in their flirting to have noticed, although I knew they did keep an eye on me as they sometimes teased me about Tony at night in the dormitory.

"She loves him, she wants to kiss him," they would chant in unison before collapsing in giggles at my blushes. Of course, they were sort of right but I was relieved he'd never suggested I ride on his bike.

However, it was only a matter of time and, although I mumbled about early starts and tiredness, Kirsty and Anne decided one Saturday that this was the night I was to join them, and that there really was no point in my protests. So, with a mixture of excitement and fear, I found myself clinging desperately to the back of Tony's leather jacket as he proudly revved his beloved Fanny Barnet and followed his brother and friend Rob at high speed.

"Put your arms around my waist," he yelled as we raced along. Initially it felt very awkward but once I held him I felt quite safe and cosy despite the wind whooshing past my ears and my flared skirt flapping painfully against my knees. Gradually we left behind the houses and shops and were

15

speeding along country roads, with hedges on each side and shapes of shadowy cows in the dark fields. Eventually the bikes were parked on a grassy verge, all six of us jumping off and stretching, the boys and Kirsty lighting up their cigarettes. After standing around in the dark chatting for a while Tony and I followed the others over a wooden gate, and then they disappeared and only giggles and heavy breathing told me they were still nearby. We did kiss briefly but it felt very dry and awkward and we both seemed to feel much happier once we sat on the top of the gate, his jacket around my shoulders, and tried to identify the different star groups. It was such a relief that he didn't want to rush anything and was happy for us just to enjoy each other's company. I had been through enough new experiences recently, and whatever the others were up to in the cold muddy field no longer seemed as glamorous as it had in the dormitory tales.

The weeks that followed felt magical and wild. My existence seemed almost schizophrenic, divided as it was between the smart and conscientious young lady who worked hard at the insurance office and the free spirit I turned into on the nights when Tony collected me on his motorbike. I could feel others from the office watching as he pressed the helmet hard down over my backcombed blonde beehive and we kissed briefly before I climbed on behind him, my skirt riding up almost to my hips. A couple of the girls were a bit jealous, because they didn't have boyfriends, but most of the staff in my office were friendly and happy for me. Apart from Dave, who sat at the next desk and suffered with acne that he treated with a strange ointment that made his whole face white, and gave him a sweet odour I could only think of as the smell of death. He'd asked me out early on, and I think he thought I said no because I considered myself better than him. Actually it was because I was frightened the smell of the lotion might make me throw up if we were too close to each other. We were expected to fill in monthly forms giving good and bad feedback on our immediate colleagues, and whilst I only ever put such things as 'taps his pencil while on phone' Dave once wrote of me 'wears her skirts immorally short'. When my boss read this out in the feedback session I had to stop myself from saying that they didn't seem to be immoral enough to stop him looking at every opportunity. In fact, they were longer than some other girls wore, but I think those moments as I climbed on the bike fed Dave all the immorality he fantasised about.

Once Tony had dropped me back at the hostel he would go and meet up with his brother and friends. Kirsty, Anne and I, and any other girls currently in our group, then went through the usual rituals of hair and make-up, puffing dry shampoo into our hair to save time on washing then seeing it reappear later as a chalky dust on leather-clad shoulders. A few of us who were similar in size would exchange clothes for the evening, to try and make our limited wardrobes as varied as possible. I was very glad Anne's feet were as big as mine, as my budget hadn't really stretched too far yet in the way of shoes. My wardrobe was easily the most limited so I borrowed a lot and even the green school skirt still featured on occasions, albeit shortened and dressed up with a fashionable top. Trying to afford office and casual clothes meant that when we roared down to Brighton for regular standoffs with the mods on their mopeds I often looked more like one of their girls. However, once I had managed to buy a fake leather mini skirt and a black pvc mac, which I belted tightly around my increasingly slim waist, I fitted in with the other rockers pretty well.

Sometimes we'd manage to cook and eat a quick meal, knowing the boys' money all went on leathers, bike maintenance and petrol and the most we could expect was fry-ups or hotdogs from one of the lay-by stands frequented by bikers. I'd never really had the opportunity to cook at home, apart from simple dishes like omelettes or macaroni cheese, so I now tried to be inventive on my limited finances. Others approached my food cautiously after disasters such as a vegetable stew containing pickled walnuts, or a cucumber baked in a batter made with just plain flour and someone's left over cooking sherry.

"It's your pretentions of grandeur," laughed Anne after spitting out the latter. "Just can't admit you're as poor as the rest of us." I guessed she was probably right and that it was a family trait, recalling how the living room of the flat we moved into after my father left had, for months, contained no sofa or chairs, but simply an expensive extending Ercol dining table that had used up all mummy's money and was her pride and joy. I was amazed when I arrived home from school one summer's day to find it had been joined by a beautiful matching polished beech cabinet that took pride of place in the bay of the window. I was even more amazed when mummy lifted the top of the cabinet and a Singer sewing machine magically arose from the interior. Infected with her enthusiasm for these items of quality I would polish them regularly and show them off to occasional visitors, while the two proudly and patiently dominated the room, awaiting the dining chairs and curtains that joined them just in time for Christmas. As mummy once told me; "Just because we might be short of money doesn't mean we have to be poor. It's all an attitude of mind."

After our lengthy preparations and rushed food we'd hear the boys revving up outside and we'd make our way past the disapproving glares of the nuns and hurry out to be greeted by wolf-whistles. On one such evening Sister Agnes had taken me into her office to tell me I should give some serious thought to my behaviour.

"I'm not doing anything wrong, Sister," I responded and saw her eyebrow raised and lips pursed.

"I don't think you realise what an underworld you are getting into, young lady. I have seen who you are mixing with."

"Do you mean Kirsty?" I asked with a small smile, sure that Kirsty and the others had already been at the receiving end of this lecture.

"Well, I think you are probably encouraging each other," she said, "but I am more concerned about these noisy ruffians I see outside several times a week. Perhaps you are too naive to realise that these sorts of people are really only after one thing, dear." I hated the insincere way the nuns all used that word 'dear' and couldn't stop myself from asking "What is that, Sister?" in my sweetest voice. I could see from the confused look in her eyes that she wasn't quite sure how genuine my question was.

"Never you mind," she said in a slightly subdued tone. "Just listen to my advice and find yourself some nice young friends." I could have argued with her but knew it was pointless, as many of the nuns seemed to make snap judgements on people without bothering to look any deeper. In fact she was way off the mark, certainly as far as Tony and his brother were concerned. Steve was all talk and, whilst he and Kirsty did kiss and cuddle a bit, nothing more developed. Despite her talk and their sometimes outrageous flirting, they were almost as innocent as I was. Tony and I never even got further than what were really just friendly hugs rather than cuddles, and pecks more than real kisses. I was aware that, at some of the impromptu parties in shared flats or squats, a few of the other couples explored a bit more but actually the majority of us were surprisingly innocent and, despite appearances, our group was pretty middle class.

Some of Steve's friends were older and more settled, although to me they were all quite glamorous, especially Laura. I suppose she was exempt from the class system, being a Canadian from Vancouver. She was a tiny bundle of energy, her sparkling brown eyes seeming to follow everything and her long curly black hair swinging as she darted around. Yet her voice was surprisingly soft and calm and, although only

19

three years older than me, she seemed to take a motherly role with us all. This made it really surprising when I learned that she worked in various clubs and restaurants as a belly dancer.

"I didn't even know there were Canadian belly dancers," I exclaimed as she showed me her two costumes. Laura's laugh filled the small bedroom.

"Nope, it's not particularly part of our culture," she said, and went on to explain how her Canadian father had met her Turkish mother while they were attending a medical conference in Paris. "Mum thought it was so cute when I learnt the dancing from her, as a child, but now she'd rather I chose any other career," Laura added with a small grimace. Laura lived with her African boyfriend Kwesi, who she had met in a club over a year earlier, and they were crazy about each other. So, whilst she might flirt with customers to boost her tips, those guys there didn't stand a chance. I initially thought Kwesi had been a customer. Tony laughed when I asked him and said I should wait till we went to their flat. On my first visit there Laura took my coat then showed me into the sitting room, saying "don't be nervous." I wasn't until she said that, but then looked around the room and saw three large glass tanks on a metal rack against the wall.

"Fish?" I asked stupidly, given that from my position by the door I could see there was no water in the tanks, just something dark on the floor of the bottom one. Tony pushed me forward and I realised all the tanks contained snakes.

"Oh, Laura, what weird pets," I exclaimed with a nervous shiver and she laughed.

"Working pets," she said and, to my horror, slid open the lid of one of the tanks and lifted out a bright green snake about 18 inches long with a long thin tail. "If you relax you can hold Bernie," she said, smiling and holding the snake towards me so I could see the bright yellow underside.

"I don't think so," I said, backing into Tony, who put his arms around me and laughed. She put the green snake back into the warm tank with its two friends and it slithered away among the plants and branches, probably as relieved as I was! We all went into the kitchen and had toast and hot chocolate while I calmed down, and Kwesi explained that he had been handling snakes since he was little and now made his living dancing with snakes in night clubs and at parties.

"How come you handled them as a child?" I asked, expecting to hear his parents had kept them in their home. I was totally amazed by the story he then told, of the village in Africa where he was born and lived with his parents until, devastatingly, his mother and father died within months of each other. At six years old Kwesi was then left to more or less make his own way in life. I had thought small communities such as he described looked after each other in time of need, but in fact Kwesi was left mostly to his own resources apart from sometimes being given small bits of food, usually by the generosity of other children.

"How could they do that to a small child?" I asked. Kwesi placed his hand on my arm.

"Do not blame them, Nicky, they were frightened of me."

"Of a six-year-old?"

"No. Of the words of the fetish priest, the religious specialist in the village. He said that my parents had both died so suddenly because the family was cursed. So how could they risk the lives of their own families by taking me in?" Little Kwesi spent more and more time exploring the jungle around the village, feeling happier among the birds, monkeys and small animals there, creating night time retreats deep in the undergrowth and strengthening his young muscles by climbing the trees. "I knew to be wary of snakes in the undergrowth," he said in a slow and serious voice. "Every village child learns to respect and fear those creatures with each baby step they take. No doubt my father would have taught me about those that hung from the trees and wound themselves around branches, had he lived. Instead I found out about those myself when I was ten foot or so up the tree." He laughed, his teeth sparkling white against his dark skin. Then his face became serious again. "It was a hard and patient journey, learning to live with these wonderful beings. Sometimes it was very painful as they protected themselves from me," he said slowly, holding up his arm to show a scar where he said a puff adder had bitten him. "I learnt my lesson, and once I truly showed them respect some of them were willing to help me."

"How did they help you, Kwesi?" I almost whispered, caught in the mystery of the tale.

"They let me hold them, dance with them, bring them to local villages where the villagers would give me food, clothes and other small things I needed in return for a performance by me. Sometimes, when I was older and could go to perform in the town where richer people lived, I was given small coins which I stored away, knowing these would one day be my way to a new, happier life." There was silence, then Kwesi suddenly jumped up from the table and shouted, "And here I am…this is my happier life!" He grabbed Laura and added, "And this is my alomo, my sweetheart. Now come and meet my friends properly."

We returned to the lounge, muggy with the heating for the tanks, and without taking any of them out he showed me his different snakes. In the same tank as Bernie were Boris and Bobby. As all three were the same vibrant green and yellow with the cutest big sticking out eyes, I supposed they could only be told apart by those who really loved them. Kwesi slid the lid open slightly to spray the inside of the tank with a light mist of water and explained they had to do this every day to keep up the humidity, and that each day they fed the green snakes with a variety of insects and the occasional small lizard. I was really glad they didn't plan to feed them while I was there as the thought of that, especially the lizard, made me feel ill even though I knew logically they had to eat and their diet had to be similar to what they would hunt in the wild. The next two tanks held Kwesi's real 'dancing partners'. The first was a Royal Python, still a youngster at only three foot but, Laura said, past the skittish stage where they are quite aggressive and need to be fed pinkie mice every week. He was curled up in the large water bowl fitted in each tank.

"Even Kwesi struggled with Paulie at first," said Laura, "but with a little handling night after night he's calmed right down."

"I suppose he recognises you now," I said, "knows you're safe."

"Hmm, not really," said Kwesi. "Snakes don't really remember, apart from instinctive stuff. No, it's more that we are used to each other's vibrations; if I treat him as he needs he will respond well to me." That made sense to me. I was learning daily that my instincts were the best way of discovering who I could trust, helping me distinguish between so called good people like some of the less trustworthy nuns and so called weird people, like a smiling, sensitive and gentle snake dancer.

"Now, finally...dah, dum!" said Tony, leading me to the last tank. "This is Kwesi's star and Laura's real love, Wally." Wally certainly was the star as far as size, being a six-foot-long Burmese Python. I was astonished that Kwesi would be able to dance with this length of what looked like pure muscle wound around his neck and shoulders.

Kwesi told me he'd had him for three years but would sadly have to reconsider when he got a bit bigger as, whilst he was docile except when feeding, the sheer weight meant two people were needed to handle a Burmese over 8 foot, and Wally could eventually grow to 20 foot and weigh over 200 pounds.

Laura suggested I stroke Wally but I couldn't face it, and was amazed to hear that when they were both at home and no visitors were expected some of the snakes were allowed the freedom of the flat. Laura said she had even woken up to find

Boris curled on the pillow by her face, staring at her with his bulbous eyes. It seemed she had come to love snakes through Kwesi and had made him promise that for Christmas he would get her an Egg Eating snake!

Other than Laura and Kwesi most of our friends were bikers. They spent a lot of their evenings racing to roadside gatherings, more for the journey than the destination, and their weekends chasing off to Brighton to ride along the seafront. They'd park up, then eat fish and chips on the pebble beach, beat each other on the crazy golf or queue at the shooting ranges and other fairground booths on the pier while eating candy floss or crunching on lumps of pink rock. More or less the same as everyone else on a daytrip to Brighton really, except that we looked different with the boys' tight jeans, leathers and greasy hair. Sometimes our little group would join other rockers at a beer party or all night barbecue on the beach. I always made Tony drive me home to meet the hostel deadline, rather than staying the night, and he didn't really mind as he was experimenting at becoming a vegetarian like me and there was nothing for either of us to eat at the barbecues. Instead we'd stop on the way home at one of our greasy spoon cafes, eat fried bread with runny eggs and tomatoes and listen to our favourite tunes on the jukebox. At such times life felt really good.

It was easy in the daytime in the office, being who they wanted me to be, and it was easy in the evening with Tony and the others, being who I liked to believe I was. But then came the night time and all the roles dropped away to leave just me. Happy me, sad me, frightened me, optimistic me. All of those but, at the end of the day, just me, a teenager trying to figure her way in life, with all the memories of how life had been so far. Nostalgia for the good memories, anger and sadness for the bad ones, and night time tears for the contrast between the two. Although I tried to pretend my life started the day I left home of course it didn't, and every so often the memories and

24

feelings would flood through me until I couldn't cope with the anomalies and would retreat into the safety of another role.

At such times lying in the dormitory listening to the breathing and night time noises of the other girls reminded me of another dormitory, a long time ago, and I felt once more like a little girl among strangers, wondering when she would see her mother again.

I was happy and excited as my mother kissed me goodbye, and I skipped after the other girls through the big front door. I was wearing my best checked red and white gingham dress, with its swirly skirt and sparkling white collar, and matching red cardigan and socks. My brown leather sandals felt a bit tight in places as we had just bought them yesterday in Clarks, but I had still polished them proudly with saddle soap before I went to bed and they shone beautifully. My long hair was shiny too, as this morning mummy had brushed it until my head ached before tying it into two high bunches with big bows of new white satin ribbon. I felt smart and pretty, and at nine years old it was an exciting adventure, going to stay in this big old house with its beautiful gardens and dozens of shiny windows reflecting the late afternoon sun.

The two nuns in their long black dresses stood so stiffly at each side of the door I thought they were statues, and I jumped slightly as they suddenly chanted in unison "Slow down, girls." I tried to, but not quickly enough as I bumped into a tall girl in front of me, who turned to poke out her tongue and flick one of her long blonde plaits in my face.

"I'm sorry," I said. "I didn't mean…" I was interrupted by the nun on my side of the door, who stared at me and said "Quiet, child." The girl in front gave me a smug smile.

Inside the door was a long dark hall with a high ceiling, big paintings and dark wooden benches with maroon cushions along each wall. On the wall in front of us was a gigantic painting of Jesus on the cross, which was scary to look up at, except that his face seemed really peaceful. An older nun sat at a table under the painting, with a big book in front of her. As each of us reached her we were asked our name and age, which she wrote in the book, and given a slip of paper. I heard that the girl with the plaits was called Miriam and her paper had C2 written on it, while mine had C3. Suitcases and bags were lined up by the wall on the left, and I could see my multi-coloured stripy one that I'd begged Mummy to buy the previous day. She'd laughingly agreed, saying it was a beach bag really but at least I'd always be able to find it.

"Collect your cases, go into that room and stand by a chair," said yet another nun, pointing at a door to the right. I dragged the heavy bag through and found myself in a large cold room with nothing in it except a circle of small chairs, two big trunks by a wall and a pile of cardboard boxes.

"Right, girls," said the nun as she took the arms of two tiny twin girls and stood them by chairs, where someone had already put their cases. "Are we all here?"

"We are indeed," said another nun.

"So, girls," the first continued "sit on your chairs and put your suitcases in front of you." We did as asked. I helped a little girl next to me whose suitcase was almost as big as her. "Good. Now open your cases." I smiled as I opened mine, seeing that mummy had put What Katy Did and copies of Bunty on top of my clothes. My favourite doll peeped through the pile of flannel vests, and next to the comics was a brown paper bag that I knew was full of the broken biscuits we bought at Sainsbury's each Saturday. I loved helping unpack the shopping then sitting with mummy at the kitchen table, her with a cup of tea and a Woodbine and me with the bottle of orange juice the milkman brought each morning, rummaging through the broken biscuits till I found pieces of chocolate digestive, custard cream or pink wafer.

"Firstly, I want you all to bring any books or toys and put them in this trunk. Any food or sweets go in this one. You first, Nicola." I jumped to hear my name and felt really self-conscious as I carried my book, comics and bag of biscuits across to the trunks by the wall.

"Good girl," said the nun with a smile and I smiled back. "But is that a doll you've left in your case?"

"Yes, miss," I said hesitantly, not sure how to address a nun.

"You must say 'yes, Sister' dear. Now, I did say all toys and food so go and get the doll."

"She sleeps with me, miss," I said nervously. "I mean Sister," I corrected myself.

"Please don't argue with me, child. I said all toys and that is a toy." A few of the girls giggled as I went and got my dolly and placed her gently in the toy trunk, desperately hoping they'd give her back soon. Mummy had told me to cuddle her if I felt homesick, and I was getting the feeling that could be very soon.

After we had all handed over the toys and food we were told to put our clothes, apart from vests and pants, in the middle of the floor. Mummy had folded everything so neatly and I was proud of my smart clothes that she'd made herself. I carefully unpacked my white rayon skirt, my spotted poplin smock dress, two gingham blouses, another cardigan and my favourite pale blue cotton satin dress which we'd had to take to the Singer shop, for them to make the button holes for the tiny pearl buttons. A variety of coloured socks balanced on top of the pile, and although some of the other girls' piles were bigger they didn't look any better.

"Now, girls," said the nun in charge, as the last case was emptied, "you are going to learn the first important lesson in life. That is humility." We must have all looked as puzzled as I felt, as she went on to tell us how humility meant realising we were not special but equal to all others. She said that we were all born with the sin of pride, which came before a fall, and that the sooner we lost that the closer we would get to goodness. I was confused, as mummy always told me I should hold my head up high and be proud. In fact, her last words to me had been that she knew I would be a good girl and make her proud. I wanted to ask the nun what she meant. I hadn't known until now that I was bad, and wasn't sure how I had

28

become bad. And if I made mummy proud did that mean she would fall over and hurt herself? However, there was no opportunity for questions as the two nuns went over to the piles of clothes, many so carefully folded and stacked, and pushed them all around with their feet until it was one big messy pile on the floor.

"Now, dears," said the nun, "go and collect one lot of nightwear, one dressing gown, socks and either a dress or a skirt and blouse. Then put them in one of those cardboard boxes and take it back to your chair. "Mind," she added as we all moved towards the pile, "you will not take any item of your own clothing and I will not have you rummaging for ages. Just take the first things you find." Unfortunately, the first thing I found was a brown tunic in a scratchy material. I tried to look under it but a nun was already there, saying "that's right, dear, that's for you then." I ended up back at my chair with the tunic, a spotted nightie, a soft woolly blue dressing gown and a pair of pink socks that were actually my own, hoping they wouldn't realise.

We were then shown to our bedrooms, which was what the letter and number on the piece of paper meant. I had room C and the third bed which, I was glad to find, was under the window. I wasn't used to sharing a room with strangers, but at least I only had someone one side of me. Unfortunately, that was the girl called Miriam, who didn't seem at all friendly. There were three more beds on the other side of the room; one of the tiny twins was in the bed facing mine but her sister had been taken off to a different bedroom. They had both started crying when they had to put their teddies in the trunk, and she now sat on the edge of her bed very stiffly, her eyes puffy and her face pale. The nun who had shown us in stood in the middle of the room, pointing out our lockers and the door that led to our bathroom. She told us all to change into the clothes we had 'chosen' and put the clothes we were wearing in a tidy pile at the foot of our bed. She then went over to the tiny girl and helped her undress, and I was glad to see she was very gentle with her.

What a sight we all looked once we had changed. My tunic was so big it hung like a tent, ending almost at the pink socks, while the white blouse I'd found to go under it felt so tight I wasn't sure I could move my arms. I saw two girls wearing my clothes. A girl about my size in the bed diagonally opposite looked very nice in my cotton satin dress, and Miriam looked slightly daft in my white rayon skirt, which was too small so stretched across her tummy and finished way above her knees. I did find it funny, but hoped the skirt wouldn't be ruined and that this humility lesson would be finished soon.

Dinner that night was, for me, more about humiliation than humility. The dining room was high-ceilinged with dark wood panels on the walls and tall stained glass windows. We were seated on either side of long wooden tables, a nun sitting at the end of each one. We were firstly given a long talk about how this was our new home, which was a complete surprise to me. Mummy had told me I was visiting here and I thought it was for a week or two, like when we visited one of my aunts. The nun's words about sin came back to me, and I realised with a shock that mummy and daddy must have sent me away from our old home because I was bad.

We were then told that although this was called a boarding school we would actually be going out to school each day, to one of two different schools in the town. I wanted to ask what about my own school and my friends there, but only the nuns seemed allowed to speak. However, after we had said grace, when the plates of food were eventually wheeled from the kitchens and I saw sausages and mash being passed along I had to speak because, like mummy, I didn't eat meat.

"Please, Sister," I mumbled.

"If you have something to say wait until we have finished eating, child," said Sister Margaret, the nun at the head of our table.

I sat for a moment staring at the two fat sausages, balanced on the mash and surrounded by peas floating in dark brown gravy. Finally, I plucked up my courage and said, loudly and nervously, "I can't eat this, Sister, I'm a vegetable." As soon as the word came out I realised my mistake and tried to correct it to vegetarian, but all the girls were laughing so loudly I don't think anyone heard. Eventually Sister Margaret quietened them down and left the table to speak to the other nuns, sitting at a table of their own. Then she went out of the room and returned with a small plate.

"Your mother did mention it. It's a bit of a fad isn't it? You'll just have to make do with the vegetables tonight." With that she speared my sausages with a fork, put them on the small plate and took them back to her seat. I sat looking in horror at the meat gravy that was congealing on the potatoes and peas, and realised I was going to be very hungry tonight. I was relieved when, finally, a trolley with plates of sponge covered in pink custard was wheeled out, and we were told to pass our plates along. Suddenly I heard my name booming out angrily.

"Nicola, we do not waste food here. Children are starving in Africa. We have accommodated your mother's strange ideas by letting you not have the sausages, but you are not going to waste the rest." The plate was passed back to me and I tried to explain about the gravy.

"Rubbish," said Sister Margaret impatiently. "A bit of gravy can't do anyone any harm. Now you sit there until you have finished it all. You had better be quick about it or there'll be no pudding tonight." My heart sank. I was in a trap with no way out, as mummy had told me quite clearly never to eat meat or food with meat in it, like gravy, that it was a poison to our bodies. I sat staring at my plate, as the others tucked into their puddings and Sister Margaret glared at me from the end of the table. Eventually dinner was finished, except mine, and we were told to stand.

"Not you, Nicola," said Sister as I got up. "You will not move from that chair until you finish your meal."

The girls filed out and I was left sitting there. I was scared of the nuns but I was more scared of breaking Mummy's rule, eating meat and possibly even being poisoned. I think even the nuns were surprised by the stubbornness a little girl like me could show. It was already dark outside the big windows when the standoff was broken, as I realised with horror and embarrassment that, for the first time since I was a tiny child, I had wet myself, the liquid creating a smelly pool on their polished wooden floor. Then I got to leave the table, firstly to clean up the mess I had made with a bucket and cloth and then to go to bed early in my strange lonely bed, wearing somebody else's nightie and missing home, my parents and my dolly. It felt like the longest night of my life as I tossed and turned, pretending to be asleep when the other girls came to bed. Listening to sobs from the twin's bed after lights-out, I tried to muffle my own sobs in my pillow as I pictured my beautiful dolly lying lonely in the box of toys. This would be our first night without each other in more than two years.

~~~~~

I'd fallen in love with her in the shop window when I was only seven, but when I'd asked Mummy to buy her she said I would have to wait until we had some money. We were living in a small house in Wales at the time, daddy working in a factory and me going to a local school, where I sat at the back of the class playing with plasticine as I didn't understand the language. I knew we never stayed in houses for long, something to do with daddy's work, so I was really scared that even if she wasn't bought by someone else we would move before we had some money to get her. Each time we passed the shop I would hold my breath, fearful that she would have gone, relieved and happy when I saw her still sitting on the small shelf, smiling at me. Although she was only about nine inches tall she was so pretty with rosy cheeks, a bright yellow dress and curly blonde hair. Sometimes I was allowed to go on my own to the bus stop near the toy shop, to meet daddy from the bus when he came home from work. One day we went as usual into the tobacconist to buy his ten Woodbines and a small bottle of Tizer for me, and I saw the lady give him some pound notes in change. He had money! As we reached the toy shop I showed him my beautiful doll and begged him to buy her for me.

"Oh, I don't know, love, that sort of thing is up to mummy," he said, ruffling my hair with his big hand.

"Mummy said I could have her when you had money," I said quickly. He stood a moment looking in the shop window and stroking his goatee.

"A pound, hmm. Alright then, little miss," he said with a smile, picking me up and carrying me into the shop. I left cuddling my beloved doll, marvelling at her shiny blue eyes and squidgy legs and arms, that wouldn't poke me in bed as my other dolly's hard fingers did. I ran into the house, so excited to show mummy, and was shocked when she sent me to my room where I sat and listened to bits of their argument. Words like 'useless provider', 'waste of space' and 'play the generous one' were shouted by my mother, while daddy mumbled stuff about sorting things out and me being a good girl. I hated hearing them argue and hugged my new dolly tightly, desperately hoping she wouldn't have to go back to the shop. Eventually I heard the front door slam, then mummy came into my room.

"So," she said, taking my doll. "You talked him into it."

"I'm sorry. You said when we had money mummy, and he did," I said quickly and she smiled a tight little smile.

"Oh to be as young and carefree as you," she said, kneeling down and putting the doll on my lap. "Here you are, you can keep her, although that pound should have paid a bill. In fact, I can tell you what our new young family member will be called. She'll be called Ubrocus, because we are certainly broke this week thanks to her!" She explained what she meant and we laughed about it together. Even daddy laughed at her name when he eventually came home and gave me and Ubrocus a bedtime kiss, his scratchy beard smelling of cigarettes and beer.

~~~~

I think Sister Margaret felt bad about the dinner episode as she was really nice to me at breakfast the next morning, putting an extra slice of toast on my plate presumably to make up for the lost dinner. We had been woken early to find a little pile of clean clothes on the chair by each bed. Not our clothes of course, but slightly better fitting than last night's mish-mash. I ended up with quite a nice blue poplin dress with puffed sleeves and a flared skirt, which a sweet girl called Kate later told me was hers. She said it suited me better than her anyway, and I felt really good until I remembered I wasn't supposed to, because of the humility thing. As it was the weekend, after breakfast we were taken for a walk around the gardens and shown where they grew vegetables. Lunch was tomato soup and cheese sandwiches, and after lunch we were marched into the big room with the trunks and told we could each choose a toy and a book for the afternoon. Again we were not to choose our own, but I did get a brief chance to stroke Ubrocus' blonde curls, before I collected a jigsaw of the Kings and Queens of England and a book about birds. Then we were all shown into the playroom which was quite nice, with big couches and bright rugs on the floor, and we kept ourselves occupied until dinner. I was really nervous going into the dining room, and was so relieved to see a hardboiled egg salad placed in front of me. While they had no idea about vegetarian food they did try to find things for me to eat, and I didn't mind that it was often just vegetables, as long as I was never again threatened with gravy.

Bedtime had what seemed a strange ritual to me. At home I was not allowed anything except water once I had cleaned my teeth. Here we washed and changed into our nighties and dressing gowns then went to the dining room, where one of the Sisters would pour us big mugs of hot chocolate and we could take a piece of bread and butter from the plate in the centre of the table. We then went out to clean our teeth and returned to the dining room to line up and file out past two nuns by the door. One of them would pour a spoonful of cod liver oil into each open mouth, the other followed this by giving each of us a spoon twisted in malt, which was thick and brown and sweet and which we would suck on like a lolly, returning our spoons next morning before breakfast. It did take away the taste of the cod liver oil but I was sure it wasn't doing my teeth much good, and wondered if mummy would be cross when she found out.

Some nights we would have pillow fights, which were safe as long as we only giggled quietly and stayed in our beds, chucking the pillows across the room at each other. However, many times someone would become over-excited, jumping from their bed and running down the middle of the dormitory in the dark to frighten her unexpected victim by landing the pillow right on their head. This would provoke inevitable shrieks of pretend horror, followed by responding shrieks of laughter, and we all knew then that we had seconds to feign sleep before one of the nuns would throw open the door and switch on the light. It reminded me of 'statues', a game we'd played at birthday parties at home. Even then I'd be caught moving when the music stopped and my timing hadn't improved much. It was only a couple of weeks before I was caught in the middle of the dorm, my pillow held high above me ready for the shot, as the light went on. I burst out laughing as Sister boomed out my name, and was still giggling when she grasped my arm and steered me through the bedroom door, turning off the light as she went. The giggling soon stopped as she opened the door of a large store cupboard along the corridor and, taking the pillow from me, pushed me inside.

35

"You will spend the night in here, Nicola. That might teach you to appreciate your bed and to stay in it when told to in future."

With that she closed the big door and strode off. I stood for ages by that door, terrified of the dark that seemed so different from the dark of the dormitory, and nervously listening to all the creaky night-time noises of the old house. Eventually exhaustion overtook me and I curled up on the lino under the shelves and fell asleep, waking up stiff and cold to the usual morning bell and the sound of the other girls heading for the bathroom.

The horror of that night should have stopped me joining in dormitory rebellions, but in time I just accepted it as part of the routine of boarding school, along with all the other strange rules and regulations. What was harder was balancing that alongside very different rules and ways of behaving at the school I went to daily, where we were encouraged more to express ourselves as individuals. Sometimes I would forget the difference and then pay the price, such as the day I stayed to help my class teacher put all the chairs up on the desks so arrived back at boarding school twenty minutes late. As Sister told me I was thoughtless, inconsiderate and not to be trusted I tried to explain that I was being helpful.

"You know you are required to leave school promptly and to come straight home," she said sternly, ignoring what I had said.

"This isn't my home," I blurted out as tears of frustration welled up. My rudeness probably increased my punishment, as I was marched to the dining room and stood in the corner, facing the wall. I was then left standing there until after all the girls had come in and eaten, and only when the room emptied was I allowed to move, to clear the tables and head off for another hungry early night.

The idea that I had been bad, even though I didn't know exactly how, played on my mind constantly and I kept looking for ways to show that I was good really. The incident of helping the teacher after school showed me how difficult this was, a good thing in one place becoming a bad thing in another. I got further proof of this when; waking early one rainy morning, I glanced out of the window and was amazed to see the twin who slept opposite me standing in the middle of the soggy lawn, wearing only her nightdress and bare feet. None of us were allowed in the garden without permission anyway, and I couldn't understand why little Sharon would be out there. I heard a sound from the next bed.

"Are you awake, Miriam?" She grunted in reply.

"Why?" she asked sleepily. I still didn't like her, as she took every opportunity to boss the children around and make fun of them, but she'd stopped having goes at me and I suppose we grudgingly put up with each other. Now I definitely needed her advice on what to do, so I told her about Sharon. As she jumped from her bed to look out of the window I thought I saw a little smile on her face.

"It's not funny, Miriam. What should we do?"

"Well, you can't go out there or you'll be in trouble. So, either you leave the kid till a nun spots her or you go and tell one of the Sisters." To me there was no choice, so I put on my slippers and dressing gown and tapped on the door of our dormitory Sister's room. Within minutes the place was buzzing with activity and as I returned to the dorm I heard the slam of the back door as Sharon was brought in from the rain. I expected her to be put back into bed so she could get warm again, but instead Sister appeared and collected Sharon's dressing gown. As she passed our beds she looked over at Miriam.

"Do you know anything about this?" she asked and Miriam looked puzzled.

"No, Sister, I was sleeping until Nicola woke me up."

"Is that right, Nicola?"

"Yes, Sister," I replied, although actually I didn't really know if she was asleep or not when I'd spoken to her. I assumed little Sharon was being warmed and comforted somewhere. So when we filed in to breakfast I was shocked to see her standing in the corner facing the wall and wearing only her dressing gown and slippers, her long wavy hair still damp. As we all took our places Sister Margaret cleared her throat.

"Some of you will be aware that this child," her arm swept out towards Sharon "decided that rules are there for no reason and can be broken to have a bit of fun. Not only did she decide to go into the garden without permission, to play with the cats at some ridiculous time of the morning, she also decided to try to blame another child for 'forcing' her to be there." There was a brief sneer from the Sister and, as I listened to something confusing about Sharon going to a place called Coventry and instructions not to speak to her, I again noticed a smile on Miriam's face.

"Little sneak," she muttered as we carried dishes to the kitchen.

"Oh no, it's true. You made her go there!" I whispered back in horror.

"Don't be daft," said Miriam. "I might have taken her on an early walk to show her the bush where the mother cat keeps her kittens, but how could I make her stay there?" The reality was Miriam could make the younger ones do anything. They were all afraid of her, although her reputation until now had been more about threats than anything she'd actually done.

"That's horrible, Miriam. That poor little thing so upset and her sister in tears as well. I'm going to tell Sister." Miriam slammed her pile of dishes onto the kitchen trolley and turned to me with a big grin.

"Tell her what, Nicola? Don't forget you are already my alibi. It was you that was awake first, you that woke me. Remember that." It was certainly what I had told Sister. I wanted to be strong and brave and explain I couldn't be sure she'd been asleep, explain about the smiles and comments, but I had no proof and I wasn't brave. I just felt that yet again I'd done the wrong thing while trying to be good. If I'd just gone down the garden and brought Sharon in no-one might have known. Something told me if I now tried to do the right thing by telling, not only would Miriam make my life hell but it would all go wrong anyway. I felt so guilty and sad for the twins but, as it turned out, after their parents' routine visit the following Sunday they took the twins away with them and they never returned.

Those fortnightly Sunday visiting days were really hard for me, as I never knew whether anyone would come. The night before we would be given some of our own clothes, and the morning would buzz with excitement as everyone tried to look their best and anticipate where their family might take them for the day and what goodies they might bring. Our chores finished, hair brushed and shoes polished, we would sit on the benches lining the entrance hall, waiting for the deep echoing sound of the brass knocker on the front door. One of the Sisters would then undertake what seemed to us girls a painfully slow walk down the hall, and open the door to reveal the new arrival. We all learnt early on to curb any instinct to run and hug our visitor, instead sitting 'like young ladies' while Sister made polite small talk with them before coming to collect their child and escort her to them by the door. They would then be shown out and the door closed, whilst we all anxiously awaited the next knock, knowing every moment we had to wait was a moment less we would have with our loved ones.

On the first visiting Sunday it was my mother who arrived, looking like a movie star in a swirling fake fur cloak over a green suit the colour of her eyes. She was wearing a bright red lipstick and her long auburn hair was swept up under a wide brimmed hat, trimmed with the same material as her coat. I thought I had never seen her look so beautiful, and I was really proud as all the girls stared when Sister walked over to collect me and take me to her. I was a little surprised by the stern look on Sister's face and the abrupt way she instructed mummy to 'return her promptly by 4p.m. please,' then closed the door without a goodbye. I soon forgot about it and just enjoyed my day with mummy, which ended with high tea in the nearby town. She told me about some things she had been doing, and asked questions about the schoolwork and boarding school. I wanted to ask her why I was there and when I could come home again but something stopped me, possibly fear of the answers I might get. Instead I found myself reassuring her that I was alright and happy and she had nothing to worry about.

"Well, as long as you are absolutely sure, darling," she said in a rather vague way as we left the tearooms. As she squeezed my hand I was tempted for a moment to tell her of the loneliness and the swapped clothes and about Ubrocus living in a box of toys, but I didn't. Instead I promised myself I would be brave enough to do so, and to ask about going home, when she came again in two weeks.

The next visiting Sunday I was ready early, and as I sat on the maroon cushioned bench I kept repeating to myself "Be brave, ask her. Be brave, ask her." Perhaps it might have worked, but I would never know as she didn't come. I waited and waited, chanting to myself as I watched each of the girls go happily out of the door, until there was just me with the two nuns in the large cold hall. One of the nuns took hold of my hand gently.

"Come on dear, let's see if we can find some juice and biscuits shall we?"

"But...she'll be here soon," I said, turning back to the door.

"I think she might not be able to come today, dear, but I'm sure you'll see her next time."

40

Next time was for me an eternity away, and it was only after reassurance that I'd be called if she arrived that I could eventually be persuaded to go to the warmth of the kitchen. Once there I fought against the tears by burying myself in a cookery book, while the two nuns mumbled in the corner. I couldn't really hear what they were saying except it seemed to be something about mummy's lipstick and clothes being the reason she wasn't there, which made no sense to me at all. When one of the nuns put her arm around my shoulder and said that naughty mummy should have let us know I found myself defending her vigorously, before rushing to the dormitory to sob into my pillow, just like my first night there.

Although mummy turned up again on the next visiting day, casually explaining her absence by saying that my father had been supposed to come "and you know how unreliable he is, dear." I wanted to tell her how horrible it had been when no-one came, but I didn't want to spoil this visit so I said nothing. Perhaps I should have, because the visits continued to be hit and miss and I continued to feel abandoned on a regular basis. Although I had learnt to cope with my new life, I still desperately wanted to leave this place, to go home and for everything to go back to how it used to be. Yet the longer I was there the less likely it seemed.

Then the unthinkable happened and part of my wish came true, rescue coming in the most sudden and unexpected way, so that I should have been really happy yet was simply terrified and even more convinced of my badness.

5

I did get some news of home. After a few weeks in the hostel I had built up my courage to go and see an aunt who also lived in London. I was worried that she would be really angry or would even somehow force me to go home. However, she was actually more understanding than I expected, and it was a relief to realise that others had become aware of my mother's extreme, erratic and often aggressive behaviour.

Over a very welcome, albeit characteristically burnt, meal of lentil rissoles she told me that mummy had reported me missing to the police, but they had said that, at sixteen, I was legally entitled to leave home, as long as I was safe and able to look after myself. Apparently that initially caused her anger and frustration, but already that had passed and she seemed to be carrying on with her usual life, minus a daughter. I asked my aunt not to tell mummy she'd seen me but she pointed out that not only was I possibly asking her to lie, I was also being cruel by not letting mummy know I was alright.

Eventually we agreed she would tell of my visit but not pass on information such as where I lived or worked. After that I got fairly regular updates, never sure whether I wanted to hear she was grief-stricken because I had gone or that she was happy, making it alright for me to be happy too. After a lot of pleading from me my aunt agreed to try to get some of my things from home, and returned with the rather odd collection my mother had put together. This included a pleated wool tartan skirt that, rolled up, had filled my stocking a couple of Christmases earlier, leaving little room for anything else apart from the obligatory mandarin orange in the toe, some brazil nuts and the usual chocolate Santa balancing on top. There too were my much coveted but now childlike patent dancing shoes, a shiny black dress with white lace around the sleeves, that I had never seen before, a few books, a couple of summer blouses and my record player. The 45rpm of Mario Lanza's *Drinking Song* given to me by my father, was still on the turntable. None of my other discs were in the bag, but just getting the record player was really exciting. We eagerly set it up in the hostel lounge so everyone could play their music, volume low and the door closed to avoid the disapproving glares from the nuns.

"We are paying for the honour of living in this dump," Anne pointed out. "It's not like they're having us here out of charity so they'll have to put up with a bit of music won't they?" Spurred on by that thought we started to have quite lively evenings with the other girls in the chilly lounge, and the repertoire of music grew to encompass all our different tastes.

Initially I spent most of my spare time with Kirsty, Anne and the guys, excited by the new world they introduced me to and feeling they could do no wrong. Inevitably however, the more I got to know them they became less perfect and more human to me, along with some human flaws. Despite the nuns' observations, I continued to think a lot of Tony and his brother but a few doubts crept in about the girls. The biggest shift came on one of our Saturday afternoons in Brighton. We'd driven down late morning and parked up the bikes before heading down the pier for fish and chips, or in my case chips. The guys had a glass of cider each at one of the bars in the arcade, while we girls wasted money on the slot machines. They always had any drinks early, on the grounds that the alcohol would have worn off before we drove back. Then we all headed down the beach, where the combination of sun and cider made the guys silly and sleepy as they lay on the pebbles among the sunbathers, looking somewhat incongruous in their leathers, which they refused to take off. With a bit of teasing we girls did manage to get their boots off and bury their feet under the pebbles, but we soon became bored with their company and headed off to the Lanes, our favourite part of

Brighton. We spent the next hour rummaging around in the antique shops, and the other two tried on clothes in several small boutiques. I didn't have any spare money and, unlike them, I couldn't be bothered getting undressed and dressed over and over if I wasn't buying. By the third or fourth boutique I was bored and decided to wait outside in the sunshine while they popped in and out of changing cubicles. I was just thinking of going in to speed them up when they suddenly both ran out of the door, shrieking and laughing simultaneously, and set off at speed down the lane.

"Come on, Nicky," Anne shouted as she ran, and I chased after her without any idea of what we were up to. Suddenly I heard someone panting behind me and a middle-aged man grabbed my arm, stopping me in my tracks.

"You little thief," he spat in my face. I was filled with panic, but almost immediately a plump woman wearing a sequinned bolero hurried past us.

"Not her, Bert, she wasn't in the shop. Come on."

"Sorry, love," he muttered as he followed her. I stood there catching my breath as I watched them turn the corner. I was pretty sure the girls would head to the beach looking for Tony and the others, so I decided to cut through past the pavilion to the pier and make my way along to where I'd be less conspicuous among the crowds of holidaymakers. Once I reached the seafront I immediately saw the dark leather shapes of the guys on the pebbles by the water's edge, looking like beached seals. I was surprised as I neared the pier entrance to hear Kirsty's voice yelling, then saw through the crowds her bright red jacket as she waved her arms wildly in the air.

"Meet you at the end of the line, guys," she yelled. Then she spotted me hurrying towards her and she started laughing as she stood for a moment, hands on hips. Anne stood behind her, pulling on her arm as she glanced back in the direction of the Lanes. "Come on, Nicky!" Kirsty yelled. Although I would have preferred to join the guys I found myself pushing past people to join her by the ticket office of the novelty electric railway, where she jumped the queue to buy our tickets and we settled breathlessly into one of the open carriages. As the train set off I was sure I saw the sequinned bolero in the new queue building up, and I turned away guiltily although I'd done nothing wrong.

"What on earth was all that about, you two?" I asked as the train trundled along. They continued giggling, while Kirsty reached under her jacket to pull out a multi-coloured tie dye scarf and Anne produced some shiny bangles from her pocket. "Did you steal them?" I asked in horror, knowing as soon as I spoke how stupid I sounded.

"Oh Nicky, you are so prim and proper," said Kirsty, draping the scarf round my neck. "That's why we never let you join in," added Anne.

"It's horrible you two. That poor couple are just trying to make a living. And it's illegal," I added, almost as an afterthought. They both laughed.

"Stop being so stuffy, Nicky. It's fun and exciting. You keep the scarf, it suits you. The wrinklies will get paid for it by their insurance company anyway." I was stunned, yet somehow the confidence in their voices made me wonder if I was making a fuss about nothing. I wanted to stand up for what I believed was right, but instead found myself muttering weakly "Well I don't want it." and reaching over to stuff the scrunched up scarf into Kirsty's jacket pocket. She just laughed and it wasn't mentioned again once we jumped off the train as it reached Black Rock. We just walked around fantasising about living by the sea when we were rich, eventually hearing the roar of the bikes as the guys arrived to drive us home.

Although I enjoyed the company of Tony and the others this incident, and a few other small conflicts, showed me that I also wanted and needed to make different friends and experience a variety of new things. Despite for years having

45

lived only a half hour train journey from London I had hardly ever been there, as far as I could remember. Mainly I had come up with my mother for occasional visits to various aunts, days that started with anticipation and excitement but gradually deteriorated. On the train journey up mummy would hurry up and down the carriage, smiling at each person as she leaned across them to close all the windows, explaining to anyone who listened that black dust would blow into the carriage when we went through the long dark tunnel just outside of town. Even on very hot days few people objected, possibly somewhat intimidated by this striking confident woman in her smart tailored outfits and large flamboyant hats. Part of me felt embarrassed by her, but I also felt proud she was my mother as I shyly pretended to be reading my book when others stared at her, men in admiration and women with looks of distaste that I suspected hid their envy. However, after a day with one of her sisters, and the usual rivalry and undermining that entailed, the journey home would be spent in a heavy silence, only broken if anyone, including myself, dared to look at her and risk the angry sharpness of her tongue. Whilst I did enjoy seeing my aunts and cousins I was never sure she did, and partly wondered why she put us through it on a fairly regular basis.

Now London was my own playground and sometimes it felt exciting just to wander around on my own, seeing what I could find and constantly discovering new things. The museums and galleries were full of wonder for me. It was hard to believe all of this had been so close to home yet I hadn't seen it before, and I was embarrassed to have to constantly ask directions in my own capital city, especially as most of the people I asked turned out to be tourists. I decided one day that the best way to avoid embarrassment was to develop a strong French accent, and I did indeed find people much more helpful. This included a rather cheeky young bus conductor who chatted to me each time he passed my seat and, as

46

requested, gave me good warning as we approached the stop for the National Gallery. I spent an enjoyable couple of hours looking at Turner's paintings, several people happily giving the young French tourist the benefit of their artistic knowledge, and it was quite a relief to drop the accent as I boarded the bus home.

"Single Swiss Cottage please, I think I've got the right money," I said as the conductor arrived, rummaging in my bag for coins.

"Blimey," said a familiar cheeky voice, "you certainly picked up the lingo quick, love!" And I could only blush and laugh as I looked up to see the same conductor who had brought me there.

On one of these exploring days I saw a long queue of young people in front of a gateway topped by a banner announcing that 'Billy Graham' would be speaking there. I didn't know who Billy Graham was but joined the queue and eventually went through to a large open air area with a central stage and tiers of seats. There seemed to be thousands of seats and, feeling the pressure of those pushing in behind me, I quickly slipped into one by the aisle near the back. Gradually the whole stadium filled and the noise of thousands of chattering people was overwhelming. Then, suddenly, music struck up and the crowd went silent and still with an air of tension and expectation. As the music reached a crescendo a man walked onto the stage and the crowd erupted with applause, which stopped abruptly as he started to speak in a deep, authoritative and hypnotic voice. It was only then I realised he was some sort of priest and I had brought myself into a gigantic prayer meeting. I wanted to leave, but knew it would draw too much attention to me. So I sat through it in a state of semi-awareness, joining in with the audience rituals as best I could and quite enjoying the rousing hymns, despite some of the messages. Then suddenly it was over, he left the stage, and I mysteriously found myself in the front row seated between two young men smiling warm smiles and talking to me. They told me I was brave, they were proud of me and that I could be saved, but most of their words were a jumble as I tried to figure out how I had not only moved from the back of the stadium to the front but also seated myself between two of Billy Graham's entourage. I leaned forward and looked along the row, and saw the same pattern repeated over and over, little groups of three with the outer two smiling and talking at the central one. An enormous panic filled me and gave me the courage to eventually stand up and rush to the exit, despite the protestations of my two friendly minders. Only in the safety of a nearby café was I able to breath properly again. I never managed to solve the riddle of what happened that day and could only put it down to some sort of mass hypnosis, but the message I took from it was that I never ever again wanted to be trapped or controlled by others.

6

Another Friday night, the bathroom full of chattering girls vying for the limited hot water and places at the mirror.

"What are you doing tonight, Nicky? Seeing Tony?" I looked up at Mary's reflection, her face full of concentration as she drew thick black lines under each eye.

"No, he's got a family thing. I think I'll just catch up on some reading."

"Boring!" she said, in one of the comedy voices she was so good at. She'd keep us entertained in the dormitory late at night as different characters from films or cartoons would appear to penetrate the dark, making humorous observations on the dormitory's occupants. Then she switched back to her usual soft Irish lilt

"Hey, come out with us, we're going to see that new band, the Kinks, in town."

"Oh wow, that sounds great. How much is it?"

Sadly, it was more than I could manage. Mary offered to lend it till the end of the month, but I had to settle for a night in as I already owed money to Kirsty.

This was becoming a regular pattern. Although my job was reasonably well paid I was only a junior clerk, and I found it impossible to stretch my salary to the next payday if I spent on much more than food and rent. After a couple of months of seeing me relying on Kirsty to help me out till payday Beth, another of the Irish girls who had come over from Limerick a few months earlier, suggested I get an extra evening job with her.

"It's easy work, it's insurance like you are already doing and you only have to do the number of evenings you want to," she said. I had wondered how she could work as a typist in an estate agent's office yet manage to send money home to her family, so I was happy to agree. She took me to a small grubby office situated above a local café, where I was given a perfunctory interview by a plump balding man wearing baggy trousers and a knitted cardigan. He puffed on a pipe as he looked me up and down.

"Yes, you could do well," he said thoughtfully, "although you'll have to tone down that make-up. The husbands won't mind, but the sweeter you look the more the women will trust you." It transpired that I was going to be 'introducing people to our insurance policies'. I soon found that what this meant was being driven by him to different streets and knocking on doors, then persuading the residents to let me in so that I could reel off an almost scripted speech intended to get them to sign up for life assurance.

"It sounds a bit scary, Beth, going into strange houses," I said as we emerged from the building.

"Well, I've been doing it a while with no problems," she reassured me, "and Mr Evans will know if you've been abducted if you aren't there when he comes to collect you." Her confidence inspired me, and any remaining doubts I had were wiped away as a group of us gathered outside the office early next evening and piled into the back of Mr Evans' van, to be driven to our destinations. Everyone seemed friendly and happy and I tried to hide my nerves. We were dropped off in pairs and whilst I had hoped I'd be with Beth, I was quite happy to find my partner was a good looking guy with a pale face and reddish blond hair. I'd already noticed him when he'd sat across from me in the van, chatting to a tall girl with a long black pony tail and sparkling blue eyes. However, it felt really awkward as the two of us stood on the cold dark street corner watching the van drive off.

"I am Lars," he said, not smiling or making any effort to shake my hand.

"Um, I'm Nicola," I said nervously.

"I know. It is my job to show you the strings," he said in a strange clipped accent. I stared at him for a moment, my imagination running wild, then burst into laughter.

"You mean show me the ropes, don't you?" He hesitated, blinked, then nodded slightly formally.

"You are correct, I am still improving my English. How good is your German?" I wasn't sure in the dim light whether I saw the flicker of a smile on his face

"Um...I only speak a bit of French. Are you German then?"

"No, I am Swiss. However, that is irrelevant, we must work. You will take that side of the street, I will take this," he said, totally business-like and formal again. "You must remember it is good for them to sign for this, and it is especially good for you as you earn nothing until they sign."

"But what if they already have insurance or something?" I said anxiously. "I'll be working for nothing." Then he did give me a small smile and nodded.

"That is what commission means, Nicola. So you must persuade them the policy you are offering is the best. Just for this first week, if you feel they are too difficult come and get me and I will help convince them." The way he said it sounded almost scary, but that was probably as much to do with his accent as anything. In fact, when I did have to ask for his help, as nerves got the better of me at my very first house, I watched with admiration as he smiled and charmed his way, until the middle-aged couple not only invited us in but offered us tea and biscuits and were almost grateful to sign. Left alone after that, I somehow found the courage to knock on the rest of the doors, and even bluffed my way into a couple more houses, although neither of the occupants agreed to sign for the insurance. So that night I earned a pittance and that only due to Lars' generosity, as he'd secured the signature. However, the pittance was more than I had before so I decided I would stick with it for a while, hoping I would improve my technique. Plus, if I was honest I did have another agenda as, whilst being with Tony felt comfortable and natural, anticipation of future evenings spent with Lars brought a sense of excitement and challenge, the challenge of getting him to turn some of his elusive charm on me.

He didn't actually take any persuading to switch his interest from the dark haired girl to myself, and after a couple of evenings of watching him settle on my side of the van, his knees under his chin and his eyes apparently closed so that I could see the long fair lashes resting on his cheek, she suddenly didn't turn up any more. For those nights I had seen hurt in her blue eyes as she looked at him and me and I felt guilty, although I had done nothing.

"Do you know why she's left?" I asked Beth and she laughed.

"Pretty obvious isn't it? He's moved on and she's hurt, so she's changed her evenings."

"But nothing's happened. He's just friendly to me."

"Oh, Nicola, who are you fooling? She can see the way you look at him, we all can, and she can see how he looks at you. After all, he was looking at her that way until a few days ago!" Her words were confirmed the following evening when, in the darkness of the van, Lars asked what I was doing after we'd finished our rounds that night.

"Why?" I asked, immediately feeling stupid as a girl on my other side sniggered.

"Perhaps we can go for coffee," he said and I found myself agreeing, although after working all day and evening sleep would have been more appropriate.

Our first kiss was that evening, in a dimly lit coffee bar in the basement of an old building, with tall candles and chess sets on the tables and a folk singer balanced on a stool in the corner. Lars did most of the talking, and his clipped accent softened somewhat as he told me of his village home in Switzerland and about coming to London to study business. I just watched the candlelight flickering on his pale skin and soaked up the atmosphere, which was so different to what I'd seen of London so far.

"Do you play?" he asked eventually, moving the chess board closer to me.

"Not really," I replied.

"But you must learn then," he said authoritatively, and for the next half-hour he reeled out the rules and tactics of the game, while I sipped my hot chocolate topped with whipped cream and hoped he wouldn't actually ask me to play this complicated game.

Kirsty was in the lounge when I got back to the hostel just before the doors were locked.

"Have fun?" she asked, surprising me with her sarcastic tone.

"Yes thanks. What's wrong?"

"If you are going to two-time Tony at least you could tell him, not leave me to do your dirty work. He's been moping out there all evening."

"Two-time him? Tony and I are friends Kirsty, we're not dating."

It was true that although we had talked about dating we'd both agreed we'd stay friends for now, rather than risk the friendship with a relationship. He was studying and working part-time in a Wimpy, so now rarely picked me up from work anymore, and we only ever went out as part of the group. I'd told Tony about the new job and, although he'd expressed concerns about me only getting commission, he'd been supportive.

"Are you going to tell him about Lars then?" Kirsty asked, after I'd babbled on for a while about my evening. "Because I'm not going to cover for you." I just laughed.

"Don't be ridiculous, Kirsty, there's nothing to hide. Of course I'll tell him if there turns out to be anything to tell! One hot chocolate and one kiss do not a romance make, you know." One of the other girls giggled and Kirsty struggled to control the beginnings of a smile.

"You had whipped cream as well," she muttered, and we all ended up laughing together.

I was a bit concerned by her remark about Tony moping and was glad I hadn't agreed to work the following evening, so could check out what was going on with him. He turned up with Steve and gave me a big grin as he saw me come out of the hostel with Kirsty.

"You ok?" I asked, settling on the wall next to him. He looked at me sideways and I thought there was a slight hesitation before he said,

"Yep, all groovy. You?"

"Just busy, with this new job and everything. I sort of met this guy that works there, quite nice but strange, bit different to us, plays chess and…" I could hear my voice babbling on mindlessly and I glanced up at Tony to gauge his reaction. He was looking at me with a slightly puzzled expression but as he caught my eye he changed it to a smile.

"Chess, huh? Oh my goodness, strange indeed," he chuckled as he stood up. "You coming for a spin or staying to read up on game strategies?" I laughed as I climbed on the back of his bike, but I knew we were both aware of the underlying question.

"I'll catch up on strategies tomorrow," I shouted as he revved the engine, hoping I'd cleared up any mixed messages. I guessed I had as, although the four of us had a fun evening, when the boys dropped us home Tony didn't reach out for the usual goodbye hug, just patted me on the arm, smiled and said "See you." before driving off.

I had little time to worry about it over the next week, working all day and a few evenings then having my first real dates with Lars on the free evenings. Although I was pretty tired, when I was with Lars I felt I could relax as he took charge of everything and made me feel looked after. Despite being only three years older than me he seemed really grown up and confident. However, I did realise early on that

54

occasionally the confidence was a bit of a bluff. We'd been to see a film and he suggested we go for an Indian meal. I'd only eaten in an Indian restaurant a couple of times so was unfamiliar with the names on the menu, especially with what was vegetarian.

"Don't worry please," said Lars. "I will choose for you." This was reassuring and I felt proud as I watched him discussing our order confidently, even assertively, with the waiter. When the dishes of food arrived on the table he was quite the gentleman, spooning the different foods onto my plate and filling my glass with water from the jug. The food smelt delicious and I started to eat enthusiastically, until suddenly my fork hit something firm and white that had been buried under vegetables. I speared it with my fork and held it up by the candle.

"Oh no, they've put chicken in my food!" I said, holding it out to Lars. He glanced up and stopped chewing for just a moment, then continued calmly.

"It is only a small bit, Nicky. Put it on the side of your plate."

"They should take it back; they've brought the wrong dish," I said, irritated. "Haven't they?" I asked, and he put down his knife and fork.

"I was not aware you would make such a performance about such a little meat," he said, then reached across the table to take my plate and place it next to his. I sat there slightly stunned as he ate both plates of food, stopping only to tell me that I should have explained more clearly what I could eat.

"Or you should have ordered yourself, Nicky. I feel rather hurt that I try to help you and you criticise me." I found myself replaying our conversations, and realised I probably hadn't really been clear how strict a vegetarian I was. I didn't even know if they had vegetarians in Switzerland. When I glanced at his face he looked sad, and I guessed he was disappointed the evening hadn't worked out as he'd planned.

"It's alright," I said, reaching out to squeeze his hand, but before I reached it he was summoning the waiter to get the bill. He walked slightly ahead of me as we made our way back to the hostel and I was quite relieved when he turned and put his arms around me as we got to the gate.

"I am sorry, Nicola," he said quite formally. "I have disappointed you."

"No, Lars, you haven't. I'm sorry I hadn't explained clearly. Thank you for a lovely evening," I added after he kissed me goodnight. As I lay in bed later, my stomach rumbling slightly, I pictured the beautiful smile on his face as I'd left him and felt relieved and happy that we'd got through the awkwardness of the dinner.

He was no longer partnering me at the job and, although we sat together in the van, Lars said it was better others weren't aware that we were a couple. The first time it felt strange as he ignored me and spoke with others, but then it started to feel quite exciting, that we had this secret life most of the others didn't know about. When he spoke to new girls and they flirted with him I got a warm fuzzy feeling, knowing that later I would be the one he'd be cuddling and kissing.

So it was really tough when one evening after our round Mr Evans took me back to the office.

"I'm sorry, young lady, it's just not working out is it?" he said, as he rummaged in a folder on his desk.

"I'm still getting the hang of it," I said "At least you don't have to pay me anything while I learn," I added with a laugh.

"That's true," he said, ruffling through papers and picking one out, "but you're taking up space that someone else could use. Someone who can actually sell insurance," he added, handing me the sheet of paper.

"I sold a few policies," I said quickly, but he shook his head and pulled a pound note out of his pocket.

"You're not making money for me or yourself, Nicola. Time to call it a day I'm afraid," he said, handing me the money. I couldn't really argue as I glanced down at the paper with the list of hours I'd worked and put the measly pound note in my pocket.

Lars was waiting outside for me and didn't seem that surprised, probably because he knew how badly I was doing.

"I'll miss you, little Nicky," he whispered as we stood embracing. "Make sure you think about your poor Lars travelling around alone those evenings, then we'll have to make up for it on the other evenings." I thought this was romantic, but when I told Anne later she just sniggered.

"So you're supposed to spend your time thinking about him flirting with the other girls?"

"Oh, Anne, you are such a cynic. That wasn't what he meant at all," I said quickly. However, once the idea was in my head it was hard to get it out, especially when I remembered the dark haired girl he'd sat with before, and how he'd asked me out just after she left our round.

I spent the next couple of evenings with Kirsty, Tony and the others, distracting myself with the continuous banter, and when Lars unexpectedly met me from work the following day I felt reassured. We went for a walk on Hampstead Heath and after a while he pulled a rug out of his rucksack and spread it on the slightly damp grass. We settled down on it, interrupting our chatting with frequent kisses, and I was struck by his intensity as we cuddled.

"Wow, you have missed me," I whispered into his shoulder.

"Of course," he said, stroking my hair. "Have you missed me?"

"Oh yes," I mumbled and reached up to kiss him, but he pulled back.

"So what did you do while I worked?"

"Nothing special," I said and started to tell him about the pub we'd gone to the night before and how the locals had been quite hostile, because of the leather jackets. Lars sat up, leaning over me slightly, and I saw the glow of the setting sun highlighting the red tints in his hair.

"Of course," he said sharply. "They choose to rebel against society, it is their choice."

"It's just clothes, Lars," I said, feeling uncomfortable with his tone of voice. "They are good people; they shouldn't be judged like that."

"If that's how they choose to appear, that is what will happen, Nicola. If you choose to spend your time with them then you will be judged too." He had stood up as he was speaking and I did the same, shaking the damp off the rug and wishing I hadn't mentioned the evening with the bikers. He was really quiet as we walked down to the road.

"Have I upset you, Lars?" I asked, and he looked down at me with the expression I was starting to think of as his sulky boy face.

"I was just reflecting that while I worked I thought of you, all alone, and missed you. Now I find you didn't think of me at all, you were out having fun." I reached for his hand and squeezed it.

"Oh, Lars, it was because I missed you that I went out. They were just a distraction," I heard myself add, and immediately felt guilty that I'd somehow betrayed Kirsty, Tony and the others. Then I saw Lars' smile appear and decided it was worth it as they'd never know anyway.

"But I like the idea of you missing me, beautiful girl," he said softly, putting his arm around me. "Next time, try not distracting yourself. It could feel good just to want me." He squeezed me tight and I found myself laughingly agreeing.

So the next evening that he was working I turned down the offer of a meal with Laura and Kwesi and settled on my bed with a library book, hoping that didn't really count as distraction. I thought Laura was trying to talk me round when, about an hour later, one of the girls called me to the telephone, but she said it was someone ringing from a callbox.

"Hello, Nicky, how are you?" It was Lars, almost laughing down the phone.

"All the better for hearing you," I responded almost automatically. "What has happened? Why aren't you working?"

"I am, but I was passing a telephone box so I just thought I'd call and see if you are missing me," he said.

"Of course," I replied and heard another chuckle from him.

"That's my good girl," he said and then the money ran out and the line went dead. I was laughing to myself as I went into the lounge, but when I repeated the conversation to Mary and Kirsty they weren't impressed.

"He was checking you hadn't gone out, I bet," said Mary and Kirsty nodded, patting the seat beside her on the sofa.

"Come and sit here and forget about him for a while, good girl," she said, almost spitting out the last two words.

"I think you two are just jealous," I said lightly as I sat down.

"Oh yes, that's it of course," Kirsty agreed, putting her legs across my lap to rest her feet on the arm of the sofa. "Nothing to do with you being taken over by a control freak." I laughed and hit her lightly with a cushion, but her words made me uncomfortable and shortly after I headed back to the dormitory and an early night.

Although it was good for my energy levels to have a few nights in, it didn't do anything to tackle the money problems that the insurance job was supposed to have solved. I racked my brains to think what I could do that would fit around my day job. I wondered briefly if I could get a Saturday job in Woolworths as I had during my last year at school. I'd enjoyed the special atmosphere and smell of arriving early before the store opened, and setting out the plants that I was responsible for, trying to remember their names for customer queries but usually resorting to reading the label. After the store closed

59

and we'd cashed up the tills I had to water the plants so they wouldn't die overnight, being careful not to overwater so the paper I wrapped them in for the customers didn't leak before they reached home. I mentioned the idea to a couple of girls in the dormitory, but they said they thought only school kids got the Saturday jobs. I was going to check anyway, but when I told Lars he said we might as well finish our relationship, because we'd never see each other. When I thought about it he was right really, as between my job and his college and evening work there was very little time to see each other, and weekends were pretty precious.

"If you need a job find one when I am working," he said and I promised I'd try.

I then remembered that just after my fifteenth birthday I'd enjoyed some weeks working as an usherette in our local cinema, having convinced the manager that I was old enough and would bring my National Insurance card in shortly. Again it was a place of atmosphere and smells and muted sounds, broken by visits to the freezer room. There I would fill my tray with a selection of ice-cream and lollies, and fix it round my neck in time to walk down the aisle and position myself in front of the screen as the interval started. Usually I could watch the B movie, apart from interruptions when I had to shine my little torch to direct latecomers to empty seats, and I would mime along to the voices in the film that I saw so many times. Yet I always missed the end when it was time to stock the tray, as the ices would have melted in the stuffy atmosphere if I'd filled it earlier. One time I didn't get to fill the tray at all, because the support feature was an unbelievably graphic documentary about hair transplants. As we watched sections being cut out of the back of a giant scalp on the screen, to be repositioned in the bald area at the front, people started fainting and vomiting and rushing to leave the cinema. I thought people wouldn't come again or the film would be taken off, but the cinema continued to fill up and the response from the audience was equally dramatic. My services were needed throughout that film, but generally once everyone was seated for the main film I could put my feet up in a small back room. There I would listen carefully for the sounds that would tell me the film was about to end and I needed to prop the door open and supervise the audience leaving, before cleaning up. While I sat back there I was knitting myself a jumper with beautiful peach-coloured wool and a fancy border at the bottom and cuffs. I was pretty proud of it and even Mr Skelly, the manager, admired it each time he popped in to nag me about bringing in my insurance number. I got away with it for quite a while, but when I was leaving one evening he stopped me to say that he was going to ring the tax office to chase up the number. I was faced with a choice then; either admit I was fibbing and was too young for a number or just leave. Lying in bed that night feeling sick with anxiety and guilt I decided on the latter, only realising much later that my beautiful jumper was lost to me forever, rolled up in its Jaeger bag in that little back room.

I went to a couple of London cinemas to see if I could get a job there, but one was fully staffed and the other only wanted someone who'd work five evenings a week. I almost applied but then realised Lars would be furious if I didn't have any evenings for him. I was pretty fed up when I got back to the hostel, hoping the couple of girls I owed money to wouldn't be around, as I was running out of excuses. I guessed I was going to have to revert to the lifestyle of my first months in the hostel, getting by on next to nothing, in order to clear my debts. I just hoped if I kept evenings free for Lars he'd at least feed me occasionally, preferably with something he didn't have to eat for me.

7

The prospect of my first Christmas alone in London was quite daunting. Everyone at work seemed to have family plans and most of the girls in the hostel were going to friends for the big day, or even for a few days. Lars was going back to Switzerland for the break, and although Tony made vague noises about me coming to his parents for the meal, I knew they had a very large extended family and didn't need extra people in their little council flat. Initially my aunt had suggested I come there for the day, but then she decided to go to an elderly friend in Cornwall.

"Obviously it'd be a bit awkward to take you along, Nicky. I do hope you understand."

"Of course I do, don't worry about me, aunty. I have lots of new friends in London now."

"You wouldn't consider going to your mother's?"

"Probably not. Not this year." I'd sent mummy a Christmas card and a small Wedgewood vase that had cost nearly a week's wages, hoping these would reassure her I still loved her. However, I didn't yet feel strong enough in my own identity to see her without getting caught up again in her craziness. Kirsty asked the same thing, feeling guilty that she and Anne were going to her parents from Christmas Eve until New Year. She'd explained that they'd already be crowded in her old room and I didn't blame her, knowing it had all been arranged before I turned up.

"I'll be fine," I reassured her. "It'll be good to have a peaceful one. I had enough Christmas dramas when I was at home." I was trying to make her feel better, but partly it was also true that Christmas at home had been pretty intense. On Christmas Eve my father would go to the pub while mummy would stay up late wrapping presents, filling the stocking and cleaning the house in the hope that all would be perfect on the big day. Then, late at night, I would be woken by the sound of him stumbling through the door, greeting her with some badly sung carol, and her responding with anger. Although she would shush him she was actually louder, and I sort of liked to hear his singing which was definitely preferable to the nasty argument that would follow, before the house fell silent and I finally drifted off to sleep. This meant that on Christmas morning we were all overtired, and everyone acted strangely to try and avoid triggering Christmas Day conflict. Although the night before I had felt angry with my father for getting drunk and upsetting mummy, the following morning I would feel sad for him as, apparently filled with remorse, his shoulders slumped as he silently prepared all the vegetables at the sink. When mummy would grumpily check he had cut the crosses in the bottom of the sprouts I would pray he hadn't missed any, for her to slam onto the chopping board in front of him.

I had actually decided to solve two problems at the same time and, after a nerve-wracking interview on the fifth floor of an imposing office building near Victoria station, had got myself a Christmas job at a seaside holiday camp. It was a bit unclear what it actually involved, as they said with it being a small camp we'd all have to pull our weight. Still, at least I knew I'd be with others in a happy Christmas environment and would start the New Year with a bit of spare money for a change. It seemed slightly scary that I wouldn't know anyone, but it also seemed I'd spent much of my life encountering strangers in new situations, and alongside the fear was an excitement at anticipation of the unknown.

I'd booked a couple of days of my annual holiday at the insurance company in order to start the camp job on time, but it still meant I'd have to travel right after work. So my borrowed case was packed early in the morning and wedged under my desk. My wash bag and all my precious make-up items were stuffed into the large handbag I'd borrowed from Anne, along with a magazine and a big bag of mint imperials for the journey. The day passed quickly with all the pre-Christmas chatter and girls from the other offices appearing with silly Santa hats and plates of mince pies. Finally, it was time to collect my wage packet, bulging slightly more than usual due to holiday pay, from the cash office and say my farewells. The bus to Paddington seemed to take forever and the queue at the ticket office was so slow I thought I was going to miss my train, but all was achieved with ten minutes to spare and I finally felt I could relax. Then I realised I had forgotten to ring my aunt as promised. I looked around frantically for a phone box and saw one across the concourse. Aunty was pleased to hear all had gone to plan and was full of advice about how to keep myself safe. It seemed rather funny that she felt I needed to protect myself in a small holiday camp, considering I was already living on my own in a city. I had just decided to point this out to her when I heard the loudspeaker announcing that my train was about to depart.

"Got to go, aunty, happy Christmas," I shouted, grabbing my case and rushing through the open barriers to board the train, just as the whistle blew.

I was laughing and breathless as I jumped onto the train, slamming the door behind me and squeezing into the only empty seat in the first carriage. I smiled gratefully at the middle-aged man in a tweed coat, who raised his eyebrow questioningly then lifted my case onto the luggage rack before sitting back down next to me. Once the train settled into its soothing rhythm I took off my jacket and folded it on my knee. This last week had been hectic at work and pretty busy socially, juggling my time between different friends, and I guessed my week at the holiday camp would be pretty busy too. This journey might well be my one chance to relax. So I didn't need the stress of the rather grubby looking man opposite, who clutched an open book but didn't turn any pages and instead seemed mesmerised by my legs in their white tights and black and white checked mini skirt.

Still, he seemed harmless, so I gave him a small smile as I tucked the jacket protectively around my knees and reached for the magazine in my handbag. Except there was no handbag! Trying not to panic, I felt between me and my neighbours, evoking another questioning glance from tweed coat man, then bent over to check on the floor. My last hope was the luggage rack but the bag was bright pink and I could easily see through the netting that it wasn't up there. Suddenly my stomach lurched as I had a vision of the bag sitting on the metal shelf by the coin slot in the telephone box, and I realised I had left it there when I made my mad dash for the train. All my money and my hard earned make-up were in that bag along with the pricey magazine. And my wash bag. And my mint imperials. Then dawned the worst realisation; that my train ticket was also in the bag, on Mary's instructions safely zipped into the side pocket so that I wouldn't lose it. Any time now the guard could appear to check our tickets, and I guessed the least that would happen was that I'd be turned off the train at the next stop. The worst? I didn't know, but dramatic visions of me spending a cold and lonely Christmas in a police cell didn't seem impossible. I suddenly felt really sick.

"Can you save my seat please?" I asked tweed coat man, surprised at how calm my voice sounded, then carefully climbed over all the feet to reach the corridor and look for the toilets. Before I found them I came to the guard's van with its caged luggage area, empty apart from two bicycles and a large brown parcel tied up with string and covered with labels of various colours. I saw the plump, balding guard sitting in the far corner reading a newspaper. He glanced up as I paused by the entrance.

"Everything alright, miss?" he asked with a smile and, although I wanted to hurry past, the effect of his gentle voice and kind fatherly face was to bring me to tears. He jumped up and took my arm.

"What has happened, girl?" he asked, looking back down the corridor I'd just come along.

"Nothing," I spluttered, my eyes stinging painfully from the mixture of tears and mascara.

"Goodness me," he muttered, guiding me over to the chair and producing a white handkerchief, with the embroidered initials JS on the corner. "Wipe your eyes, girl. Underneath too, you look like a ruddy panda," he added, picking up a large grey bag in the corner and producing a shiny vacuum flask. He unscrewed the two cups from the top of it and balanced them next to him, as he sat down on the large brown parcel. "Now, have a brew and calm down, missy, then tell Jerry what's up and I'll see what I can do." Jerry proved to have a very calming effect and I gradually came to realise none of this was the end of the world, especially when he told me that because he believed I had bought a ticket he wasn't going to report me. "You're going to the end of the line anyway, so just wait by the barrier until I've closed all the train doors then I'll come and explain to the ticket collector there. Probably be Steve, very reasonable fellow. Could be you've avoided prison on this occasion," Jerry said laughingly. I laughed too, not minding that he was making fun of me and all the fears I'd poured out to him. "Well, I haven't got any make-up to sort out those eyes," he added, "but you can have the paper to read. I've got to do my rounds now, so off you go before you lose your suitcase too. I'll see you by the ticket barrier later." So I returned to the carriage somewhat calmer and, after a quick glance through the paper, I dozed for the rest of the journey.

It was drizzling and already dark when we finally pulled into our station, and it seemed to take forever for all the passengers to leave the train and Jerry to make his way along, slamming the doors as he passed.

"Hello, Steve," he called loudly as he approached the barrier, and the young ticket collector raised his arm in greeting. "This one's alright, Steve," said Jerry, taking me by the arm and lifting my case through the barrier. "Saw her ticket before she lost it."

"Oh yeah," said Steve with a grin, "touched your soft spot did she?"

"Cheeky bugger," said Jerry, guiding me through. "Right, love, how you going to get to the holiday camp?"

"Um, they said there's a bus out in front of the station. I've forgotten the number but I can check on the board."

"Forgotten something else too it seems. These country buses are pricey and you don't have any money, do you?" I hadn't thought of that. "I could give you the fare I suppose," he said before I could answer. "Or, better still on a rainy night like this, why don't I just drive you? I've got the car in the car park and I go that way anyway." I couldn't believe how kind he was and looking at the cold dark puddles outside the station I was really grateful.

The car park was at the back of the station and there were only a couple of cars in it. We dashed through the rain to his blue Ford Escort, him carrying my case which he put in the boot, while I thankfully climbed into the passenger seat. He switched on the overhead light as he settled behind the wheel, then leaned over towards me. Assuming he was reaching for the dashboard, I sat right back in the seat and was horrified as his plump face closed in on mine.

"What are you doing?" I squeaked nervously, as I felt squidgy damp lips on my cheek.

"Just a quick cuddle, girlie, you can't begrudge an old man that when he's done you a favour," he mumbled. I turned my face away sharply and was horrified to feel his wet tongue licking my ear, at the same time as his pudgy hand squeezed the top of my thigh. I grabbed his arm with both hands to push it away from me, feeling his watch scratch my knee as he pulled it back. Then suddenly his hands were gripping the tops of my arms and pressing me back in the car seat. As he pulled his head back I saw an expression that almost seemed like hatred in his eyes, and for a moment my body felt paralysed as we stared at each other. Then I remembered one of mummy's nutty days when she had slapped my face calmly and repeatedly until I managed not to cry or flinch, explaining that it was for my sake because you were a victim if you showed fear so, whatever happened, you must appear to be in control. As this memory came I felt strengthened, not so much from her weird tuition but from the anger that bubbled up inside me.

"Stop it, Jerry," I said as firmly and loudly as I could through my fear, shocked to hear the authority in my voice. Amazingly he did stop, shifting back into his seat and wiping the back of his hand across his drooling mouth. I pulled my mini skirt back down and reached for the door handle.

"Don't get yourself in a state, girl, I can't even get a hard one anymore," he said, his hand on my arm. I shook it off. "You can't blame me for wanting to cop a feel can you? That skirt almost invites it."

"It is not my fault," I heard myself say, almost petulantly, as I finally managed to open the door. "I was stupid to get in your car, but you're the dirty old man." He actually looked guilty as he came around the car in the rain and opened the boot.

"I could still drive you," he said. I gave him what I hoped was a withering look and lifted my case out. "I'm sorry, love," he said in a really quiet voice, grabbing my hand as I strode off, and somehow forcing a half crown into the clenched fist. I wanted to throw it back at him, but in reality knew I needed the bus fare so amazed myself by thanking him for it as I hurried off through the station.

Sitting on the bus as it drove through dark country roads, I reflected on it all and felt stupid and ashamed. I could hear my mother's voice asking why I didn't think before I acted. If I'd been more thoughtful I wouldn't have left my bag in the telephone box and set the whole situation in motion. Having done so, I could at least have realised it would be pretty stupid

68

to get into a strange man's car in a dark deserted car park. "Idiot!" I heard myself mutter and quickly glanced up to see if anyone had heard me, but no-one seemed to have noticed. I guessed I was too trusting, but Jerry had been really kind when I was upset and had helped me as far as the ticket. I suddenly recalled Steve's comment about "She's touched your soft spot," and felt sick, wondering if Jerry had done this before and Steve knew what was going to happen. Perhaps I should report him when I came back to the station next week. I wondered if they would believe me and decided they probably wouldn't, not against someone who said he'd worked for them all his life. I also realised there was a part of me that didn't really want to report him, especially as I'd managed to stop him before he really did anything, that I actually felt sorry for the pathetic old man that he was. I guessed it was hard for me to reconcile the kindly father figure with some nasty abuser, and reducing him to a pathetic loser was the best way I could deal with that contradiction right then.

Once I arrived at the camp there was little time to reflect further on any of it. Along with another new girl called Helen, who turned out to be almost fluent in cockney rhyming slang, I was shown to a tiny prefab cabin in a row of identical cabins. Despite its smallness we were to discover that the one bar heater on the wall seemed to have no effect on the temperature of the room, which remained constantly cold, and the water heater over the sink in the corner ran out after a couple of washes. So we had to rinse both our hair and our underwear in cold water and drape bras, pants and tights over any available support in the hope that they might dry. The hair was even more challenging, as we would rub it wildly with towels then balance precariously on the foot rail of my bed to get our heads as close to the heater as possible, laughing almost hysterically as we crashed yet again to the floor.

That first evening, once we'd unpacked and stored our clothes in the boxes under the grey metal beds, it was the blind leading the blind as we made our way through the darkness, trying to avoid the muddy puddles as we headed for the brightly lit cafeteria. Once there we each handed over one of the tokens we'd been given on arrival, and filled ourselves up on stodgy mashed potato and overcooked vegetables. In my case this was topped off with a fried egg, and in Helen's with what she assured me was a very tasty pork chop. We were told we could have as many helpings as we wanted but one was more than enough, and we struggled to manage a portion of jam roly poly and custard that reminded me of primary school. While we ate I laughingly told Helen about losing my handbag, although not about the Jerry incident, and she was really sweet, quickly reassuring me that I could share her toiletries and make-up if I couldn't get an advance on my camp wages. It was embarrassing to be back where I'd started when I arrived at the hostel, but at least now I had my case of clothes and didn't have to steal toothpaste in the early hours!

After the meal we braved the rain again, searching for the staff offices as instructed. We passed wet shadowy figures we knew must be staff, because the campers wouldn't arrive until the next morning, but we were too shy to ask for directions. Finally we found it, tucked away behind all the public buildings, and we were shown into a large room where we were each issued with two uniforms and an overall. It was explained to us how one combination, which included a blazer, was for our daytime activities which would vary between serving food, directing campers or involving them and their children in various activities.

"Quizzes, sing-songs, knobbly knees, all the usual," said our instructor brightly. When she said the overall was for our cleaning chores I prayed I'd be assigned to those, as I felt far too shy for the activities. She went on to explain that the other outfit, a dress with pleated skirt, frilly neckline and short sleeves was for the evening. It was then I discovered with horror that we were expected to 'circulate' in the main ballroom, making sure the campers had drinks at all times and encouraging them to get up and dance.

"You'll be like the hostess at a party," she said. "It's up to you to make them feel really welcome and get them up on their feet, even if you have to dance with them. We want people to come back, and remembering a dance with a pretty girl is certainly encouragement for the old blokes, even if their wives did cut in and dance themselves to stop any hanky-panky!" She laughed as she said this, but the Jerry incident was too raw for me to laugh with her. I was also reminded of my Court School of Dancing days and the thought of all the bruised toes I'd probably caused put me in a mild panic. I just prayed my campers would turn out to be full of confidence.

Which they were, generally. Most evenings the reality of our role was standing around smiling, indicating towards the clearly marked toilet doors with a gracious hand gesture and collecting endless trays of drinks from the bar. Having started our day in the icy cold darkness before the campers were woken by the loud speakers, and having moved almost seamlessly all day between cleaning the bars, calming and reuniting lost children, reading out quizzes and treasure hunt clues and marching around camp followed by motley children all singing out of tune, I had little energy by evening. Yet when collecting the drinks, I did find the energy to laugh and joke with the gorgeous blond barman, who was called Bob and lived not far from me in London. I was probably sustained by the tiny shots of various spirits he would slide across the bar when nobody was looking, and certainly as the evening progressed everything took on a much rosier glow. Helen was very keen on him too, but although he slipped her drinks as well he made it clear that I was the one he was interested in. Finally, as the camp closed down for the night, music would blare out, campers would depart to chalets and we would clean up the mess they had created.

Then, despite our exhaustion, the three of us and a chef called Colin would all go back to our tiny chalet, Helen rushing ahead to hide all the damp underwear under the mattress. There we would spend most of the night chattering inanely, playing cards and filling our tooth mugs with smuggled cider which we mixed with orange juice. Colin shared Helen's mug and Bob shared mine. The boys would creep out in the early hours, often to bangs on the wall from neighbours awoken by their giggling and stage whispers, and Helen and I would drop off into romantic dreams before her alarm woke us a few hours later. Although we were only there a week, I felt by the end of it that I'd known Bob for years and when he said he was driving back to London I accepted his offer of a lift gratefully. It was a wonderful excuse not only to spend more time with him, but also to avoid the train and the possibility of encountering Jerry again.

It was almost eleven o'clock when we finally reached the hostel, both happy but exhausted. Suddenly it felt as if we were strangers who had just met.

"Well, um, thanks for the lift," I said self-consciously as Bob put my case on the pavement. He was equally awkward, smiling rather dopily.

"Do you have a telephone number? I could ring you. Only if you wanted," he added before I could answer, and as I gave him the number at the hostel I wondered where the confident, almost brash, young bartender had gone. Stuffing the scribbled number in his jacket pocket he gave me a quick peck on the cheek and, almost before it registered, I saw his car disappearing into the distance. As I sleepily dragged my case up to the dormitory I wondered if the kiss meant he saw us as more than the chums we'd been at the camp and, if so, how that would add to the already muddled situation with Tony and Lars.

It was really lively at work the next morning, people rushing from room to room to exchange Christmas stories and

New Year wishes. I told the girls in our office about the camp but only mentioned Bob in passing, knowing they already thought I was mean to Tony by seeing Lars. I was just going to tell them about the lost bag when Peter arrived from the post room, carrying a bundle of letters and a parcel.

"Looks like a late Christmas pressie for you, Nicky," he said, putting the parcel on my desk. I briefly felt a surge of hope that mummy had sent me something, but immediately realised she didn't know where I worked.

"Come on, open it," a couple of girls chanted, bringing a sharp "Shush" from our manager. I ripped off the paper impatiently and inside found the lost handbag!

"You dropped this," said the girl at the next desk, passing me an envelope she had picked up from the floor. Inside was a letter telling me that the writer had found the bag in the station telephone box, just as they were about to board their train for Scotland. 'So I took it with me as I couldn't think what else to do. Luckily the address of your company was on the payslip so I am able to get it back to you. You will find everything is still intact except I have to confess it was a long journey and I ate your mint imperials. Sorry. Happy New Year'.

I found myself almost in tears at the goodness of this person, as I explained it all to the girls. I wished I could thank them but there was no address and only a scribbled and indecipherable signature. This is a sign I thought, as I settled down to my work. A sign that people like Jerry and all the other bad stuff belong to last year, and that now it really would be a happy new year, filled with good people and good experiences.

8

That evening one of the girls at the hostel called me to take a phone call from Laura, whose voice sounded flat and distant.

"Did you hear?" she asked, almost coldly. Laura and I had become close friends as I loved spending time with her and Kwesi, but I hadn't had time to speak to her since before I left for the holiday camp.

"Hear what?" I asked nervously.

"Kwesi's in hospital. He's bad, Nicky, really bad," she said, and I could hear that the barrier had come down and she was trying to hold back tears.

"Where are you?"

"The flat. I've just got home."

"I'm on my way over, Laura. It'll be ok." I ran up to the dormitory and stuffed a few extra necessities like pants into my borrowed handbag, still full of make-up and things from its Scottish adventure, then hurried down to the front door. Sister Josephine was just coming in as I reached it.

"Off out as usual?" she asked disapprovingly.

"I'm going to see a sick friend, Sister. I might be late or even need to stay the night." I thought I heard an apology as I hurried off but might have imagined that; one habit the nuns were not in was that of apologising. Sitting on the bus I reflected on my earlier idea that this was going to be a year of good experiences.

"Talk about tempting fate," I thought wryly. I found myself remembering a joke someone had once told me;

'How do you make God laugh? Tell him your plans.'

Laura looked totally exhausted as she let me into the flat and broke down in tears as I hugged her.

"What happened, Laura?" I asked as I made us hot chocolate and settled down beside her on the sofa in the muggy room full of snakes.

"He was chased and beaten, Nicky. He was beaten so hard they said he was unconscious when the ambulance got to him. He still is," she added, looking at me with a stunned wide-eyed expression.

"Oh my god, Laura. Where, who did it, why?" I babbled.

"Because of me," she shrieked. "Because I'm white and he's black. Because we love each other. Because he kissed me." Gradually she managed to tell me what she knew. When she'd finished her work the night before New Year's Eve she decided to surprise Kwesi where he was performing at a small venue in Soho. When she arrived he was standing at the bar, while a heavily made-up and exotically dressed woman was dancing on the small stage. He had smiled in pleasure at seeing Laura, then explained that his spot was delayed so he hadn't performed yet.

"I'll wait for you then." Laura had said, settling on a bar stool, but Kwesi shook his head.

"No, I'm not sure how late I'll be and you look really tired, my sweet. It's a lively crowd tonight too, not nice for you." Laura said it was true that there was quite a rowdy group of young blokes, who'd obviously had enough to drink and were trying to impress their girls with lewd gestures and remarks to the dancer. "Ask the doorman for a taxi to take you safely home, Laura, and I'll see you soon," Kwesi had said with a smile. She reluctantly agreed, and reached over to give him a hug and kiss which brought whistles and loud jeers from the noisy table.

"It was my fault, Nicky. They saw me kiss him and they waited for him outside when the club closed. The doorman said they made racist remarks about him and me as he left, and called him a pervert. Kwesi of all people! He should have got a cab too. The doorman offered to call one for him but Kwesi said he'd be fine and went off down the road. They followed him and…" She broke down in tears again, before explaining how she'd been at the hospital ever since the police called her.

"I should be there now but I felt so alone. He's not aware of anything Nicky, doesn't know if I'm there, doesn't even know yet that they took the bag with Paulie!"

"Oh goodness, I'm so sorry, Laura. I'll come back to the hospital with you. But if he's unconscious perhaps you should get a few hours of sleep first? You look shattered. I'll stay with you. They've got your telephone number haven't they?" She nodded tiredly and although she wouldn't get into the bed, because it made her miss Kwesi more, she did snuggle down under a blanket on the sofa while I curled up in an armchair. I dozed lightly, fearful I wouldn't hear the phone if it rang.

It did ring, early the following morning, when we were already up, giving the snakes fresh water and spraying the tanks before heading off to the hospital. Laura was white-faced as she lifted the receiver, then started giggling slightly hysterically.

"I'm on my way," she said, replacing the receiver and rushing over to hug me. "He's awake, Nicky, he's awake! Let's go!"

Kwesi tried to smile as he saw us approaching his bed, but his lips and one cheek were really swollen and it came out more as a twisted grimace. He was lying flat in the bed, with his left shoulder and arm in a sling type bandage that held the arm on his chest. A frame over his legs kept the bedding off them. Laura leaned over and kissed him on the forehead then stayed close, gently stroking his head and whispering into his ear. I saw a twinge of pain cross his face as he slowly lifted his right arm to touch her face, his eyes closing momentarily. I felt like an intruder on a very intimate moment so I went quietly out to the corridor, horrified by the sight of Kwesi but not wanting to show it. Laura came to get me just as I finished telephoning work to let them know I wouldn't be in. Back on the ward I held Kwesi's 'good' hand for a moment, then babbled what sounded like really trite words. Luckily Laura was dealing with the situation much better, giving him

76

reassurance that it would be ok, that it would take a while but he'd be fine.

"He said I'd never dance again," Kwesi mumbled out of his swollen mouth and a flash of anger crossed Laura's face.

"Who, the doctor?"

"No, the young man, the blond one. He was laughing," he added, his eyes squeezing closed again momentarily. When the doctor came on his rounds a little later Laura took him aside, to mention this memory of Kwesi's. She told me afterwards that the doctor was reassuring, explaining that, as hard as it might be, the fact that Kwesi had some recollection of the trauma indicated that there was probably no damage to his brain, and he should make a full recovery in time.

"But we mustn't push him to remember before he's ready. They said the police will ask him some questions later and they will get someone from the psychiatric team to talk to him. He said it could take quite a while for Kwesi to get over this."

Kwesi needed his rest so the nurse suggested we go home and come back in the evening. Back at the flat Laura seemed a lot more positive. After checking the snakes again, pausing sadly at Paulie's empty tank, she took a long bath, washed her hair and changed into clean clothes. I made us sandwiches and big mugs of tea, and we sat at the kitchen table making small talk. Suddenly Laura leaned across the table and grabbed my hand. I glanced up at her face, its calmness belying the panic in her grasp.

"Nicky, I need your help."

"Of course, Laura, anything I can do to help I will."

"Firstly I need you to promise me that you can keep a secret, even from Kwesi. A big secret." I couldn't imagine her having secrets from him, they were so close, but I agreed anyway.

"Kwesi and I had special plans for New Year's Eve," she said. "We agreed neither of us would work this year, and we were going to spend the evening together, cooking a special meal together and just enjoying each other's company." Her voice faltered as she added "Of course it didn't happen, because he was in hospital." I started to express sympathy but she said matter-of-factly "No, it's not that, Nicky. I had a surprise to share with him at midnight." She paused. "I was going to tell him I am pregnant."

"Oh, Laura, congratulations!" I was shocked but also really happy for them. "So you haven't told him yet? Wow, I'm sure that will raise his spirits. The two of you will make wonderful parents." Laura got up from the table and walked to the window, staring out.

"Yes, we will," she said calmly, "one day." The silence seemed to last an eternity as I struggled for meaning in her words. She turned to face me. "It will take months for Kwesi to heal, Nicky, and in that time he will need me to look after him. To say nothing of our extended family," she said, waving an arm towards the living room and its three tanks. I started to babble about helping, but she cut across me. "Even once the bones in his legs mend he probably won't be dancing for a long while, perhaps never. So I need to support us both, and the snakes, and I can't see me prancing around in my belly dancing costume at six months pregnant, can you?" She was right of course.

"There are other jobs, Laura." She laughed softly.

"Not that I can do, or that we can all live on. Those tips are my lifeline, not the wages. Anyway, no-one will employ a pregnant woman. As I waited for a special time to tell Kwesi I'm over two months gone already. I'll be showing soon."

"So what happens now?" I asked, almost in a whisper.

"That's where I need your help, Nicky. I've got an appointment to see a psychiatrist tomorrow. I need to convince him I'll go bonkers if I have a baby. If he agrees I've got to see another one, then I can have an abortion. When that happens I'll need someone to be there with me, to make me strong."

"Oh, Laura, this is terrible. What if they don't agree?"

"They must, Nicky. If I have to I'll even play on their prejudices, tell them the father's black. That should do it," she said coldly.

"And if not?"

"Then I'll be paying through the nose to some back street doctor. Either way I'll need your support, Nicky."

Of course I tried to suggest alternatives to her, as did the second psychiatrist who she saw at the hospital we went to in South London a few days later. He was much tougher on her than the first had been, but eventually he agreed. I never asked if she'd had to use Kwesi's colour to persuade him, knowing that would have made her pain even greater. I was relieved, although I still wished I could change her mind. Yet, as wrong as it seemed, the reality was that Kwesi had no family and Laura's were over in Canada, so they were very alone with this. I could see how painful the decision was for her, but also that in a way there was no decision, her love for Kwesi overriding everything else. I suggested she talk to him but she shook her head vigorously.

"This is too much for him right now, Nicky. It wouldn't be fair. I will look after him and support him through this, and when he is really strong again we can go to Vancouver and get married, like we always intended to one day. Then we can have our little urchins," she added with a gentle smile.

A few days later I yet again called into work sick and together we went back to the hospital where, after tedious paperwork, Laura was taken to a cubicle to remove her clothing. She looked very young and scared when she emerged dressed in a pale green hospital gown that barely tied behind her, stretching as it was over the really slight curve of her tummy. I was filled with sadness and, as she smiled weakly at me, I couldn't stop myself from asking

"Are you really sure, Laura?"

"Yes, absolutely," she said, blinking rapidly. We followed the nurse into a nearby room with four beds in a row, women of various ages already in all but one of them. The nurse helped Laura into the empty bed.

"You'll be having a small injection shortly," she said, "and then soon after that you'll be taken through to theatre. It'll all be over before you know it," she added brightly. She turned to me. "If you wait out there, dear, we'll let you know when she's ready to leave." I was stunned by how matter of fact it all seemed, and tried to distract myself with the out-of-date magazines in the waiting room. Nearly an hour later the nurse appeared and beckoned for me to come through.

"Is it over?" I whispered in the doorway and she shook her head.

"No, I'm afraid not. We've tried to take her through twice but she starts crying hysterically. Mr Martin says he can't operate while she's like that. Apart from anything else, her pulse is racing. I think you need to check if this is really what she wants dear." I was horrified to indeed see Laura sobbing in her bed.

"Come on, Laura, let's go home. You can't put yourself through this."

"No, Nicky," she said firmly though the tears. "I have to do this and you have to help me."

"How can I?"

"I don't know, but I do know this is right, Nicky. If I can just not think about what's happening, then I can get in there. I need you to distract me…anything!" I sat holding her hand for a moment and she stopped crying. There was desperation in the silence as we sat there, both feeling helpless.

"I know," she said suddenly. "What was that long poem, the one you told me you recited in that talent competition?" My mind went blank for a moment, then I remembered telling her how at school we were expected to perform in the end of year show. I was scared silly, knowing I couldn't sing or play

80

an instrument, so in the end I persuaded another girl to dress up as a small boy and sit at my feet on stage while I recited Rudyard Kipling's poem 'If'.

"Nurse, how long before I go in again?" asked Laura.

"About ten minutes, love, but if you're in a state again…"

"No, I'll be alright this time, if Nicky can wait with me," Laura reassured her. "Just don't keep me waiting much longer than that, please." When the nurse nodded and walked away Laura turned back to me. "That poem was really calm, Nicky, about being strong and doing the right thing, keeping your head when others are losing theirs. If you recite it and I repeat it we'll get through this. Please, Nicky, please."

It felt totally surreal to be sitting in that room full of frightened and grieving women, who for whatever reason had just lost or were about to lose their baby, reciting a poem about a father telling his son how to be a man. Yet for Laura's sake I did it and she repeated each line after me, a look of complete concentration and focus on her pale face.

"Meet with triumph and disaster, and treat those two imposters just the same," she recited firmly as the nurse took her off to theatre, and I retreated to the waiting room, drained and relieved that it was over.

From his position on the bed Kwesi didn't see how Laura shuffled into the ward that evening, and I suspected only I noticed her wince as she bent across to kiss him on his forehead. Steve and Tony turned up soon after we arrived, and as having too many visitors at once was frowned upon I waited out in the corridor, glad not to have to make small talk with Kwesi whilst knowing what had happened to his child that day.

9

The experiences Laura and Kwesi endured had a pretty profound effect on me over the following days. Although I'd been through quite a lot for someone of my age, I'd had little opportunity to reflect on big issues. So it was quite overwhelming to suddenly be forced to confront, albeit through others, the potential for life and the potential for death. It was also very intense to encounter the deep love involved in Laura's sacrifice, alongside the hatred in the racism of Kwesi's attacker. I had heard racist remarks before, but never realised that such bigotry could lead to almost killing another human being without any provocation. Probably like others of my age, I never really thought about death and despite being vaguely aware that it could happen to anyone I had considered myself immune, relegating it to the realms of sickness and old age.

Faced now with the memories of Kwesi's injuries and how easily he could have been killed, I found myself selfishly looking for a safe place to resort to, a place in my head where I was safe because I wasn't sick, I wasn't old, I wasn't black. Yet I found myself wondering what would have happened if Laura had waited for Kwesi, and they'd left the club together. Would the group still have attacked; would they have beaten Laura as well? Laura, who was full of life and love. Laura, who was just like me. I momentarily felt guilty, hearing in my own thoughts the idea that somehow Laura dying would be worse than Kwesi dying, but I quickly realised that this wasn't about them at all but about how fragile and potentially temporary my own life was. I tried to talk with Anne and Mary about this in the lounge one evening, but they just told me not to be silly.

"You're sixteen, for goodness sake," said Mary. "Stop being such a pessimist. Unless you walk under a bus you've got about another fifty years to get through." I laughed along with them, because I could see they weren't yet ready to confront the stark reality that experiences had thrust upon me. I guessed they joked about it to stop it being frightening for them, and it was true that I too found it frightening. Yet at the same time it felt somehow really exciting, as if knowing one day I would die made living all the more valuable. I felt a great sadness about the potential little baby who would never experience life and, whilst respecting Laura's choice, I couldn't help wondering how it might have worked out if there hadn't been a choice. Would they somehow have coped, and lived happily ever after as a family? Would Kwesi have felt guilty not being able to support them, would Laura have ended up resenting all the demands on her? Would the stress of it all have split them up? All of these thoughts constantly preoccupied me, but I also realised that I would never have the answers to these questions. Again, I knew I could only take what I could from the experience, which at that time amounted to three things. One was the practical resolve to try and ensure I never put myself in that situation. However, the second was that I should never judge others because I could never really know their reality, what had created it and what influenced the way they dealt with it. I supposed I might need to extend the lack of negative judgement to myself at times as well. The third realisation was a reinforcement of recognising the value of life and, perhaps more importantly, living it in a meaningful way.

All of which led me to reassess what I was doing with my own life. In the initial euphoria of these realisations I was ready to make dramatic changes, the first being to stop living life on the superficial level by dying my hair and wearing make-up and fashionable clothes. I also decided to stop socialising so much, and instead enrol in evening classes and join some, as yet undefined, organisation in order to do voluntary work with the poor and needy.

My resolve wavered slightly on seeing people's reactions when I turned up at work the next day, devoid of make-up and wearing the calf length pleated tartan skirt that had been forwarded from home. The school summer skirt I'd left home in had been shortened and altered so much that this 'Christmas stocking' skirt was now the only really unfashionable item of clothing I had.

"You look terrible, are you alright?" asked my boss, which wasn't a great start to the day.

"I just thought I didn't need to wear make-up," I said, slightly defensively.

"You don't need to, dear, but like most of us you certainly look a lot better with it than without it!" I wanted to argue with her about nature versus superficiality, but hadn't really formalised my ideas enough to share and defend them yet. My aunt wasn't very supportive either, when I decided to visit her after work. Given that glamorous make-up and flamboyant clothing was very much her style I probably shouldn't have been surprised, but still the laughing comments about plain Jane and orphan Annie upset me. She must have noticed, as when we settled down in front of the fire after dinner she suddenly said "So what's happened?" I thought she was asking for news and started to tell her about the holiday camp, as I hadn't seen her since I'd got back. She listened to my babble for a few moments then interrupted me.

"No, I mean what has happened to bring about this change, Nicky? The scrubbed face, the clothes, the pinned back hair. You haven't been..." she paused, poking the fire then turning back to me "you haven't been assaulted or anything, have you? I've heard girls can react this way." Jerry's plump face loomed in front of me for just a second, but I knew I wasn't reacting to what had happened with him. Aunty might be wrong, but the very fact that someone wanted to know what was going on for me right now was such a relief I burst into tears and, as she hugged me, I told her about

Kwesi's attack. She made tea for us then she asked various questions about his recovery and even about Paulie. I was happy to tell her the police had found him, still in his bag, on an area of wasteland where the louts must have dumped him when they realised what the bag held. He'd been returned to Laura the day before. I didn't feel I could tell her about Laura's abortion, sworn as I was to secrecy, but I did share some of the bigger issues about life and death that had come up for me and the resolutions I had made.

"It's tough being confronted with such things so young," she said, smiling kindly. "I do know, because our generation faced death constantly during the war." I was surprised this had never occurred to me, that I had somehow assumed a youth of innocence for everybody but the unlucky few.

"Different people coped in different ways and a minority couldn't cope," she added and her eyes squeezed shut momentarily. "I thought you said you reached the conclusion that life was valuable and there to be lived?"

"Yes I did, aunty."

"So why the austerity, the plans to abandon all your friends in pursuit of knowledge at classes? Living life fully doesn't mean you can't include joy and the frivolous, it means experiencing all the range of things life has to offer, meaningful and superficial. Otherwise you might as well become a nun," she added with a laugh, "and while each to their own I don't see them having much of a life at all!" I thought of the nuns I'd encountered at boarding school and the ones I currently lived with, some gentle and kind but many of whom seemed to see quashing impulsiveness and enthusiasm as their main mission in life, and knew that was not my calling.

After my talk with aunty I got things a bit more in perspective and was helped by seeing Kwesi make a steady recovery. Laura too was calmer than I expected and seemed fairly happy. Getting Paulie back had been really important to her, not only because they both truly loved those snakes but also because she hadn't yet told Kwesi he was missing and now didn't need to burden him with that. I watched her fussing over all the snakes before rushing off to visit Kwesi, then on to work at the clubs until late before sleeping for a few hours, only to start the whole thing again the next morning. She seemed reluctant to accept help from anyone and I guessed that maybe mothering Kwesi and the snakes helped with her loss, while the manic busyness kept the grief at bay. We never talked about what we had shared. I felt she was at peace with the choice she had made and was learning to live with it. I very much hoped I was right.

I realised that, whilst a bit of extra study and perhaps some volunteer work might not go amiss in the not too distant future, sorting out my current priorities was probably more urgent. Work was fine, albeit lowly paid, and I was making good progress there so, apart from continuing to look for extra sources of income, that area of my life was fine. The hostel wasn't ideal, but with my limited resources I accepted I wasn't going to be moving anywhere else in a hurry. As far as friends in general I felt I was quite lucky, having casual friendships with girls at work and with some of the bikers, and a great friendship with Kwesi and Laura. I also enjoyed a variety of different friendships within the hostel, which were good as long as I kept away from certain aspects, such as what Kirsty and Anne got up to in the shops of Brighton and possibly elsewhere.

Another important area was family. I knew one day I would have to go and see mummy, try to sort out what level of relationship we could have, and I had talked at length about it with my aunt. She felt, as I did, that there was no point in me going to see her until I felt strong enough to deal with what might follow. I almost did feel strong enough, and was pretty sure, with the recent realisation that life can be short, that I would be going there quite soon, but not just yet.

Which left relationships. With visiting Kwesi, supporting Laura and catching up on my other friends I didn't get a chance to meet up with Bob, although he rang a couple of times. I reassured him it was just because I had a lot to do and that I'd get back to him soon, but I suspected I needed to get a clearer picture of what I wanted from relationships before I added a third to my collection. After a lot of thought, what I did eventually find time to do was to tell Lars, when he rang to say he was back from Switzerland, that I didn't want to see him anymore. I knew it wasn't very nice to finish with him over the phone but I also knew how persuasive he could be, and that if we met up he'd get me to change my mind. That was the main problem with our fledgling relationship: just because he was a bit older and studying I felt he saw himself as more intelligent and a teacher, feeling he had to educate and guide me. Even in decisions that were totally mine, such as what to wear or who to like, he tried to convince me of his superior wisdom. Kirsty had only met him once and decided he was a control freak which, although judgemental, was far more objective than his judgement of her, Tony and my other biker friends.

"These are the losers in society, Nicola, they will drag you down to their level."

Kirsty just asked why I put up with him trying to influence everything I did. I could understand why it seemed like that to her, but in a way I didn't just put up with it and we argued quite a lot. Yet somehow he always talked me around to his way of thinking. I reflected on the irony of the first conversation we'd had, when he said it was his job to show me the strings. It was a mistake on his part yet had actually proved prophetic; he did try to pull my strings. Partly I was in awe of him and how clever and knowledgeable he was, and flattered that he was even interested in me. I knew I wasn't stupid, as he made feel at times, but I was younger and had no qualifications so perhaps he was right in feeling superior to

87

me. There was also something romantic about him coming from a foreign country and speaking in a different accent, and I had thought that as well as being an attraction perhaps the cultural difference was part of the problem. I suppose I'd hoped as we spent more time together he would change. But if anything he had become worse, questioning what I did when not with him and why I spent time with other friends rather than him. Although he claimed it was because he missed me, I suspected it was because away from him I was more able to do and say, even think, what I wanted to and somehow he couldn't bear that. I thought it made him fearful that I wouldn't want to be with him.

"Hmm. He'll get you to prove you care by having sex with him next," said Kirsty, and I suspected from the bitterness in her voice that she was speaking from experience.

"He knows that's not going to happen," I said "He knows I'm not ready for that and to give him his due he never pressures me in that way. He's not all bad, Kirsty, or I wouldn't be with him," I added laughingly. She grudgingly agreed but couldn't stop herself from muttering "Wait and see." Actually he was quite a puritan in that respect, and had told me he also wanted to wait until he was sure the woman he was with was the one he wanted to spend his life with. The thought of any lifelong commitment to anyone filled me with total panic, although I knew deep down that the woman he chose wouldn't be me. As far as our current relationship I tried to give him a lot of reassurance but it had little effect. Probably because he was right, that time spent with Tony and the others was a reminder of how simple life had seemed with them and how exhaustingly intense it was beginning to feel now. Perhaps that was because despite our fairly innocent flirtations the relationship with Tony was much more based on friendship, which was why we could still see each other while I was dating Lars.

Kirsty said that Tony was hurt when I first went out with Lars, but he never told me that and he continued to be as nice and as friendly towards me as ever. Back in the flirting days Tony and I had discussed the idea of a girlfriend and boyfriend relationship but never pursued it. In a way it seemed more comfortable that we didn't name it, just enjoyed our time together. I'd briefly had a boyfriend when I was fourteen and I supposed a small part of me wanted to feel the excitement I had felt then, but I also knew how painfully it could end. It was a time of extreme emotions that I tried not to dwell on too often but that I would never forget.

10

When I was first aware of him looking at me the laughter and babble of my school friends seemed to fade away, and as our eyes met I felt suspended in time. It was hard to miss him when he came upstairs on the bus and sat across the aisle from me. You didn't see many Asian people in our small town, and you didn't usually see guys as handsome as him either. With his smooth dark skin and shiny black hair, which curled just above his collar, he made the noisy grammar school boys at the front of the bus look pasty, spotty and incredibly immature. While they entertained the girls with their usual tomfoolery, laughter and smutty comments his beautiful dark eyes just studied me calmly, a slight twinkle of confidence in them drawing me back each time I glanced away. I was confused. Why me? I could have understood if he'd paid attention to Sally or Janet, or almost any of the group, but I was never really the one who boys flirted with. Partly because I was a bit clumsy and unsophisticated but also, I suspected, because I was one of Sally's acolytes and nobody got much attention from boys when Sally was around. Although only fourteen, she had a wonderful figure and knew how to make the most of it. She wore the same school uniform as we all did, yet on her it looked like she was in a magazine. The white blouse was always crisp and spotless, the top button casually left undone, providing an occasional glimpse of the lace edging her bra, and the spray-starched collar turned up at the back, framed by her long blonde hair. The green cotton skirt, that on me hung limply just past my knees, was on Sally a halo for her long slim legs. This was achieved by her rolling it up at the waist and pulling it tight with a black patent leather belt, while the hem stood out all round supported by the three stiff net petticoats she wore. I had asked my mother for a petticoat, but she didn't think it 'appropriate for school'. Likewise with the stockings Sally wore, which made her legs smooth and shiny while my white ankle socks seemed to shorten my legs and reinforce the message that I was still a child. Of course in many ways I was, more than any of the other girls in my class, apart from Melanie who was fat and geeky without any friends. I would occasionally lie in bed feeling guilty about having been mean to Melanie during the day, especially as we were really both in the same boat, but I'd still do it again every so often. Teasing her had become a habit the first couple of years in grammar school, possibly because it was the only way I could reassure myself I wasn't at the bottom of the pile. It didn't really work, as she actually seemed quite happy as she was and would just look at me with a slightly patronising smirk on her face. Then suddenly there was no need for me to prove anything as, for some reason that I could not fathom, Sally, the most popular and envied girl in class, had decided last year that I could be her friend! So she, Janet and I would hang around together and, as a group, we were treated with respect by all. Even by the teachers, as Sally not only had the looks but also had brains, and the three of us would chat about schoolwork as well as make-up and fashion. As part of her trio I felt like somebody, alone I felt like a nobody. So to be singled out for attention by this handsome guy was incredible and unnerving. So much so that I moved downstairs two stops before mine, in order to jump off quickly and hurry home.

The next afternoon he appeared again, but this time he actually sat on the seat next to me, behind Sally and Janet. He smiled at me and held his hand out formally.

"Hello," he said softly, "my name is Nazir." I heard the pause in the chatter around me, followed by a loud jeer from one of the boys, as I automatically put my hand out to shake his. Neither of us said any more and I stared out of the window till we neared my stop, aware of my burning cheeks and his partial reflection in the glass.

"You coming, Nicky?" Sally asked as she jumped up. "Or you staying with your friend?" She and Janet giggled as they headed for the stairs.

"Excuse me," I mumbled and he smiled again as he stood up.

"I think this is my stop too, but ladies first please," he said, then followed me off the bus. Of course it wasn't his stop, as I found out a few days later, but with his looks and his charm I was too flattered to care as he walked with me to the end of my road. That first time we walked as a group, and when he introduced himself to Sally and Janet they smiled and asked him a few questions about himself. He said he was nineteen, worked early shifts in a local factory and lived with his family the other side of town, by the common. When we reached my road he asked if he could walk with us again tomorrow and I smiled and nodded. The others said nothing, but as he walked away Sally turned to me with a strange look on her face.

"I can't believe you, Nicky. What are you doing?"

"I'm not doing anything, Sally. He sat next to me then followed us off the bus. Probably you he's interested in anyway."

"Better not be," Sally said, grimacing. "Not my type actually, and he shouldn't be yours either. Your parents will kill you."

"Why?" I was totally confused. "What do you mean, he shouldn't be my type?" I asked, secretly thinking I should be so lucky.

"Nicky, you are so naïve. I'm sure he's nice enough, but my mum has told me about them. There's lots of them up in London," she said, "and they all stick together. They don't mix with us."

"Well, he wants to be friends with us," I said quickly, feeling uncomfortable as I listened to her, seeing Janet nodding in agreement.

"Does he?" she asked." I think it's just you. Sorry, Nicky, but mum says Paki boys see getting a white girl as a challenge. They just want them for *that*, she says, then they marry one of their own. Oh, and he's nineteen!" I felt my cheeks burning, a mixture of anger and embarrassment.

"I don't think that's fair of your mum, they're just people like us," I retorted, walking away towards my house. "And I'm not nineteen so he's not going to get *that* anyway, is he?"

I'd never argued with Sally before and I felt shaky and anxious. I had been excited to tell my mum about him, but after what Sally said I decided it was better not to yet. After all, he might just disappear and there'd be nothing to tell anyway.

Far from disappearing, the next afternoon he was at the stop outside the school and, after enduring the stares and comments for a few stops, he suggested we got off and walked the rest of the way. I was happy to agree, especially when he took my hand as I jumped off the bus and didn't let go. He told me he lived with his mother, brother and sister and that they'd come here from Pakistan six months ago, soon after his father had died. His eyes looked misty as he spoke of his dad, and I tentatively squeezed his hand in what I hoped was a gesture of comfort. I told him about my parents, how sad it made me when they argued as they seemed to do often lately. He nodded wisely and said he thought that must be very difficult for me, trying to keep them happy. I was amazed that he understood.

"Would they be happy about me being your good friend?" he asked in a rather quaint way.

"I don't know really. Sally said they wouldn't, but I'm not sure." He squeezed my hand tightly.

"It might be that your friend is right. It might be that you should keep our relationship a secret until we are sure it will not cause them trouble. We must not make them unhappy."

93

The word 'relationship' threw me completely. It sounded so grown up and safe and exciting.

"You're very considerate," I said, smiling up at him. "I wasn't sure it was me you were interested in you know. Sally and the others are so much prettier and..." He leant over and placed a finger on my lips.

"You must not talk this way," he said softly, staring into my eyes with a very serious expression. "There are lots of girls like them, but I could see you were different."

"In what way?" I found myself whispering back.

"They are all show but you are sweet and innocent, a good person." I felt myself tingling all over, amazed and flattered that he could see all that in me from our brief encounters. "The innocence and beauty of a child, even though you are a young woman. How old are you, Nicky?" I was astonished to hear myself say I was sixteen, as I crossed the fingers of my free hand behind my back to cancel the lie. "As I thought," said Nazir, letting go of my hand and putting his arm around my shoulder. "Already I know you deeply, Nicola, we are a kindred spirit." I wasn't quite sure what he meant, but I felt so comfortable with him it seemed he was right. When we passed a group of girls from my class their disgusted looks meant nothing. I was proud to be with him and stared right back at them.

Spending a bit of time walking alone with him after school some days was quite easy. My mother knew I sometimes hung around chatting with the girls or even went with them to the local coffee bar, where the grammar school boys teased us while flicking cigarette ash into their coke and claiming drinking this disgusting mixture made them high. It was a bit more difficult when Nazir asked me to spend Saturday afternoon with him, as I had to tell my mum I was going to Sally's house. I was glad we hadn't yet had a telephone installed, so she couldn't ring and check. I felt guilty, but it proved well worth it as we headed off to an area near the local lakes, where there was a friendly cricket match. The sun was really warm and the grass smelt wonderful as we lay there, me with my eyes closed, listening to the increasingly distant sounds of the match, whilst Nazir rested on his elbow and watched it intently. He had brought biscuits and orange juice, so after the game we had a mini picnic by the lake, watching the rowing boats.

"This is almost perfect," I murmured and Nazir turned sharply towards me.

"Why almost, what have I done wrong?" he asked sternly. I laughed at his serious expression.

"Nothing, you're sweet. It's just telling my parents lies, it's not something I like to do." He took both of my hands in his.

"You must not be selfish, Nicola." I must have looked surprised, as he continued "don't you realise it is selfish to upset them by telling them, just to make you feel better? We have already discussed this. We will tell them together when the time is right, and then I will make them love me as well." He showed me the discussion was closed by kissing me very gently on the lips. It was so unexpected I had no chance to see how it happened without us banging noses, which had always been my fear.

Lying in bed that night, I replayed our conversation and was struck by his saying he would make my parents love him 'as well'. He was telling me I loved him! Perhaps he did know me better than I knew myself, because that hadn't occurred to me in the short time I had known him. I didn't actually know what loving someone felt like really, apart from family love of course. Yet as I thought about how I'd felt lying on the grass with him, how I enjoyed listening to him talk and the feeling of my first kiss, I realised he could well be right.

A few days later it started raining as we walked and Nazir, sounding somewhat reluctant, said we should go to his house. I was really excited as we made our way there, thinking I couldn't wait to tell Sally that her mother was wrong, that he'd introduced me to his family. I wasn't quite as confident when we arrived and the door was opened by a young woman he would later introduce as his sister. As she looked from him to me and back again, and they exchanged a few curt words in their own language, I wondered if the prejudice did work both ways. Then she stood aside to let us pass and smiled at me as she murmured "Welcome." We went into a large kitchen with a wooden table in the middle, at which sat an elderly lady in a sari.

"This is my mother," said Nazir and there was a similar exchange to that at the door. I was invited to sit at the table, and served several dishes of food that smelt very strong but tasted much less spicy than in the local Indian restaurant. Amazingly, all but one was vegetarian so I just ignored that dish. Nazir disappeared and I was left feeling very awkward, as neither of the women seemed to speak English. Although they spoke to each other they ignored me, apart from serving the food. It was a relief when Nazir returned, but he immediately said "Come, we will go to my room." His room was on the ground floor at the front of the house, a large room with a big double bed. I felt a bit awkward but he sat me on the edge of the bed, then put some music on a record-player under the window. "This is from my country," he said, smiling, and I found myself relaxing to the beautiful sounds. I was touched to see empty shiny spaces in the fine dust on the top of the dressing table and chest of drawers, and guessed he had come in and tidied up for me while I sat in the kitchen. I wasn't sure most men would have bothered. He was proving so sweet and thoughtful, I felt very lucky to have met him.

Over the next couple of weeks popping to his home for a while became a regular occurrence and, gradually, his mother and sister became more welcoming. One time his mother pulled her daughter's sari tight to show me the bump of her stomach. "Baby?" I asked, miming rocking one in my arms, and his mother nodded, smiling. I felt flattered that she would share this with me, especially as I had seen no husband, and I was sure being a single mother was frowned upon in their culture even more than in ours. I asked Nazir and he explained that she was married, but her husband had to stay in Pakistan.

"He will come later," he said, "before this baby is born."

Although Nazir was only nineteen, his mother and sister seemed to look up to him. He told me that after his father died he became the head of the family. "They must show me respect," he said. "I am a man." Often there would be brief disagreements which I couldn't understand, but Nazir would always have the last word, then we would retire to his room. Sometimes his mother would try to continue the argument, knocking on the door and coming in as we lay together on the bed chatting, laughing and occasionally kissing. He got very moody when she did that, and would often get up and suggest we went out, slamming the door as we left. I felt a bit bad leaving without saying goodbye, especially as they always gave me food, but I realised it wasn't wise to argue with Nazir at those times. It would quickly pass anyway, and he'd be back to his smiling, loving self.

I certainly didn't need any more conflict, as my mother had found out about him. A neighbour had seen us together in a coffee bar and, horrified, had quickly found an excuse to visit. I arrived home one evening feeling happy and contented, to find my mother sitting on the edge of a chair, a very serious expression on her face.

"Is it true, Nicola?" I feigned innocence.

"Is what true, mum?"

"Have you been going to coffee bars with a black boy?" My nervous giggle probably wasn't the best response.

"A black boy, mum? He's not black, he's ..." I was going to say brown, but realised the conversation wasn't about shades of colour. "He's from Pakistan, mum, and he's really nice, very polite. He has a nice family."

97

My mother raised her eyebrows.

"So he's taken you to get his family's approval has he? Yet it seems our approval wasn't considered important."

"Of course it is, mummy." I wondered how to explain my thinking, but didn't get the chance.

"Well, you won't get it, my girl, I can tell you now. We did not struggle to give you a nice comfortable home, and a grammar school education, just to have you waste yourself on a foreigner." Actually I got myself the grammar school place by passing my eleven plus, I was tempted to say, but this was no time for flippancy. Despite Sally's warnings I couldn't really believe my mother was showing this blind prejudice.

"Mummy, I'll bring him home to meet you. You'll like him, I promise." She shook her head.

"Nicky, I want you to be happy but this boy is not right for you. I'm assuming boy; how old is he anyway?" Yet again I heard an instant lie come out of my mouth, as I told her he was seventeen, knowing him being older just added to the problems. We continued to argue for a while, then mummy said "Look, dear, I won't tell your father if you promise me you will finish this." I felt some small relief, not only because I could avoid his anger for a while but also because the longer I could stall, the longer the rows between them about me could be postponed. My fingers were firmly crossed behind my back as I said "I can't believe you are asking me to do this, mummy, just to make you and my father happy." She took this as my agreement and hugged me then, telling me I was making the right decision. Nazir hugged me too, as I sobbed uncontrollably the next afternoon. I thought he would suggest meeting them as he'd previously spoken of, but he explained that the time wasn't right yet.

"So we have to stop seeing each other," I wept.

"This cannot happen," said Nazir, holding my shoulders and staring into my eyes, the way he often did when he wanted to get his point across. "If you finish this, Nicky, you will break my heart. I will have no reason to live. I will throw myself off the railway bridge." I was so shocked by his words my tears stopped immediately. I felt so mixed up. On the one hand it was amazing to think someone loved me that much, on the other the responsibility for his life as well as my parents' happiness was overwhelming. Part of me just wanted to run away from it all, but I also knew the only person who really understood me in all this was Nazir. I reached up and stroked his face.

"I won't leave you, we just have to be really, really careful."

However, ours was a small town and I suspected my mother had further reports, as she took to questioning me closely each time I went out. Sometimes, as I returned home I would meet her coming down our road, agitated and often not dressed appropriately for outside and I knew she was having one of her bad days. It was as if she peered out of our door till she saw me turn into the road, and then rushed out. I felt guilty at the distress I was causing her, but I couldn't see any reason for giving up Nazir except her prejudice. I so wished she would meet him, so she could see as I did how charming and caring he was. Maybe it was that wish that made me take more risks, letting him walk me right to the corner of my road, standing chatting to him there instead of rushing home. It was probably inevitable that when I was late home one afternoon she came round the corner, looking for me, and found the two of us sitting on a wall, his arm around me. The drivers at the taxi rank laughed and cheered as my mother ran and grabbed me, pulling me away from Nazir, who hurried off with fear on his face. At almost fifteen I felt like a small child, belittled, humiliated and angry. Not with her, that would take much longer, but with those men leaning on their cabs, smoking cigarettes and enjoying the show. My sad crazy mother in her smart tweed suit and bedroom slippers, my handsome boyfriend, one scared dark face among so many hostile and mocking ones, me with tears streaming down my cheeks. It felt we were all just characters for their entertainment.

"I'll show you," I vowed silently. "One day I'll come back here in a fur coat, then you will see I am not a nobody."

And eventually I would fulfil that promise, the day of my mother's funeral. Although the coat was second-hand and slightly mangy I wore it as I travelled from London in my uncle's car through the blinding rain, arriving hours too early. I laid it on the chair beside me as we ordered lunch in the café where I used to meet my school friends, and where that day I dug a dead fly out of my cheese omelette. The hem dragged on the wet pavement as I bent to retrieve the hankie I'd dropped, which was floating away along the gutter. I wrapped it tightly around me as I locked myself in the car outside the church, hysterical and unable to face what lay ahead. But face it I did, the coat dripping as I stood watching that tiny coffin being lowered into the ground, shocked that the woman who had held so much power over me was so small. And afterwards I chose to walk through the rain back to my old home, past that taxi rank, my head held high as if I really was somebody of importance, even though it would be many years before I discovered that was true.

Ironically, I think these attempts on my mother's part to break us up actually perpetuated the relationship with Nazir longer than if it had just plodded on in what had become a fairly routine pattern. It was no longer as exciting, just comfortable and familiar. However, my mother's anger made me feel I had no choice, I had to support Nazir, I couldn't give in to such unprovoked hostility. At home the atmosphere was cold and angry and I felt very lonely, whilst with him and his family I felt noticed and cared about.

So we continued to meet, but there were few walks or outings for fear of being seen, and we spent more and more time in his house, in his room. Although I still enjoyed talking with him and the kisses and cuddles on the big bed made me

100

feel special and important, I got somewhat restless and found myself spending longer with his mother and sister, lingering over the meals. I could tell he didn't really like me spending much time with them, but I simply teased him about wanting me all to himself.

"I do," he said. "You are my precious thing, I cannot share you." I laughed but felt uncomfortable at his words. I felt even more uncomfortable a couple of days later, when he came into the bathroom as I was washing my hands, locking the door behind him.

"Nazir, what are you doing?" I asked, half laughing with embarrassment. He stood behind me, staring at me in the tall mirror above the sink, and put his finger to his lips.

"Shush," he whispered, "this is our secret time." Before I could ask him what he meant he put both arms tightly around me, lifted the front of my skirt and started to put his hand inside my pants, as we both watched in the mirror.

"Stop it, Nazir, that's too much," I said with a small embarrassed smile. I saw his eyes darken as they did when he was angry, then he suddenly turned me around to face him and began to unzip his trousers.

"No!" I said, shocked. "We can't do that, Nazir. I'm only fourteen," I added desperately as he persisted. A look of pure hatred appeared on his face momentarily.

"You lied to me," he said bitterly. Before I could respond there was a frantic knocking on the door, and his sister's voice was saying something urgent. I took the opportunity to unlock the door and walk out of the bathroom, not able to look at her as I wondered what on earth she would make of us both being in there.

I wasn't sure how I felt about Nazir after that, but when I saw him near the school a few days later the familiar tingles returned. As we walked along the back streets to his house he was very apologetic, but made me realise that it had all happened because I had lied to him about my age. He was right of course, I had. It seemed I was lying to everyone lately and I was messing things up all round. My parents, Sally and Janet and now Nazir; all were angry with me and I felt very alone, trying to sort it all out. It was a relief when we arrived at his house to find his mother and sister, smiling and friendly with the usual dishes of delicious food in the warm cosy kitchen. There was also a new person at the table. Nazir's brother was a year younger, taller and darker than him, with muscular arms and a big smile. He introduced himself as Malik as he shook my hand, telling me he worked the late shift at the same factory as Nazir. His English was very good and it became a really sociable time as he translated what his mother and sister were saying. Nazir had never done that and I could tell he wasn't happy about it now, but I could also tell his brother had a much closer relationship with their mother than he did. Then the two of them had a brief exchange, Malik sounding authoritative, and after a while Nazir disappeared to his room.

We four continued our conversation, discussing their home in Pakistan, the forthcoming baby, hopes for the future.

"What do you want for your future, Nicola?" Malik asked and I smiled shyly, shrugging my shoulders.

"I'm not sure really. Good job, my own home. Just to be happy I suppose."

"We can be happy once we are sure of our future," Malik said, repeating my words to his mother and sister. "They ask if you have ever been to a fortune teller such as you see on Brighton pier." I laughed.

"No, I'm not sure about them being genuine. Anyway, they're really expensive." Again he exchanged words with the others.

"You are right," he said. "They might not be genuine. It is a gift given to the wise." He hesitated then smiled at me. "I will share a secret. In our country my mother told many fortunes that came true."

102

I was amazed as I looked at the little old lady, nodding smilingly at me. She spoke to her son again.

"She is asking if you would like her to tell you your fortune." It was exactly what I needed right then, some sense of where I was going, and I agreed gratefully as I held out my palm. She looked up at her son. "No, not your hand," he said. "She has her special way that is more accurate, but I cannot be in the room." I was confused as he went out, shutting the door behind him. The sister came to me and stood me up, then pushed each of my feet with hers until my legs were apart, while the mother watched with a smile on her face, nodding wisely. Then the sister placed a cushion on the floor in front of my feet and helped her mother to kneel on it. I could not believe what happened next, the mother pulling aside my pants leg as her daughter gripped me firmly from behind and then…

"Ow, stop it," I yelled as the mother's fingers probed.

"Little hurt, it quick," said the sister, her rounded stomach pressing into my back as I tried to pull away.

"There," said the mother, removing her hand from under my skirt and waving it in front of us. "All good yes?" she said, as her daughter released me and helped her to a chair. Her younger son came in immediately, and I flushed to think he had been standing right outside the door while it happened. I wanted to run out, but as they were all acting in such a matter-of-fact way I realised it must be because I was young, and from a different culture, that I found this embarrassing. To them it was nothing. They spoke among themselves for a few minutes then he turned to me smiling.

"All is good," he said. "My mother tells me you will have a good future and all your dreams will come true."

It was rather vague but at least it was positive, so I was thanking her as Nazir returned from wherever he had disappeared to for the last hour. He seemed restless and angry, and instead of the usual cuddles he said he must walk me home because it was too late. Which was true. I knew there

103

would be questions when I got home but I now also knew it would all be ok one day.

As we walked along I took his hand. "Nazir, don't be sad. It's all going to be alright. Your mother told me so, she read my fortune." He let go of my hand and turned towards me with a scathing expression. "Did you believe all that?" he asked sneeringly.

"Yes, your mother said..." The ugly look on his face stopped me.

"You silly girl," he muttered, "she was not telling your fortune, she was checking to see if you had sex yet. She is wanting to protect her son from you, not believing when I tell her we do not do that."

I don't know how long I stood there just staring at him, partly numb, partly flooded by a confusion of feelings. Mainly I felt so incredibly stupid, naïve, gullible. Angry, embarrassed, humiliated...so many different feelings...and to top it all, disgust. Disgust that he must have known what was going to happen, what was happening while he skulked away in his room. Yet he didn't warn me, protect me as he'd always said he would, he just let it happen. Finally, my pride fought its way through the turmoil.

"No, we didn't do that, Nazir, and we never will, because it is over." His arms were immediately around me but I pushed them off.

"No, Nicky, that is not necessary. Now she has checked my mother will be happy..." I couldn't believe his words.

"This isn't about your scheming mother," I found myself yelling. "It's about me. I lied to my parents, lost my friends, all for you and you put me through this. And to top it all, as usual it is you that gets upset and moody and me that reassures. No more, Nazir, I can't take any more of all this." He couldn't stop himself. Even as I turned to walk away, tears flooding down my cheeks, I heard his voice telling me this

104

was because I had shouted in the bathroom, that he had told me to be quiet.

I never heard the end of his explanation of how yet again I'd brought everything on myself, his voice becoming fainter as I ran towards my home and burst in the door sobbing loudly. My parents were in the front room and sat me down between them, demanding I tell them what had happened. Of course I couldn't tell them what had happened with Nazir's mother, but his name kept breaking through my sobs and I heard my father asking my mother what the hell was going on.

"Later," she snapped at him, then she took me to my room. "Has he done anything to you, Nicky?" I knew what she meant and shook my head vigorously.

"Not that, mum, just broken my heart."

"Oh for goodness sake." She stood there looking lost. "I told you, Nicola and you've been lying to me it seems. Now your father knows and...oh for goodness sake," she repeated as she flounced out of the room. She left the door slightly ajar and I could hear the arguments between them going on well into the night, knowing that I'd caused it all.

I was woken the following morning by my father tapping on the door and calling my name. I struggled awake, realising I'd fallen asleep fully dressed.

"Why aren't you at work, dad?" I asked as he came in.

"Because I've got to sort out the mess you've made, young lady. So, give me his address." I tried to argue, telling him it was all over and they had no need to worry. He was insistent, pointing out he could hardly be expected to believe me or my mother, with everything that had been going on under his roof. All my protests were in vain and eventually I told him where Nazir lived, pointing out that he wouldn't be there because he was working.

"We'll see," my father muttered and I watched from the window as he stormed off down the road. I wasn't sure if I was supposed to go to school, and my mother didn't appear from her room, so I just curled up on the bed crying as I thought over all the dramas of the last few weeks. Later I heard my father return, and the shouting started again, to eventually be followed by a slammed door and long ominous silence. My mother opened my door. "We need to talk, Nicola," she said gently, and sat beside me on the bed. Although I listened to what she said and nodded as if I understood I couldn't really take on board the meaning of her words. "So, dear, your father has talked to his brother and, through him, to those poor women. To all of them at the house, apart from him. Lucky for him he was at work or goodness knows what your father might have done. That poor family is as shocked as we are. Can you imagine what all this has been like for his wife?"

"Whose wife?" I asked stupidly, and that was when she explained that the young woman Nazir had told me was his sister was actually his wife.

"So the baby?"

"Yes, it is his baby yet he expected her and his mother to put up with him bringing home a young girl. I understand they even had to cook for you." I was horrified at what I was hearing.

"I thought they wanted to cook for me, mum, I thought she was his sister." Mummy ignored my protests.

"Not only that, they told your father he was taking you into their bedroom, onto their bed. How could you, Nicola? After you left each time that poor young woman would find her brushes and creams and things all stuffed in a drawer."

"The empty spaces," I gasped. "I thought it was his stuff he'd cleared up but it was hers." No wonder there were always curt exchanges when we arrived, no wonder his mother kept interrupting us in the bedroom, and his poor wife banged so hard on the bathroom door. No wonder they subjected me that final indignity, needing to know for sure what was going on.

"Oh, mummy," I sobbed. "I am so stupid and so sorry."

She hugged me then, for the first time in ages, and did try to be supportive of me in my grief. But she had enough to deal with, as the rows with my father continued, until he left us a few weeks later.

For me, the grief and guilt merged into one and I withdrew into myself, until my mother's increasingly erratic moods forced me to put my feelings aside, in order to try to support her.

11

I was surprised that, when I called him, Bob invited me to his flat for lunch, rather than us going out somewhere on a date. He offered to drive over to pick me up but there was a bus that went straight there, so I said I'd make my own way. It was a smart street that I found myself on when I got off the bus, lined on one side with terraced four-storey Georgian houses that looked as if they had flat roofs. Number six was very smart, the green painted panelled door topped by an oblong window, and colourful flowers in boxes on the ground floor windowsills. As I pushed the bell I suddenly felt nervous about seeing Bob. The door was opened by a short elderly man who seemed to be expecting me, smiling as he welcomed me into the hallway.

"Is it someone for me, Mr Cazian?" I heard Bob's voice ask from above us. As the old man turned towards the stairs I saw he had a big curve at the top of his back, his chin tucked into his chest like a tortoise. "No, Robert, this young lady is for me please," he said laughingly, his accent quite guttural. I heard Bob laugh in response, then saw him leaning over the banisters at the bend on the stairs. Even from a distance his high cheekbones, blue eyes and blond hair looked as handsome as I remembered. "Nicky, come on up," he called and, after thanking the old man, I climbed the stairs to be greeted with a hug from Bob.

"Behave yourselves, young folks." I heard Mr Cazian say as he disappeared through a door off the hall.

"Hello, you," said Bob with a warm smile. "I'm afraid we have a lot of stairs to climb; I'm right at the top of the house." It was indeed a long way up before we reached the open door of Bob's flat, which seemed slightly pokey and quite dark considering the apparent opulence of the house. We walked straight into the sitting room, which had a patterned carpet, a settee along one wall and a narrow dining table with two chairs under the surprisingly small window, which was very unlike the grand ones on the first floor that I had admired from outside. There were two doors off the sitting room, the open one leading into a small kitchen and the other, I was to discover, into quite a large bedroom with a double bed and dark wardrobes so big you had to squeeze past them to get to the tiny bathroom. Another door in the bathroom led to an equally tiny box room, with space for only a single bed and a chest of drawers.

There was a slight smell of burning from the kitchen, and Bob's calm sophistication wavered slightly as he rushed to grab a pan off the stove, dumping it quickly on the worktop as the heat from the metal handle reached the palm of his hand.

"Oops," he said with a grin, "just in time I think." The vegetable sauce in the pan was thicker than intended he said, as he spooned it over very well cooked spaghetti and carried the heaped plates to the dining table.

"Shall I take my coat off?" I asked, giggling, and he was slightly flustered as he took it from me and hung it on a hook inside the bedroom door. I was soon to learn that Bob liked everything to flow calmly and smoothly, but wasn't always as laid back as he tried to appear. The pasta was quite tasty and was followed by a slice of chocolate swiss roll over which he'd poured cream, which had soaked in and made it all rather mushy. Nevertheless, he was the first young man I'd known to cook a meal so I was pretty impressed, and told him so. By the time we finished eating we had both started to relax, and to feel comfortable with each other in the way we had at the holiday camp. As we settled on the settee with cups of tea I asked him about the old man who had shown me in.

"Oh, Mr Cazian is lovely," he said, "albeit very old fashioned in his way of thinking. He and his wife are from Armenia. They came over years ago with very little money, now they own this house and let it out in flats, while they live on the ground floor."

"So he's your landlord? How does that work out, having them there all the time?" I asked. Bob laughed.

"It's ok, although they could possibly tell you the exact times that I go out and arrive back home, her sharp eyes miss nothing. They like to be sure their tenants are respectable," he said with a grin, "so we might even see him later." Sure enough, once I'd persuaded Bob to let me help and we were in the kitchen washing up, there was a knock on his front door and when he opened it Mr Cazian was standing there, breathless from climbing the stairs.

"My good lady asked me to pop up, Robert, to say if you and your lady friend would like to come in for tea, before she leaves, you are very welcome. She has made a cake," he added, glancing over at me standing by the kitchen door holding a tea towel. I was surprised to hear Bob say "Thank you that would be lovely," and to see Mr Cazian raise his hand in a small wave to me, before setting off on his long journey back down the stairs.

"Phew, tea with the landlord. Heavy stuff already," I said half-jokingly as Bob returned to the sink.

"It'll only take ten minutes, more a formality than anything. It's sort of become a ritual really. You don't mind do you? It's just they like to show an interest and I think he sees me almost like the son they never had." It seemed a bit odd to me, but I'd never had a landlord, so I wasn't to know, and reassured Bob that it was fine. We went on to have a relaxed chatty afternoon, discovering all the things we had in common as people do in the early days, with a couple of hugs and one hesitant kiss thrown in. I went into the kitchen to get a glass of water and saw from the clock on the wall that it was already half past five.

"Bob, I thought on the phone you said you had to start work at the bar at six?" I said as I went back into the sitting room. He glanced up, startled, then looked at his watch.

"I do. Whoops, we need to make a move or I'll be late." He jumped up and disappeared into the bedroom, returning only moments later changed from his jeans into a smart white shirt, black trousers and shiny black shoes, my coat over his arm.

"You look great," I said, admiring how the outfit set off his chiselled good looks.

"Flatterer," he responded flippantly as he helped me on with my coat, but I could see he appreciated my comment. He apologised for the rush as we hurried down the stairs, Mr Cazian magically appearing at his door as we were halfway down the last flight. "Oh, Mr C, I am so sorry, I misjudged the time. Please give my apologies to Mrs Cazian." I saw the old man's lips purse, and he glanced briefly at me with what momentarily looked like hostility, although he then smiled and shook my hand as we left.

"Do you want to come with me?" Bob asked as we walked towards his car. "We could chat in between me serving." I didn't really fancy spending my Saturday evening conspicuously sitting in a hotel bar, even if he was there, and anyway I felt we'd talked enough for our first London meeting.

"I promised Kirsty and Anne I'd be back," I said, for some reason not adding that we were supposed to be going to a biker party that evening. My reticence was probably a leftover from the Lars days, when such an innocent statement would have evoked questions and sulks.

After apologies for not having time to drive me back to the hostel, a quick hug and the promise of a phone call, he drove off and I made my way to the bus stop. I felt really good on my journey home, happy and relaxed and fairly convinced Bob and I could have a fun relationship, if I didn't have to encounter the Cazians too often.

Bob must have enjoyed the afternoon as well, because I was called to the hostel phone at nine the next morning, encountering a disapproving look from one of the nuns as I descended the stairs wrapped in a towel, another around my wet hair. His voice was brighter than I felt. The party the night before had been pretty lively, with lots of dancing, and we had only just made it back in time for lock up. We'd then chatted until the early hours, the three of us curled up on my bed, until a normally quiet girl called Sarah threatened to throw a shoe at us if we didn't shut up and let her sleep.

"What are you up to, Nicky?" he asked. "It's a beautiful day. I thought maybe we could go out. I thought we could go to London zoo." It all came out rather breathlessly and it took me a moment to think. "We don't have to, we could do something else if you want," he added before I could speak.

"No, that sounds great, Bob. Um, thanks, I'd love to." I could hear the pleasure in his voice as we arranged when and where to meet, and I felt very flattered.

"Wow," said Kirsty, back in the dormitory. "He's keen. So are you, judging by the sickly smile on your face." I laughed.

"I've never been to the zoo. I can't wait to see all the animals," I said.

"Yep, yep," said Anne, flicking my wet hair. "We all know which animal you want to see!" Everyone laughed and I felt myself blushing.

"He's not an animal, he's a gentleman," I said defensively and they all laughed again.

I was excited to be spending more time with Bob, and when I saw him by the zoo gates I had to restrain myself from running and hugging him. I was unnerved by my own emotion, as I hadn't felt that way in a long, long time. However, it must have been mutual because as soon as he spotted me Bob came forward with a big grin and outstretched arms. We laughed as we swapped a muddle of polite questions about journeys and the evening before.

"Whew, shall we go in?" Bob suggested as we both paused for breath. I nodded and pulled out my purse, but he showed me two tickets he had already bought and we made our way through the gate. "Where would you like to start?" he asked as we stood looking at the various pathways leading away from this central area.

"Wow, it looks bigger than I imagined," I mumbled. "I don't know. I've only heard of the aviary that some member of the royal family just built, and Guy the gorilla."

"Ok, let's start by finding Guy then," said Bob, grabbing my hand and pulling me after him through the crowds of family groups in their Sunday best. The crowds were even denser as we reached the gorilla's cage, and it took a while for us to work our way through to the front. Which made the first sight of this amazing creature even more incredible, as we suddenly spotted him on the other side of the bars. Almost instinctively I moved closer to Bob when I saw how enormous this gorilla was, and he put his arm around my shoulder as he told me that Guy was a silverback and weighed almost 500lbs.

"And he looks almost as tall as me," I added. Guy was sitting on the ground looking out at his audience with a calm but seemingly slightly amused expression, absentmindedly scratching his arm with what looked like a large beautifully manicured finger. I had a mixture of feelings about staring at such a magnificent beast trapped in a cage, wondering how he felt about it all. I wanted to stay and watch him, especially when a sparrow suddenly flew into the cage and landed on the hand that Guy stretched out. A gasp went up from the crowd, and I think we all expected him to hit out or to squash it. However, he just seemed to study it, turning his head at different angles while focusing his bright intelligent eyes on the little bird. Then the bird flew off, and he glanced after it briefly before returning to his scratching. I couldn't believe an animal so large could be so gentle, and that added to the discomfort I felt about Guy not living free in his homeland.

113

"Shall we move on, Bob?" I asked and once we were away from the crowd I told him how I felt.

"Yep, I know what you mean, Nicky. I'm a bit ambivalent about zoos too, but they also do a lot of research and apparently some species wouldn't survive without them. Guess these poor animals are the draw to get our money to support that work." I vaguely remembered learning some of that at school but hadn't thought about the last bit so, once we decided to stay, I felt slightly less guilty about my voyeurism. We spent the next couple of hours chatting as we visited other animals, such as the elephants in their concrete castle and the penguins, shuffling along on the cement around their pool before several of them gracefully slid into the water.

Over a sandwich lunch I did tell Bob about the party the night before, and he seemed genuinely interested, laughing with me at various incidents, rather than being resentful in the way I feared. He then told me a bit about his family. I had guessed from his slightly posh voice and his general demeanour that he came from a fairly well to do family, and was surprised at his current career as a barman. However, this made more sense when he told me his parents owned a large and very smart hotel in Dorset that he was one day expected to run.

"Father's plan is I should get experience in all areas of hotel life before I get involved in management. My plan is I should enjoy my freedom in London as much as possible before they reel me in!"

"So you'll be going back to Dorset?" I asked nervously and he squeezed my hand reassuringly across the table.

"Not for yonks, Nicky, anything could happen by then."

"I was only asking," I said flippantly, glancing away to hide my blush. We were sitting outside, despite the chilliness, and I felt proud as I saw a couple of girls glance at him as they walked past, seeing their appreciation of his good looks. He seemed unaware of them, and as I turned back I saw a small smile on his face.

"Shall we make a move?" he asked tactfully and I nodded. I walked ahead but he caught up and held my hand, and almost immediately the awkwardness passed, as we stopped to look at the rhino.

The afternoon was full of the same mixed emotions. Although some distance away, the polar bears on the Mappin terraces looked large and magnificent and totally out of place in that bleak man made environment. The darling chimps looked like they were happy, yet I wasn't sure they should be having tea parties and performing for us. However, despite any sense of guilt, I really enjoyed my day, partly thanks to the wonderful animals but largely due to the company. As the closing bell rang through the zoo we both realised we hadn't been to the aviary. I was about to reassure Bob that I wasn't too bothered, when I heard him say

"We can come back and see it in a couple of months, when it's warmer," and I felt myself tingle with excitement. So he really saw a future for us!

"That'd be nice," I said, as casually as I could, as we headed off to a coffee bar. It was one of the ones Lars had taken me to, but with Bob it was a totally different experience, our focus being on relaxing and enjoying the singer rather than learning the intricacies of chess. I wondered how long I'd be comparing him to Lars, fearful of another controlling relationship, and surprised at the effect Lars had had on me in such a short time.

As well as the coffee bars and the zoo, Bob showed me yet another side of London over the next few weeks, and I fell even more in love with the city. Whether it was the smart new boutiques of Kings Road, where the mods hung out and bought the latest fashions, or the noisy bustling Portobello road market, I loved it all. I couldn't afford the fashionable boutique clothes and, despite his parents being fairly affluent,

Bob couldn't afford the guys' stuff in Carnaby Street either. Nevertheless, it was great fun, not only to look in the shop windows, but also to watch the strutting of self-conscious young people, whose main aim seemed to be getting noticed. Although I still saw myself as more of a rocker, I was a little bit envious of them with their style and confidence. Portobello market also had loads of stuff we could never afford, especially in some of the antique shops and stalls, but we had fun rummaging among the goodies in the vague hope of finding an amazing bargain that would turn out to be worth thousands. On one stall I found a really cheap original Charleston dress complete with fringes and, with some encouragement from Bob, I bought it with the money that would have paid for the following week's lunches. So, although the market was less than a mile long, it took us ages to explore it before Bob whisked me off to a local macrobiotic restaurant. I found the idea of macrobiotic pretty strange, but it was great to know that despite being vegetarian I could choose anything on the menu, and what I did eventually choose was very good. What I really appreciated was the fact that he'd given thought to what I would enjoy.

As a contrast to the busy shopping areas we also spent quite a bit of time walking in the parks, making the most of the limited together time we could fit around our different work schedules. Despite the winter chill that turned the grass a frosty white and put a silvery sheen on the railings, I loved walking round the lake in St. James Park trying to identify the different water birds or standing on the bridge to look at Buckingham Palace. Bob preferred the grandeur of the Serpentine, in Hyde Park. He was impressed by the design of the newish restaurant, which was mostly made of glass and had an unusual roof that looked a bit like four umbrellas. We couldn't afford to eat there but did go in for a drink and, because it was raised above water level, we could see right across the Serpentine. When I marvelled at the view Bob gave me another reminder that he saw a future for us, telling me about the bandstands and how we could come back in the summer and laze in deckchairs while listening to the music.

"You in your summer dress and me in my shorts, showing my knobbly knees."

"I can't wait," I said lightly, but although we both laughed, remembering the holiday camp competitions, I knew we were serious. We were quite tactile with each other and jumpers, coats and gloves didn't make close touching very easy. Of course we did have that opportunity in his flat, yet ironically we spent very little time there. I think we were both a bit scared of what could happen, having on one occasion carried our kisses and cuddles a bit further than intended. We'd been interrupted by Mr Cazian's knock on the door and, although I had started to find his persistent monitoring really annoying, on this occasion I was rather relieved and suspected Bob was as well.

Bob was much more romantic than Lars or Tony, and after only a few dates was sharing his dreams of a family, home and children. I guessed this was understandable given that at twenty he was so much older than me, and although I didn't have such plans for the foreseeable future, I did feel it showed that he was a sensitive and caring person. Although he didn't put any pressure on me it was also pretty clear from both the passion of our kisses and the roaming hands that he wanted us to sleep together, but respected that whilst he had experience I didn't. When we were together I certainly felt that, given I was going to one day lose this intangible thing called virginity, Bob could well be the one. However, right now I still wasn't ready to rush into that kind of involvement.

Then, to my astonishment, he came up with the idea that I should move in with him. "Bob, that's daft," I said as I snuggled closer to him on the sofa. "We've only been going out for a few weeks."

"Perhaps it is, but what have we got to lose?" he asked, hugging me excitedly. "You're living in that rubbish hostel and I've got a great flat, so it makes sense to pool our resources."

"Oh, this is an economic strategy is it, you're after my money," I teased him. We had both talked about how expensive London was and perhaps a tiny part of me really did wonder if this was a strategy to save on his rent. Then one glance at his face reassured me there was more to his suggestion than monetary considerations.

"Don't be daft," he said. "We get on great together don't we? And it works for Laura and Kwesi so why not us?"

Bob's idea did seem crazy, but also very tempting. As he said, we did get on really well and I felt I could truly be myself with him. Whilst the friendship with Tony was about a sense of wildness and rebellion and the relationship with Lars had been a process of learning, with Bob it felt it was about laughing together, dreaming dreams, chattering as we walked barefoot along rainy streets, and me discovering what it could be like to be a teenager. He also got on well with my friends, and I was particularly relieved to see that he had no issues with Kwesi in the way I suspected Lars had, despite his denials. We were at Laura and Kwesi's when the subject of my mother came up.

"We will miss you," I said as Bob and I snuggled on the sofa in their humid snake dominated sitting room, glad of the warmth as sleet splattered on the window.

"Ah bless. You too, Nicky," said Laura, "but you can come and visit us." They were both moving to Vancouver shortly, and I laughed at the idea of me ever managing to get there.

"You just never know what's possible," said Kwesi and when I looked at the crutches resting against his chair and considered how much he had overcome, I guessed he was right. It would still be a while before he was totally back to his old self physically and even longer before his confidence returned fully, but I knew he'd get there and perhaps Canada would be the place he'd do it. Nevertheless, I pouted childishly and said, half-jokingly,

"Don't go, please don't leave me." Laura ignored my silliness.

"I'm really looking forward to seeing all my folks, that's for sure," she said with a big smile.

"Yep, family are really important," said Bob and I glanced briefly at Kwesi, wondering how he felt hearing this, given that he had no family, but he just nodded his head and added "This is very true." Funny enough I didn't connect Bob's statement with myself at all until Laura said "That's what would make me really happy, Nicky, if you tried to start again with your mum."

"I'm just not ready, Laura, not strong enough. Aunty says she's become even weirder and I can't deal with it yet."

"Maybe, but you can't really know perhaps until you try," said Kwesi, reaching across to squeeze my hand.

"Mothers are so important, Nicky," said Bob softly, a concerned look on his face.

"I know, Bob, but you haven't met my mother. In one way she is lovely, but she can just make me feel so squashed, so bad. And I never know which mother I'll encounter," I added, trying not to show how upsetting the conversation was becoming.

"That's tough," Bob agreed, "but maybe now, if you saw her, things would be different." I got up to go to the kitchen and found myself snapping at him.

"I will when I'm strong but…"

"Hey," he suddenly shouted, jumping up from the sofa and grabbing my arm. "Let's go and see her together, we can tell her about our plan of sharing the flat."

"What?" Laura and I chanted in unison, and I couldn't help laughing at his intensity.

119

"I haven't even agreed to living together," I said quickly to Laura.

"Oh, you will soon I'm sure," Bob laughed, and Kwesi and Laura laughed with him. "We can go in my car," he continued excitedly. "It'll be good to meet her and surely she'll be nice to you if I'm with you?" I didn't answer him, recalling how when mummy's moods took her she didn't care at all what others thought, like closing all the windows on train journeys regardless of others. Yet he made everything sound so simple and even Laura agreed the trip could be a good idea.

"There's never going to be a right time, Nicky, but at least this way you'll have support."

"True," I said hesitantly and found myself reluctantly agreeing to go the next Saturday.

"Do you want us to come as well?" Laura asked as she and I prepared a salad in the kitchen. I almost said yes, but then I recalled mummy's attitude towards Nazir and realised I couldn't risk submitting Kwesi to even more prejudice.

"I'll be fine," I said and Laura smiled.

"We can do all sorts of things we never thought we could, if they are the right thing to do," she said softly and I hugged her, knowing she was referring to the abortion as much as the proposed trip home.

I hardly slept the next couple of nights, feeling both excited and anxious, as mixed memories of mummy and home filled my thoughts. Several times I was tempted to cancel but Bob had booked the time off work to take me, so it felt I had to go through with it. Kirsty thought I was daft.

"After all the stuff you've told us," she said grumpily, "I don't know why you'd bother."

Mary called across from the other end of the dormitory; "She's hardly told us anything." She was right, I'd really said very little of my mother's cruelty and massive mood swings. I had always tried to keep it hidden and defended her to those who criticised. As the roomful of girls discussed the pros and cons of my trip, I wondered if Kirsty was just fearful of me making up with mummy and leaving the hostel. So, as very often happened, I found myself putting my confusion to one side and reassuring Kirsty that we'd always be friends.

As I waited for Bob on the wall outside the hostel the following Saturday morning Tony, Steve and Rob pulled up on their bikes.

"Hiya, stranger," said Tony, walking over to give me a leathery hug. "What are you up to?" I explained about the trip and he hugged me again. "That's great, Nicky. Good luck with it." Just then Kirsty, Anne and another girl came rushing out of the front door, and although Bob's car pulled up nearby I felt a bit strange as I saw the new girl climb on behind Tony. However, at that moment he turned to give me a smile so warm and intimate that I felt sure he'd always be there for me, whatever happened. Bob was smiling too, from where he stood by his open car door and I thought how lucky I was, and that if so many people cared about me perhaps mummy would too, like she once did.

12

My head throbbed and it was a struggle to open my eyes, which felt as if they had been glued together. For a moment I felt like a tiny girl again, waiting for mummy to bathe my sticky eyes as she had each morning. When I finally managed to open them a little I saw a high white ceiling and, as I tried to look sideways, a tall metal stand that hovered over me. I struggled to lift myself on my elbows but my head and neck hurt too much, so I relaxed back into the pillow, wondering what was happening. My whole body felt stiff, as if I'd been stuck in one position for ages, and I tried to stretch. My neck pain eased as my arms reached beyond my head, my hands touching the cold of the metal bedstead, but my legs didn't seem to be stretching at all. I tried to move my feet sideways in the bed and realised I couldn't really feel my legs and feet, just a vague sensation of heaviness from my waist down. With a struggle I managed to raise my head from the pillow enough to look down at my feet, to see if they were tied down as they felt, but all I could see was the outline of my lower half beneath a greyish green blanket. It was tucked in tightly at the bottom and I guessed this was what stopped me moving. My head dropped back onto the pillow and I was trying to summon the energy to pull the blankets loose, when I heard a door open and some sharp footsteps on a hard floor. A round puffy face, topped with a small starched hat on pulled back blonde hair, hovered above me, green eyes peering into mine and a large hand resting heavily on my forehead.

"Hmm, cooler. You've decided to wake up then." The voice was slightly muffled, coming as it did from behind a white cotton mask that covered her mouth and nose and looped behind her ears. I wasn't sure if it was a question but it didn't matter as, before I could consider replying, the face disappeared, and I felt hands gripping my arm and pushing me sideways. As I stared at a bare wall I felt coolness from the blanket lifting and something hard move down my back, then the hands were under my arms, pulling me back and upwards and the face appeared close to mine. "Now do your business, child, and don't take all day. You're not the only patient I have you know." Patient, business…the words struggled in my mind.

"Patients are in hospital," I heard my voice say, quietly and hesitantly.

"Well, where do you think you are, Buckingham Palace?" asked the woman, with a half chuckle. "Have you done yet?" She leaned closer and I peered down where she was staring, embarrassed to see my legs splayed as I sat on a sort of metal bowl.

She pressed her large hand on my stomach, moving it round in a clockwise direction, and the combination of this and the awkward way I was balanced made me feel nauseous. "Come on, girl, get those bowels opened," she said, quite gently yet impatiently. I wanted to do as I was told so this would be over, yet I felt my stomach muscles tense even tighter, despite hearing a small trickle of wee hitting the container. Just then another, younger, woman came into the room pushing a noisy trolley, and out of the corner of my eye I saw a blue bowl with wafts of steam coming from it. Between the two of them they removed the bowl, wiped me with scratchy paper then lay me back down and took off my nightie. I still felt confused and embarrassed, but they were very matter of fact as they washed me all over with a slightly scratchy flannel soaked in the warm water and covered in a smelly soap that made my nose tickle as they washed my face. They chatted between themselves as they worked, the younger woman describing a film she had seen the night before but her eyes twinkling each time she caught my eye. I guessed she was smiling at me behind the mask that she also wore. After a rub down with a towel the first woman, who I now knew to be a nurse, went out with the trolley while the younger one dressed me in a clean nightie then, after propping me up with pillows, sat on the edge of the bed and gently brushed tangles out of my long hair.

"Why am I here?" I asked nervously. "Why can't I wash myself?"

"Oh, you poor little chicken," she said, squeezing one of my hands, and asked me whether I remembered the injection at school. I did and found my right hand automatically moving to the top of my left arm where the puncture had been.

"I wasn't ill though," I said quickly. "I went to class afterwards. I went home..." I hesitated. "I mean to my boarding school home, not my mummy home. I want my mummy," I added and felt tears trickling down my cheek.

"Aah bless, of course you do, poor mite. She'll be coming to see you soon I'm sure." She gave me a quick hug whilst nervously glancing at the door, then resumed the hair brushing. She explained how the morning after the polio vaccination I'd gone to school as usual, but then suddenly developed a terrible headache and stiff neck. "The teacher was very good, she called the ambulance straight away and they brought you here."

"But what's wrong with me?" I asked and heard her tut loudly.

"It's a reaction, dear. I'm still training as a nurse, so don't understand it all, but it happens sometimes." She went on to explain that I couldn't feel my legs properly because they were paralysed, but that they could get better in a few weeks or so.

She spoke so brightly I felt I should be grateful or something, and I didn't speak anymore in case she saw that I was really sad and frightened. She stroked my hair with her hand as she stood up.

"I'll leave you propped up for now and I'll come back soon with a comic, dear," she said. "I'm Nurse Evans, but you can call me Julie when it's just us," she added and I heard the door close quietly behind her.

Propped up on the pillows I could see I was in a high square room painted a pale sickly green colour, and that there were no other beds. In fact there was nothing really, apart from the bedside table and a dark green plastic chair against the wall opposite. I found myself thinking about green being mummy's favourite colour, but not these ugly greens. Hers was a soft olive green that looked smart and elegant and matched her eyes. These thoughts brought more tears and I had to use all my strength to pull the bedding out from where it had been tucked in so tightly, in order to wipe my eyes on the corner of the sheet.

"This wasn't what I meant," I heard myself whisper, remembering how I'd longed to get away from the boarding school. "I wanted to go home, I wanted to be with mummy." With these words came further sobbing, which was how Julie found me when she returned with a comic and a book called Heidi, both balanced on a tray that slotted over the bed. She wiped my eyes gently, murmuring soothing sounds and adjusting the pillows slightly.

"Come on, chicken, you show me what a big girl you are," she said and I gave her a weak smile. There was a bowl of tomato soup, some crackers and a cup of orange juice on the tray as well, and now the nausea had passed I felt really hungry. "Take it easy today, dear. Maybe tomorrow you'll be on the meat and vegetables." I explained about being vegetarian and could tell by her expression that she thought it a bit daft, but she said she'd make sure it was in my notes. She showed me a cord hanging by the bed that she said I should pull when I'd finished eating. "Or if you need that horrible old bedpan again," she added as she left the room.

So began long tedious days of boredom and frustration, the monotony of the long lonely hours only interrupted by meals, bed baths and a little elderly lady who came in twice a day to move and massage my legs. The frustration of having to wait for a nurse to respond to the bell pull for the slightest thing was awful, and led to situations that for a nine-year-old were really embarrassing. It was bad enough when the juice upset and I had to try and throw off the soggy blanket, but still sat in the soaking wet nightie for ages because the nurses were busy. What was far worse was when no-one responded to my need for a bedpan one night, so that when the nurse did eventually come I had soiled the bed, the air in the room full of the awful smell. I had never seen this nurse before, and from the way she was rubbing her eyes when she arrived I suspected she had been sleeping.

"You filthy child," she hissed from behind her mask as she pulled back the blanket to reveal my shame, and although I couldn't see anything from where I lay I flushed to imagine what she was seeing. "Disgusting!" she kept barking harshly as she wiped me with the hard paper and pushed me roughly onto my side, so that she could drag the soiled sheet from under me. I started to apologise but she took no notice. She left me balanced like that on the rubber-covered mattress and went out of the room. She was gone so long I had begun to think she was going to leave me like that all night, but then she returned with some linen and a bowl of water and washed me really roughly.

"Don't you ever do that to me again, you naughty girl," she said, as she pushed a clean sheet under me and pulled me onto my back. "We'll make sure you don't tonight anyway," she added, fumbling below my line of vision. It was only when she'd slammed out of the room that I could explore with my hands, and discovered she'd put some sort of nappy on me. I lay awake the rest of the night, feeling both humiliated and guilty, fearful that the nurse might return. The next morning Julie found me exhausted, my eyes swollen from crying and my back hurting from the way the thick nappy had raised my hips. Initially she gave me the usual reassurances and comforting noises, but when she pulled back the covers and found the nappy I saw anger in her eyes.

"I'm sorry, Julie, I tried to hold on but…"

"Oh no, chick, I'm not cross with you," she said quickly. "These things happen, it's not your fault. But you won't be wearing one of these again." I knew then that it was the other nurse she was angry with, but still couldn't help wondering if she'd be as nice if she'd had to clear up the filthy mess I'd made.

On the third day I was propped up slightly, reading Heidi, when the door opened. I glanced up to see the same doctor who'd visited the day before, together with Julie and another woman. It took a moment for my brain to register the eyes above the mask.

"Mummy!" I yelled, all my instincts trying to get my body to jump out of the bed to get to her. Instead I grasped the metal stand to help pull myself to an upright sitting position, the way Julie had shown me. I was so happy as she crossed the room towards me, pausing to check with the doctor before leaning over to hug me, and despite my useless legs I felt everything was now going to be alright. Which made it all the lonelier when, after an hour of sitting by my bed on the green chair telling me her news, she got up to leave in response to a nurse popping in to say visiting time was over.

"Will you come again tomorrow, mummy?" I pleaded.

"I don't think I can make it tomorrow, darling, but I'll be back soon." I was about to plead, desperate that it shouldn't be like it had been at boarding school, when she added "I need you to be a strong brave girl, Nicky, because mummy has lots of other things to worry about as well." I wanted to ask her what she was worried about, apart from me, but I didn't want to upset her. So I pretended I really was brave and strong as she squeezed my hand goodbye, explaining she couldn't give me a kiss because of infection.

Julie popped in before she went off shift, to check I wasn't too upset, but she found me angry rather than sad.

127

"I don't care if she doesn't come," I muttered. "Guess other stuff is more important as always." She listened to me rant for a while until I calmed down, and after she went I just felt guilty talking about mummy like that. "Sorry for being selfish," I whispered as I drifted off to sleep, exhausted by the emotion of the day.

She did visit several more times over the next few weeks, the fact that it was always unexpected making it exciting, but leaving me with a mixture of sadness and anger in between. Even daddy visited once, which was a big surprise. My certainties were based around the hospital routine, which made me feel safe as I gradually got stronger, so that even when Julie went on holiday I didn't get too upset. I was getting physically stronger too, as sensations gradually returned to my legs. It was really strange to see mouths moving, when it was decided I was no longer infectious so people coming into my room didn't have to wear masks. Even stranger was when Nurse Jones turned up with a wheelchair, and I was given a tour of the corridors and a brief visit to the great big windy world just outside a door. Julie was over the moon, when she returned from holiday to find I'd been moved from isolation to a ward with other children, although she said she missed me. I sort of missed her too but it was fun to be around other children, to be taking more and more wobbly steps each day under the guidance of my elderly physiotherapist and to be looking forward to going home. Home! That was the big one, especially when on one of her visits mummy told me I wouldn't be going back to boarding school, but to the new house she and daddy were living in.

13

For the first part of our journey Bob managed to relax my nerves with funny stories from his childhood, creating for me Enid Blyton type scenarios of scrapes and adventures with his brothers and sister. They were funny but also they sounded so warm and loving, my fantasy being that they all ended with the whole family devouring crumpets and warm milk in front of a log fire. As we got nearer and nearer to my home it became harder for him to distract me, familiar sights bringing back memories so different to his anecdotes.

"Down there's where we lived when I came out of hospital," I murmured, indicating a turning we had just passed. The confused look on his face as he turned sharply towards me reminded me I hadn't even told him I'd been in hospital.

"Do you want to go and see it?" he asked, pulling into a lay-by.

"I'm not sure. It doesn't hold great memories," I said hesitantly.

"Would it help exorcise some demons, do you think?" Bob asked, raising his eyebrow quizzically.

"I guess it might," I agreed, and as soon as there was a gap in the traffic he did a U turn then crossed into the road I'd indicated. After only minutes we came to the small estate with its neat little identical houses and, having shown Bob where to park opposite what had been my home, I found myself remembering the first time I'd come there, clutching daddy's hand tightly and still slightly unsteady on my feet from the months in hospital. I was so excited and thought mummy would be too, standing at the door waiting for us. But when daddy opened a gate and we went up a short path, I saw the dark green door was shut.

"We'll surprise her," I whispered to daddy, and he gave me a small smile as he ruffled my hair. I never knew whether she was surprised or not, as after rushing into the house I eventually found her in the bedroom at the top of a narrow staircase. She was buried deep under the blankets, her long dark hair spread on the pillow and her face turned towards the window on the opposite wall.

"Mummy, I'm home," I whispered, and she responded by lifting one arm from under the blankets and reaching out towards me. I was shocked to see her face as she turned to look at me, the eyes appearing gigantic and the rest really bony. Her other hand emerged and she touched her cheek with the index finger.

"Kiss," she mumbled, her voice sounding flat and tired, matching the sleepy look in her eyes. I leant over and hugged her, planting a big kiss where she'd indicated, but pulled back as I heard a small moan.

"Be gentle, dear," said Daddy, just behind me. "Mummy's not very well you know."

I started to ask her what was wrong, but she wiggled the fingers of one hand in the air and disappeared back under the blankets and I felt daddy pulling on my arm to guide me out of the room.

I never did really find out what was wrong with her, although later I would reflect on that time as the beginning of her depression and mental illness. For some reason I didn't ask many questions. I guess I was taking my cue from daddy, who appeared to carry on as if everything was normal, enrolling me in the local school and taking me into town to buy the uniform whilst constantly reminding me to 'be a good girl'. On mummy's bad days he would take food up to her on a tray, and I would add a glass with primroses I had picked from the railway bank at the bottom of the garden. On her good days she would wander round the house lethargically, dressed in sloppy clothes and summoning me to help her with even simple chores. Meanwhile he would disappear, often not returning until after I was in bed when I would be woken by their rows. They had labelled the days as 'one of mummy's

130

good days' or 'mummy's having a bad day' but to me they were all bad. I really hoped when she got stronger the apparently carefree mother of my early years would return, but she never did and life just adapted to the increasingly dramatic swings between the good and bad days.

"Are you ok?" Bob's gentle question and his hand on my arm jerked me back to the present.

"Yep, of course, I'm fine," I babbled, blinking rapidly to control the tears that had been threatening. Although he knew I now had a difficult relationship with my mother, I wasn't ready to betray her by sharing the past with him or anyone else.

"Let's drive that way," I said brightly, pointing to the right, "that's where I went to school."

The single story school was still there, like an island between two roads, the trees around the edge of the large playground seeming smaller than back then. I laughed as I told Bob how we used the fallen leaves to divide the playground up into rooms, and would jump from one to the other in a series of complicated games. He grinned as I added "then when the bell went we would kick them all over the place before running into class, so we could create them all differently next time." I found myself momentarily reflecting that I had been doing that most of my life, trying to discard the past so I could create a brand new better future.

"Sounds like fun," Bob said and I nodded enthusiastically, going on to tell him about my first day there, when mummy told me to keep my uniform clean and daddy told me I would be collected when the bell rang.

"I was so careful all day, Bob, my tunic was spotless! Then I waited what seemed like ages for one of them to come but no-one did. Most of the other children were collected, some lived locally so just walked home, then there was me. I should have said something to the teacher but for some reason

131

I didn't think of that. So, as we'd come on a bus, I got on a bus that stopped near the school. I kept looking out of the window for my house but didn't see it. I think the conductor assumed I was with one of the adults so he never asked for my ticket and he seemed pretty shocked when I was the only one left on the bus at the end of the route. Then he took me to the police station and they had to call the school and everything." I started laughing at the recollection. " They told me to sit down while I waited for my father, but when I saw the chairs were dirty I refused to sit in case my uniform got dirty. Apparently I stood there for over an hour!"

"You poor kid," said Bob gently, his arm around my shoulder. I looked at him in amazement.

"It was funny, everybody laughs when I tell them that story," I said, disconcerted by his response.

"Oh, ok," he said quickly. "I just thought it sounded scary, no-one coming to get you and then being so worried about getting dirty." I hadn't seen it that way and I suggested we drive on, unsure whether him saying what he did made me sad or annoyed me because he spoilt my funny anecdote.

We were both really tense for the last few miles, Bob trying to cover his nerves with his characteristic tuneless whistle. As we went through the town things somehow looked different, but suddenly we were at the end of the road and passing the taxi drivers who'd mocked me just a couple of years before. As we parked outside the flats I looked up at the big window of the sitting room, picturing the smart dining furniture inside and wondering if she yet had a sofa or comfy chair.

"Shall I come up with you?" Bob asked as I climbed out of the car, but I shook my head.

"Give me a few minutes first," I said, hearing the nervous croak in my voice. "I'll come and get you shortly." I leaned into the driver's window to give him a peck on the cheek and he whispered "Luck."

132

I was flooded with memories and anxiety as I climbed the steps to the main door and pushed it open. I noticed the large hallway had been redecorated, the ugly brown below the dado rail now deep blue and the front door of our flat painted to match. I knocked nervously, silently practicing different greetings as I waited. I knocked again, listening for any sounds of movement within and remembering the sickening feeling of coming home from grammar school and waiting for that door to be opened, not knowing what mood she would be in, dreading the claustrophobic evening ahead dominated by her constant talking.

There was still no response and I had to accept that, after all the build-up, nobody was at home. As I settled back in the car next to Bob I wasn't sure if I was disappointed or relieved.

"What about neighbours?" Bob asked, turning to look back along the street. "Might they know where she is?"

"She didn't mix with the neighbours," I said briefly, not wanting to tell him about the paranoia she developed that convinced her they were all against her. Then I suddenly remembered that she had become a bit friendly with the mother of Caroline, one of my classmates.

"She lives up that passageway," I told Bob, pointing. "We can walk there." Mrs Morrow answered the door almost immediately and looked shocked to see me.

"Oh goodness, come in, dear," she exclaimed, backing up to make room for us in the small hallway that smelt of air freshener. "Did she tell you then?" she continued as she showed us into the front room. "I'm afraid you're a bit late."

"For what?" I asked. "Is it Caroline's birthday or something? She and I haven't really been in touch since school Mrs Morrow."

She told us to sit on the flowered sofa then stood in front of us, nervously chewing her lip.

"Oh no, not Caroline, she's out at work. No, it's your mother, dear, she…" I saw her look towards Bob, almost pleadingly as if he could help her, and I started to feel faint.

"What?" I almost shouted. "What has happened to her?"

"Oh no, dear, nothing like that, nothing really bad," she babbled, smiling nervously. "Well, no other way to say it really. Fact is, she's down the Town Hall getting married!"

I stood up, totally stunned. None of the fantasies I might have had as to what was going on for mummy came close to this. I became aware of Mrs Morrow speaking again.

"Actually, it'll be all over by now," she said quietly, staring at the grandmother clock in the corner. We were all standing there in silence, just looking at each other, when there was a loud knock on the front door. Mrs Morrow went out into the hall, there was a mumbled exchange and a moment later my mother rushed into the room and fell to her knees in front of me.

"I'm so sorry, please forgive me," she sobbed, tears pouring down her heavily made up cheeks. I reached down to pull her up, smoothing her hair back into the chignon under a little white hat that matched her suit.

"It's alright, mummy, why should you be sorry?" I asked, feeling tears on my own lashes.

She perched on the edge of the sofa and peered up at me, the shine of smudged wet mascara making her green eyes look really bright.

"It's a big mistake," she said between gulps of breath. "I'm so stupid. He's not one of our sort at all!" The words kept coming, gradually becoming more and more rambling, while her voice veered between that of a helpless little girl and the deep bitterness of an angry woman. My head felt like it was going to explode with the confusion of thoughts and feelings as her voice babbled on, and I was reassured to suddenly feel Bob's arm around me offering comfort and safety. I saw

134

mummy glance up towards him and was shocked by the look of hatred that crossed her face.

"Who is he?" she demanded.

"He's with me, mummy," I started to say and she let out a laugh that almost sounded like a sneer.

"So you have turned into the proverbial loose woman have you? I always thought you would, living it up in the big city."

"Loose woman?" I exclaimed. "This is Bob, he's a friend." I stopped mid-sentence, suddenly aware of a slim middle-aged man in a brown suit standing just inside the door.

"Oh, you're here, Derek," said Mrs Morrow, sounding relieved. "Good, I'll make us all tea then," she added, bustling out to the kitchen.

Derek stared at me nervously, but Bob went forward with his hand outstretched and Derek reached out to shake it and then mine. I responded automatically, introducing myself and Bob.

"Pleased to meet you," he said in a strong cockney accent.

"Is it true?" I asked. "Did you and mummy just get married?"

"Oh yes, we did, dear," he said, holding out his left hand to show me a narrow gold ring. "So I suppose we're related now," he added nervously, and mummy looked up sharply, as if this was a new idea to her.

"Did your mother tell you how we met?" he asked with a smile. I was about to say she hadn't even mentioned he existed, let alone sharing details, but he wasn't really looking for an answer as he went on to tell us how she had approached him in a café a few months ago to tell him off for eating a pork pie. At that moment Mrs Morrow came back into the room carrying a tea tray, which she placed on the coffee table.

"He hasn't eaten meat since," she said with a forced cheeriness. "Has he, Elizabeth?" she asked, handing my mother a white napkin. I saw the look of hatred return to my

135

mother's face as she stared at her momentarily, then she suddenly stood up.

"Derek, we are going home now," she barked, taking hold of his arm, "and don't you try following, young lady, because you and your fancy man are not welcome." With that she pushed Derek out of the door and I just heard him call out a stammered goodbye before the front door slammed shut.

I think we were all equally shocked in the moments that followed, and then I heard that familiar phrase as Mrs Morrow held out a cup of tea. "I'm sorry, dear; she's obviously having one of her bad days. I haven't seen her like that in a while. Probably the stress of the wedding. If you come again tomorrow, I expect she'll be fine."

"She needs professional help," Bob said and I instinctively wanted to defend her, but instead just nodded, while Mrs Morrow said something about mummy being on medication but not always taking it. The words just spun around until I heard my own voice telling Bob we had to go. He made all the necessary polite noises and then held my hand tightly as we walked to the car outside my mother's flat. I looked up, wondering if I would see them at the window.

"Do you want to try and talk to her?" Bob asked quietly.

"No, I can't, Bob, I just can't," I said, feeling my body start to shake as I climbed into the car. "Please take me away from here, please!"

Back in London I withdrew into myself so much that even people at work started asking if I was alright.

"Of course, I'm fine," I'd respond brightly, with a smile, as I'd learnt to do throughout my life. I quickly realised that Bob must have broken the family code of silence as Laura, Kirsty and the others didn't ask me what had happened at the visit, just fussed around me more than usual. I think Laura in particular felt bad, partly because she had encouraged me to go but also because she and Kwesi had now fixed a date for leaving and they were caught up in trying to find good homes for Boris and the others. They had already said tearful farewells to Wally and Paulie, who had gone to a snake dancer in Brighton.

To be fair to Bob, he did try to talk to me about it all but I shut him off quickly, telling him that although it was shocking to him it was no big deal for me.

"I'm used to it," I said. "The impetuous decisions, the drama, the mood swings, they are what make her special. And special is better than boring," I added with a laugh, seeing the puzzled look on his face briefly, before he hugged me.

As Bob had predicted I decided he was right, that it made sense for us to live together in his flat, and the excitement of that pulled me out of my torpor a little. I could hardly believe I would have my own home, where I could feel safe and which we could fill with fun and happiness.

"You sure you know it's just as flatmates, Bob, that I'll be sleeping in that little box room?" I checked before finally committing and he nodded agreement.

"All in good time," he said, smiling.

We were in his flat when I agreed so, perhaps because he was worried I'd change my mind, he suggested we go straight down to the Cazians to get their permission. It hadn't occurred to me that would be needed, but as Bob and I stood nervously at their flat door it made sense.

"Come in, come in," the old man said effusively when he saw us, grabbing hold of Bob's arm and glancing briefly at me. As on the previous couple of times we'd visited Mrs Cazian was stretched on the sofa, her swollen feet raised on a cushion, but she sat up quickly when she saw us and was soon bustling about getting tea and biscuits. Everything was very warm and friendly until Bob told them the reason for our visit, when a distinct chill settled on the room. I saw them exchange brief glances, then Mrs Cazian leant forward to take both of Bob's hands in hers.

"This is quite a surprise, dear, we'll have to give it a bit of thought," she said, apparently ignoring me altogether.

"Of course, Mrs C, that's fine. We can pay a little more rent if you want, to cover the extra water used and so on." I could hear in his voice the calmness and confidence of someone who usually got what he wanted, but seeing their faces and sensing the atmosphere I didn't share the confidence.

When Bob rang me at the hostel the next day, I assumed he was about to tell me their decision. Instead his voice bubbled with excitement, as he explained that his parents were going to be in town the following day.

"They're staying at their usual hotel," he said, naming a smart one in central London. "So I'm joining them there for dinner tomorrow, and it's a brilliant chance for you to meet them."

"Did they invite me?" I asked and heard him chuckle.

"No, but we can surprise them. They won't mind one more at the table and I know they'll love you."

Although I agreed to go I was really apprehensive.

"That's natural," said Anne, as she and Mary rummaged through piles of clothes, looking for something suitably smart for me to wear. "After all, one day they'll be your in-laws!"

"Don't be daft, anything like that is years away," I said quickly, although the words gave me a warm tingle. "What if they hate me?"

"Why would they?" asked Kirsty, holding a pair of black velvet trousers against me to check the leg length. "They'll love you, especially when they see you in my trouser suit."

She was right that the black velvet trouser suit looked pretty good on me, fitting snugly at the waist and hips and flaring out slightly at the bottom.

"You just need a trendy blouse, and I've got the perfect one somewhere," said Mary, rummaging through a plastic bag she pulled from under her bed. She was right too, the black and white geometric patterned blouse she dragged out was perfect and I looked pretty smart, apart from the blouse being crumpled. I hung the outfit on a rail, and as I got into bed that night I made a mental note to iron the blouse in the morning.

I should have known better than to hope for use of the one hostel iron before work, when everyone was rushing around, and I managed to be twenty minutes late to the office despite eventually giving up trying to get possession. This meant I had to work late to make up the time, and was even more rushed than expected when I got back to the hostel that evening. I headed straight for the bathroom to wash my hair, as Kirsty had promised to blow dry and backcomb it for me. Then she and Anne took me over just as they had back in the early days, working their magic with foundation stick and blusher and creating giant spider eyes that dominated my face. They had just finished their creation and sprayed half a can of lacquer on my hair, when another girl shouted that Steve was outside.

"You look amazing," said Kirsty. "His parents will be knocked out." Anne nodded, smiling proudly at their handiwork, then the two of them rushed off for their biker evening while I started to get dressed. It was then that I remembered the blouse needed ironing, so I switched the iron on and left it to heat while I rummaged under Anne's bed for the high-heeled black evening shoes she had said I could borrow. I was still in trousers and bra when someone called that Bob was outside, so it was a mad rush to iron the blouse. Which was probably why I didn't check what heat the iron was set at, and why an iron shaped brown scorch appeared right on the front of the blouse.

"Noooo!" I yelled, so loudly one of the Irish girls rushed into the kitchen.

"Oh my giddy aunt," she exclaimed when she saw what I had done. "Don't start crying with that much mascara, you'll be blind for a week," she added when she saw my face. "Sure, you'll have to wear something else."

"Mary will kill me! And there isn't anything else! I'm going to be late as well."

"Tell you what, girl," she said, picking up the blouse and looking at the velvet jacket I'd hung over the end of the ironing board. "Just put it on back to front and, with the jacket, no-one will ever know."

"You're a genius," I yelled, sliding my arms into the blouse and waiting patiently while she buttoned it up from behind. It felt a bit high and restrictive under my chin, but once I had the jacket on the effect was almost smarter than when it was the right way round. With a yell of thanks I grabbed my bag and rushed out to Bob's car.

The foyer of the hotel was pretty imposing, and I was glad to have Bob leading me through to the crowded dining room, where a very formal waiter in a bow tie asked our name then guided us between the tables to one in the far corner.

"Parents dear!" said Bob loudly, throwing his arms out in an all-embracing dramatic gesture that caused people nearby to look over. An elegant blonde woman and a rather pudgy balding man looked up from the table and tried to appear disapproving.

"Robert, do sit down," said his mother but her lip twitched with a suppressed smile as he bent over and hugged her gently, before sitting on the chair the waiter had pulled out.

"Oh gosh, sorry!" he said as he realised I was still standing there. The fourth chair at the table was already occupied by a girl, probably a few years younger than me, who was staring at me quite openly. Hasty introductions were made all round while the waiter went off, rather grumpily it seemed, to find another chair and table setting. Eventually I was seated between his father and what turned out to be his sister Rachel. Although the family greeted me very politely I felt like a fish out of water, the situation not improved by me being unable to find anything vegetarian on the overpriced menu.

140

"Could the chef perhaps create a lovely cheese omelette for our young guest?" his mother eventually asked the waiter, and after a brief trip to the kitchens we were advised that 'chef would be happy to oblige'. I could see where Bob got his calm confidence from and I smiled my thanks at her.

"Aren't you hot?" Rachel asked as the other three chatted of home. It was really warm in there, and most of the women seemed to be wearing silky sleeveless evening dresses.

"A bit," I said quietly, "but I'm ok."

"Why don't you take your jacket off?" she asked. "The waiter will hang it up for you," and she raised her hand to summon him. I had actually started to remove it when I remembered the back to front blouse, so made some mumbled confusing explanation as I straightened it up.

His parents asked me a few polite questions, but mostly talked with Bob. So I was surprised when his father turned to me and asked me to remind him where I lived.

"A hostel hmm. That sounds a good idea, other girls around so you can help each other."

"Yes, it is but..." I was about to mention about sharing Bob's flat, but wasn't sure if he'd want me to. I glanced over at him and sensed he was relieved I had stopped when I did.

When Rachel said she was going to powder her nose I gratefully followed her. I hadn't wanted to try and find the toilets on my own, but the dining room had become increasingly warm and I was convinced if I didn't splash my face with cold water I would pass out. In the cubicle I gratefully removed my jacket, swinging it around to create a cooling draft.

"Are you alright in there?" Rachel asked, probably confused by the sound of the buttons hitting the wooden door.

"I'm fine thank you," I said, reluctantly putting the jacket back on and joining her at the sinks.

"Are you a model or something?" she asked, looking at me in the mirror as I carefully dabbed my face with damp tissue. Before I could answer she added, "My parents would never let me go out with all that make-up. Mummy says anything more than powder and lipstick is too tarty for a young lady." The cheeks I had just cooled became hot and red with embarrassment as I heard her words.

"It's just for special occasions, like tonight," I heard myself babbling. "I wouldn't wear all this to work or anything. I just wanted to look my best."

"I like it and I expect Bob likes it," she said with a little smile. "Mummy says he's got a bit longer to sow his oats and then he'll come home and marry. Probably one of the girls I go to school with." I was stunned by the bluntness of her statement.

"He's not sowing his oats, as you put it. We are just going out."

"I didn't 'put it' as you say. I'm just telling you what I heard mummy say to daddy. I don't even know what it means really, but it will be lovely to have him home again."

Lost for words, I went to the door and she followed me back to the table, where I was now convinced everyone was judging me. The waiter had brought desert while we were gone, so I hoped we would be leaving shortly. However, when his father ordered another bottle of wine I realised we'd be there for a while, and I made a quick decision.

"I'm really sorry," I said, "but I'm not feeling very well, so I think I'm going to have to leave you all." I started to push my chair back but his father took my hand.

"What is it, dear? Do you need a doctor or anything?"

"No, no, I just need to lie down."

"You are very hot, my dear, why don't you take that jacket off. You might feel a lot better. Help her, Robert," he added, as Bob stood up and came round the table. I was horrified to feel him easing the jacket off my shoulders.

"No, I have to go," I almost shouted, jumping up and pulling the jacket tight around me. The other three looked shocked at my outburst, but they voiced various pleasantries and Bob walked to the foyer with me.

"I'm sorry to spoil your evening, Bob. I just need you to take me home." I saw a brief look of panic on his face.

"Um, Nicky I can't really do that to my parents. I mean, if you were really, really ill then... You're not are you?" I was so used to being able to rely on Bob I was a bit shaken when, after my reassurances that I wasn't about to die, he rummaged in his pocket and handed me some coins for a taxi.

"Ring you tomorrow, hope you feel better," he whispered, as he gave me a quick hug before returning to the restaurant. The concierge must have heard it all, as he summoned a taxi from the street for me, but I just ignored him and walked to the nearest bus stop, my eyes clouded by the black swirl of wet mascara.

14

When I met Bob at the coffee bar the next day he assured me that of course his parents liked me, and were only concerned that I became unwell. I wondered whether to tell him about the blouse or what his sister had said, but decided against it, not wanting to split his loyalties between me and his family.

"Ok, so today's the big day when our future is decided," he said brightly and I nodded nervously. "I can't see they'd have a problem with us sharing," he went on. "It doesn't really affect them." I was less confident, given how dismissive of me Mr Cazian seemed to be. After last night's conversation I wondered if he and his wife also saw me as tarty. So it was with trepidation that I followed Bob into their front room later that day, and perched nervously next to him on the sofa.

"So, Mr C, are you going to make me a happy fellow?" Bob asked and the old man made the most of his moment of power, rocking on his heels and twiddling with the lobe of his left ear. The way he glanced at me before he spoke gave me the answer a moment ahead of Bob.

"Sorry, son, I'm afraid it's just not on."

"What?" Bob was genuinely shocked. "Oh come on, Mr C, how would it bother you?"

"Sorry, it's just a no," said Mr Cazian. Bob started to protest but I stood up, knowing the discussion was over. As I reached the door Mrs Cazian hobbled over to me. "I'm sorry, dear," she said quietly, "but we have to go along with his parents' decision. Even you must see that girls like you don't belong in his world."

"Are you sure that's what she said?" Bob asked as we walked back to his car. I hadn't told him what she had said about me, just about it being his parents' decision.

"Oh shoot, that's the downside of having landlords that are friends with the parents. I didn't even know they'd talked," he said sulkily.

"I didn't even know they knew each other! You could have told me, Bob, I might have made more effort with Mr C if I'd realised he was feeding back to your parents. Didn't they mention about the flat at dinner last night?"

"Nope. Don't worry, it's probably just mum being overprotective as usual and getting Mr C to be the baddy." He spoke confidently but I could tell he was bluffing.

"They don't like me, Bob, simple as that. Mr Cazian has always resented me taking your attention away from him anyway, so if he's been telling them about me all this time I never stood a chance."

"I told you, they do like you, Nicky. They said so. In fact, they said...oh no, I think this might be my fault."

"How, Bob?"

"Um, I guess over dinner, after you left, I told them about our trip to see your mother, about her acting weird. To explain your dramatic exit, how you'd been under stress and that."

"You thought you had the right to tell them about my mother?" I shouted angrily. "Great! So I'm being judged by them on the basis of a miserable possessive old Armenian and a crazy parent!"

"See," Bob retorted confidently. "Even you say it, Nicky, so how can you be angry with me for telling them she's a bit crazy?"

"You told them what?" I shrieked. "How dare you. How can you judge her, are you a psychiatrist? Even real psychiatrists can't make her better," I added, tears flooding down my cheeks. Bob touched my arm gently.

"What are we arguing about?" he asked, sounding genuinely puzzled. "We are both saying the same thing."

"No we're not," I yelled. "We might be using the same words but we are saying different things. Only I can call her crazy, because she's my mum and I love her. Because I knew her before, when she was happy, before she sent me away."

"What the hell has that got to do with it?" asked Bob angrily, kicking out at the tyre of his car. "Are you saying you going to boarding school caused her to become cr...," he hesitated, "like she is?"

"Doesn't take a genius, Bob. She was fine, she was happy, then while I was away she became weird and sad."

"For crying out loud, Nicky. You didn't abandon her! It was her that sent you away."

"Exactly! She sent me away because I was bad, then I got ill and caused more problems and..."

"Oh for goodness sake get a grip, Nicky, you're sounding as nuts as her."

The sound of my hand slapping his face echoed in my head as I ran down the street, blinded by the tears and the rage. Part of me expected him to follow and I was automatically rehearsing angry rebuffs for when he tried to put his arms around me, but I was still alone when I reached the hostel and lashed out angrily at Mary instead of him. She finally gave up trying to comfort me, simply leaving a cup of tea by my bed as I pulled the blankets over my head to shut out the world, even in my misery recalling mummy doing exactly the same all those years ago.

When I awoke late the next morning, grateful that it was the weekend, my head throbbed and the cold tea still sat by my bed. Next to it was a scribbled note from Kirsty, saying that Bob had called early but she hadn't liked to wake me. The dormitory was unusually empty and quiet as I lay there, remembering how angrily I'd treated Bob and wondering why I'd lost it like that. I still felt annoyed that he had talked to his parents about my mother, but also felt sorry for him being caught up in all this. I was used to it all, the family dramas and secrets, but I could understand that for an outsider coming into it crazy might seem an appropriate word.

146

He was trying to reassure you, Nicky and in return you slap him and behave like a nasty spoilt child, I told myself as I washed and dressed, rubbing extra pancake under my eyes to try and cover the puffiness. My finger hovered nervously over the A button on the phone, ready to press it as soon as his voice answered, but the ringing tone just continued until I pressed the other button and retrieved my coins. I made a cup of tea and planned my apology before dialling again, but there was still no reply. I wondered if he was really out, or just guessing it was me calling and too upset to answer. I dialled my aunt's number instead. I hadn't seen her since breaking the news of mummy's marriage, which was as much of a shock to her as to me. She answered on the second ring, and I was reassured by her bright chirpy voice telling me she was all alone and would love me to come for lunch.

"I was really horrible, aunty," I said as we prepared salad and omelettes in her kitchen.

"Sounds like you were upset, Nicky. Probably disappointed about the flat."

"That's true, but it's no excuse. Aunty, why do you think mummy sent me to boarding school? Was I a really difficult child? Did I throw tantrums like this then?"

"Goodness, no. The opposite. You were really quiet and you became even more withdrawn when she became pregnant, so I guess she thought..."

"What! What do you mean 'became pregnant'? Who? When?"

"Well your mother of course," said aunty matter-of-factly, as she put the knives and forks on the table. "It was hard on you because she was always tired and your father... Nicky, why are you staring at me like that?"

"I never knew she was pregnant," I heard myself say quietly. "If she was pregnant where's the baby?" I felt panic rising as I remembered reciting poetry with Laura, dreading what I might now hear.

"Oh my goodness," said my aunt, switching off the gas flames under the omelette pan. "I think we need to go and sit down. You're as white as a sheet," she added as she guided me into the sitting room and sat me in the armchair by the open fire. "You were told about her being pregnant, Nicky. At first you were really excited about having a brother or sister to play with. But it's hard for small children, seeing mummy changing, tired all the time. Those things are difficult for children. I think that's why she thought you'd be happier at boarding school, with other children."

"Was it because I was horrible to her, aunty?" I asked nervously.

"Oh bless you, no. As I said, you were happy and excited at first, and it was only later you were withdrawn and a bit cross with the baby for making your mummy unhappy and ill. Little bit of sibling rivalry I suspect. Perfectly natural, dear, not horrible at all."

"The baby though, where is the baby?"

"Sadly, mummy lost it when you were away at school. That's why she couldn't visit you much in hospital and why…well, that was when she started to be a bit strange."

Why she hid under the covers, why she forgot to collect me from school, why she hit me to 'keep me safe'. I found myself filling in the blanks, trying to rewrite my childhood from nine years old to incorporate this new information.

I felt aunty's arm around my shoulder.

"Are you alright, Nicky? I'm sorry if it's all a bit of a shock. I thought you knew. You did know."

She was peering into my face with a questioning half smile on her red painted lips, and I struggled to smile back reassuringly.

"I'll be ok, aunty, just a lot to take on board. Perhaps I did know but I don't remember any of it. Except I sort of do vaguely remember her with a rounded tummy, now that you've reminded me. How could I forget? I'm sure I was never told she miscarried though."

"You're probably right, Nicky. Your mother never spoke about it, to me or anyone as far as I know. I think she felt guilty, a failure. That's probably why you forgot the pregnancy. If you'd remembered, you would have needed to know why there was no baby. By forgetting it just got mixed up in the unmentionable family secret."

I went and got my jacket from the stand in the hall, feeling slightly unsteady on my feet.

"I'm sorry, aunty," I said, as I fished my gloves out of the pocket and put them on. "I don't think I can eat lunch. I need to think. You say she felt guilty but she made me feel guilty somehow. Perhaps she remembered me being cross with the baby, couldn't forgive me," I said tentatively. My aunt shook her head firmly. "She seemed to blame everyone else for her life, aunty. And I think I'm turning out the same. Yesterday I was blaming Bob when he was trying to support me. I need to explain, apologise to him."

"It's alright, dear, with my terrible cooking I'm used to people bailing out of meals," aunty said with a nervous laugh, as she followed me into the hall. "Just promise you'll come round if you need to talk more about all of this."

I agreed I would, and after a quick hug I hurried to catch the bus to Bob's flat, deciding if he wasn't going to answer his phone I'd just park myself on his doorstep until he let me apologise. As I stood ringing the bell I remembered the excitement I'd felt the first time I'd come here, meeting up with my holiday romance, and how handsome Bob had looked as he leant over the banisters. I just wanted to hug him and for him to hug me and make it all alright.

"Hello, Mr C," I said brightly when the old man opened the door, determined to ignore the issue of moving in and what Mrs Cazian had said. "Is Bob upstairs?" I asked as I stepped

149

past him into the hall, and I saw the familiar half smile appear on his lips.

"You're about three hours too late, my dear," he said and I detected a smugness in his voice. Perhaps he had heard our argument in the street, perhaps he thought he wouldn't have to share Bob with me anymore. I smiled in what I hoped was an equally smug way.

"I'll wait till he gets back then, Mr C. Don't worry about me, I'll just sit on the stairs here," I added dismissively, settling myself on the third of the thickly carpeted steps.

"It is Mr Cazian to you, girl," said the old man, the hostility no longer disguised. "And you'll have a very long wait, considering Robert is in Dorset for the foreseeable future."

His hand reached out to open the door he had only just closed. I guessed he thought I would just leave.

"What do you mean, Mr Cazian? Bob wasn't planning to visit his parents. He rang me earlier."

"Maybe he rang to say goodbye, he is a well brought up young man."

"No, it's not possible," I said, starting to climb the stairs. "I'll wait by his flat door. You don't have to wait with me."

"Actually it is my flat door, young lady, just as this is my house. As I just told you, Robert's mother collected him and most of his belongings over three hours ago and he is not expected back in the near future, if at all."

My dizziness returned, together with a tremendous churning in my stomach, until I was convinced I was going to throw up all over the hallway. What I was hearing just wasn't possible. Our argument hadn't been that bad, for him to run home. Unless it was that bad in his world, unless I was so bad that he had to get away from me.

"Do you have the phone number in Dorset?" I asked as I came back down the stairs, hearing my voice trembling as I fought back tears. I felt the old man's bony hand grip my arm as he guided me towards the now open door.

"If Robert wanted you to have that I am sure he would have given it to you," Mr Cazian said, looking me up and down with an expression of disdain. "If you want the advice of an old man, I suggest you find someone of your own type and forget about dear Robert and his family."

As the door closed behind me the increasingly familiar tears made their way out, and I almost wished the nausea hadn't passed so I could throw up all over this nasty old man's front doorstep.

15

"Nicky, this is ridiculous. It's two days now, you have to get up." From my hiding place under the blankets I felt Kirsty stroking the top of my head, then light flooded in as she pulled the edge of the blanket back.

"You've already missed a day's work without even ringing them. You'll get yourself sacked if you don't get it together. Then you'll never pay Mary for that burnt blouse."

"I can't help it, Kirsty," I said, forcing my eyes open to look up at her. "I'm just so shocked and hurt that Bob went off like that. Not a word!"

"Maybe you should start respecting yourself and get angry with him instead," said Anne's voice from the other side of the bed. Kirsty nodded in agreement.

"Any guy who'd just go like that doesn't deserve two days of your life, Nicky. You have to get up anyway, it's Laura and Kwesi's farewell party tonight, and it's nearly six o'clock already," she said.

"Oh god, no, I can't go to a party feeling like this, Kirsty. Tell them I'm sorry and…"

"I'm not telling them anything, Nicky. I cannot believe you can consider not being there for them, after you've been such good friends."

"But I feel like rubbish."

"If you let them down you are rubbish," said Anne, pulling the covers off me with a sudden move.

"She's right," said Kirsty. "The show must go on, so just get up. Wash off the gunge, slap on the magic make-up and be ready by the time the bikes arrive to drive us there. Oh, Tony's driving you by the way," she added brightly as she flounced off to the kitchen.

I followed her in there, all my limbs aching from lack of activity and my mouth stale and dry. The tea Kirsty was making was really welcome, the hug she gave me even more so.

"Isn't Tony seeing someone, won't he be taking her?" I asked nervously.

"Yep, he's taken Christine out a couple of times, nothing serious. But she's not coming tonight, so it'll be just like the old days."

It did feel like it as, hair done, make-up and best clothes on, we walked out of the hostel to where the guys were sitting on the wall. Tony's smile was almost shy as he stood up to greet me, arms outstretched for a quick hug. It felt so good and reassuring to ride pillion on his bike again, my arms around his waist and my face buried in his smelly old leather jacket. I was so grateful he was going to be there to help me through the evening, and take my mind off Bob.

The flat was cooler than I had ever known it, with no need for the humidity now all the snakes had been rehomed. I felt really sad as I hugged Kwesi and Laura, giving them a mumbled apology on the absent Bob's behalf. I guessed from the look of sympathy on Laura's face that they already knew about his disappearance but, as much as I would have liked her support, I wasn't going to let their special evening be dominated by my latest drama.

Without the snakes and their tanks, the lounge seemed eerily spacious and empty, despite about a dozen people chattering away in there. The furniture was pushed back against the walls, leaving the floor free for dancing to great music such as Freddie and the Dreamers and The Four Seasons. It was a struggle to know how to be, a real challenge for my chameleon self. Although I was overwhelmed by the sad realisation that this was probably the last time I would see them, Kwesi and Laura seemed to have moved on and they spoke excitedly of seeing her family and their plans for the new life in Vancouver.

"The folks will hardly recognise the new sophisticated me," Laura laughed "I've turned into a real coastie!" There was a lot of chatter and laughter, interspersed with brief silences while Kwesi, still unable to dance much, changed the records and watched us all with a big grin on his face. Tony had been flitting from one person to another, dancing with Kirsty and Laura and chatting to Kwesi. Suddenly he came over to me and stared into my eyes, looking serious despite the smile on his lips.

"I think they're playing our song," he said, taking me into his arms as The Kinks and '*Tired of Waiting*' filled the room. Part of me wanted to make a joke in response, just as we'd always done, but a much bigger part just wanted to relax into his arms. So we swayed together to the music, for precious moments oblivious to those around us. As the tune finished and we each moved off to talk to others, I was surprised at what I had felt during that dance. Yes, the comfort and safety I always felt with Tony but there was something else, something new yet vaguely familiar. A warmth in the cheek that had rested against his, a tension and tingling in my stomach. An excitement and anticipation. I was shocked to suddenly remember standing in the bathroom with Nazir, both of us looking at ourselves in the mirror. That wonderful momentary rush of sensation, smothered as Nazir tried to act on it, but somehow treasured to be reignited not by Lars or Bob but by Tony, of all people.

I was really confused by my feelings and could almost hear the girls whispering about rebounds, about me stringing Tony along. So I was relieved that it was raining heavily as we drove back to the hostel, making long farewells, or even conversation, impossible.

I was glad to be back in the dormitory before Kirsty and Anne got home and quickly changed into my nightie, snuggling into bed without bothering to clean off my make-up or brush my teeth. I was just about to pull the sheet up and recreate the safe little cave I had hidden in for the last two days, when I saw a folded sheet of paper on my bedside cabinet. 'Someone called Bob rang for you. Told them you were out' it read, followed by a number and a scribbled signature I didn't recognise that probably belonged to one of the new girls. I was momentarily filled with excitement, wishing I hadn't gone to the party and missed the call. Then it occurred to me that Bob knew about the farewell party, that they'd been his friends as well and that he should have been there. This thought brought some of the anger that Anne wanted me to feel; it was bad enough that he should mess me around but he had absolutely no right to treat Laura and Kwesi like this.

"Are you going to ring him then?" Anne asked when she and Kirsty returned, way past the curfew so that even some of the girls already sleeping had been woken by the clang of the hostel bell.

"Don't you dare," said Kirsty slightly drunkenly, reaching out to grab the note from me and tripping over the end of my bed in the dim nightlight of the dormitory. The three of us laughed and were quickly shushed by several sleepy girls. "He can't just disappear, then click his fingers and you come running," Kirsty continued in a theatrical whisper, louder and more penetrating than her usual voice.

"Just shut up," came an angry voice from the other end of the dormitory. "She's hardly going to ring him at this time of night anyway, is she?" Several others muttered agreement and, despite Kirsty's attempts to climb into my bed and continue the conversation, I whispered that I was too tired to decide, that we could talk in the morning. She reluctantly agreed and eventually fell asleep in her own bed, after treating us all to a half-sung half-hummed rendition of Cilla's *Anyone Who Had A Heart*.

The song continued to run through my head as I lay there, my body wanting sleep yet feeling wide-awake and flooded with such a mixture of emotions. There seemed so much to process, so much new, with Laura and Kwesi leaving, my mother's recent wedding, the issues with Bob, what aunty had told me about mummy's pregnancy, the new feelings triggered by Tony. Yet it also seemed nothing was really new, that I had spent my whole life dealing with sudden changes and endings such as boarding school, my changed mother, the discoveries about Nazir, leaving home. Daddy leaving, I heard a little voice inside me add to the list. Don't forget daddy. Yet I had, somehow I had deleted him from my life just as my mother appeared to have done. He had come back once after he moved out, and I suddenly remembered the shock and sheer joy I'd felt when I had opened the door and seen him standing there, smiling his familiar smile. I had reached out to hug him but he was already reaching out towards me, his hands full of packages. I hesitated, unsure what to do or say, then I stepped back to let him into the hall and found myself bumping into mummy. "Sorry, but look, it's daddy!" I said excitedly, for some reason expecting her to welcome him in. Instead she pushed past me, blocking his way and my view of him.

"What are you doing here?" she asked coldly. I heard him respond but his words were lost in my memory, drowned out by her shouting angrily that we didn't want to see him and we didn't want his presents either. Then the clang of the brass knocker as the door was slammed shut. I remembered staring at her in horror and her telling me not to look at her like that, then the numbness creeping in, occasionally punctured by phrases such as 'you should have said I, not we' but eventually becoming all permeating until the questions and conflicts disappeared. Until he ceased to exist for me as he did for her.

I suddenly realised that they must have got divorced, for mummy to remarry, yet nobody had told me. How do you get divorced, I found myself wondering, do you both have to go to court, did that mean they'd seen each other? Yet nobody had told me anything, I hadn't seen him at all. Of course she wouldn't tell me or even mention him, but why didn't he find a way, write to me, come to my school, anything. He wasn't the crazy one so he had no excuse, no excuse for giving up on me. Despite the wetness on my pillow I didn't want to cry, I was sick of crying. I wanted to smash up everything. I wanted to strangle the girl in the next bed, who snored and snored and didn't care that when she broke the rhythm I was momentarily filled with the hope of peace, only to have that hope shattered by her next sudden slightly bubbly emission.

It was a long, long night and the first glow of light around the ill-fitting curtains brought relief that I could now be surrounded by others, by distractions. And perhaps get some answers by telephoning Bob.

Kirsty, Anne and Mary all hovered round me the next morning, as I dragged the stiff dial round on the more private phone downstairs at the back of the house, breaking a nail in the process.

"Go away, I'm fine," I whispered as I listened to the ringing tone, but they just ignored me.

"You need to be firm," said Mary, Anne adding that I shouldn't let him know I was upset. I slammed the still ringing phone back down and retrieved my coins.

"I'll call later," I said, "when you lot leave me in peace." They were all hugs, reassuring me that they were trying to look after me.

"I appreciate that, but I don't want to play games anymore," I said firmly. "I just want to tell him how I feel, then he can decide what he's doing. If I don't tell him I miss him why would he bother to get in touch again?" I knew I was partly talking about my father, but that didn't stop it feeling right with Bob as well. I remembered reading that Ghandi had said you must be the change you wish to see in the world, and I really wanted my world to be honest and open, without all the mysteries and secrets of the past.

They did eventually accept what I said and leave me in peace. However, what I might or might not have said to Bob became irrelevant when, after ringing for what seemed like hours, the phone was answered by a rather curt female voice purporting to be 'Sherbourne Library'. We had a brief slightly muddled conversation, then she asserted firmly that my Bob or Robert definitely did not work there, she'd surely know if he did, and that I must have the wrong number. After apologising I decided I must have misdialled and tried again, but when I heard her voice answer almost immediately I put the receiver down quickly and just stared at the paper in confusion. I was tempted to try variations on the number written there but, short of coins and already late for work, I rushed out, indulging myself in a bus ride to the office instead of my usual long walk.

Distracted by the mystery of the number, I mentioned it to Shelley on the switchboard at work, without telling her who I was trying to ring. She decided to call for herself, and laughingly confirmed she also reached a rather grumpy lady at the library. She flicked through a book she pulled from under her desk. "According to the directory Sherbourne is in Dorset, it seems. So if the person you're trying to reach is in Dorset, then the first part is right at least." I thanked her and guessed it partly helped, except I already suspected Bob's mother had taken him home to Dorset. I just didn't know where, or have the correct number.

To my surprise Tony turned up outside the office after work, as he used to when we were sort of seeing each other, and through the window I saw him waiting patiently as I made up the time I'd lost by coming in late. I'd already decided the feelings I'd experienced at the party were probably brought on by my two glasses of wine, so hoped him turning up like this didn't mean I'd given any mixed messages.

"Did you get through to him?" he asked as he handed me the spare helmet. I was going to ask what he meant, then realised that Kirsty must have already told Steve about the number Bob had left and that he must have told Tony. Hard to have any secrets in our little world!

"No, it's the wrong number. Whoever took that message must have written it down wrong."

"Oh well, "said Tony as he revved the bike. "He'll call back if he's got any sense."

Except that he didn't. The gang were going for a ride out that evening but I asked Tony to drop me off, as I wanted to be in if Bob called. I surprised myself by worrying that Tony would take Christine instead, then felt guilty that I was happy when he drove off alone, the others all in couples.

The phone seemed to be ringing constantly, but none of the calls were for me and the tension had exhausted me by the time the others returned.

"Hey, we had a great idea," said Anne as soon as she came into the lounge.

"Actually it was Tony's idea," said Kirsty, draping herself across the small sofa and kicking her shoes across the room. "Guess he realises he won't stand a chance until you get Bob out of your system."

I started to protest, but Anne cut across me.

"So tomorrow we're going to that hotel where he worked, get his number or address."

"They won't give it to us, that sort of thing is confidential at work isn't it?" I asked.

"They won't give it to you, perhaps," said Kirsty, laughing, "but I tend to get what I want, you might have noticed."

It was true that she generally did so, although I knew rules about personal information were strict, I couldn't help feeling an optimistic excitement when she and Anne set off for the hotel the following evening. I stayed in the lounge, jumping each time the phone rang and trying to distract myself with a book, but glancing frequently at the clock as I awaited their return. It was nearly ten o'clock when they finally stumbled in, giggling and more than slightly merry, Anne waving an envelope at me.

"Got it!" she exclaimed "It was hard work. Well, some of it was hard, some fun, but I got it!" They went on to repeatedly interrupt each other as they described their evening, which seemed to have mostly involved flirting outrageously with a middle-aged bar manager, and had ended with Anne being given the envelope, after whispering suggestive promises of future liaisons into the poor delusional guy's ear.

"He said there was no way he could give Bob's telephone number, but he's scribbled down his address! Now this can all be sorted once and for all!"

My hand was shaking as I opened the envelope and pulled out the piece of paper inside. Then I burst into almost hysterical laughter, a complete release of days of tension.

"What? What's so funny?" the girls kept asking, at first laughing along with me but becoming increasingly impatient until eventually Kirsty grabbed the paper from me.

"Oh, what a load of poppycock that turned out!" she exclaimed, bringing more laughter. "All that work for his ruddy London address!"

Everyone reassured me that he would ring again, but the reality was that he didn't. After a couple more days passed I started to feel angry again, wondering what I had done that was bad enough to deserve this.

"Do you think I was a really bad girlfriend?" I asked Tony as we sat on yet another gate, gazing out across muddy fields. I knew as soon as I spoke the words that it was unfair of me to ask him.

"I would say you need to ask Bob, except he's proving pretty elusive. Did you see a future for it?"

"I thought so, we even talked of moving in together. Except not in that way," I added quickly, glancing up at Tony. He still stared into the distance. "Yet the funny thing was, I'm not sure either of us was that upset when Mr C wouldn't let us. It was almost like we were playing a game, and the grown-up said to stop so we did."

"Do you think you love him, honestly?"

"It's interesting you should use that word, Tony. I mean honestly. After I told the girls I wanted to be honest with Bob I realised it was about missing him, but the word love never occurred to me."

"Kirsty said you'd decided to be open and honest about your feelings. Perhaps I should do the same," he added, swinging one black jean clad leg back over the gate so he sat astride it, facing me. "Do you want me to, Nicky?"

"About how I treated Bob?" I asked with a nervous giggle, knowing very well that wasn't what was going on here. He placed a hand on each of my shoulders, making it hard to look away from him.

"About how I feel. You already know it, Nicky, I'm asking if you're ready to hear it yet?"

"Phew, heavy stuff!" I exclaimed, laughing nervously and seeing a flicker of irritation cross his face. "Truth is, Tony, I just don't know. Except I do know you are really, really important to me and the thought of losing your friendship is really scary."

"I don't want to put pressure on you, Nicky. I guess I'm just scared that pretty soon another Lars or Bob will come along, and that we'll never know if we had a chance."

"Oh, Tony," I said softly, touched by his words, and I leant forward to hug him. Unfortunately, he chose to do the same, letting go of my shoulders, and before either of us were quite sure what happened we were both laughing together in the mud below. Which felt so good and easy that perhaps the kiss that followed was inevitable.

"Shall we give it a try?" Tony whispered as we heard Kirsty and Steve approaching across the field and, although I knew it was all too much too soon, it just seemed so easy to snuggle into his shoulder and whisper "Yes."

The weeks that followed felt so relaxed and natural, reminiscent of those early carefree days with Tony, enhanced by the excitement I now allowed myself to feel when we held hands or kissed. Those around us, including his mum, spoke of how well suited we were and how relieved they were that we'd finally got it together. Neither of us voiced any doubts or reservations we might have had, although I occasionally saw the question in Tony's eyes. As much as he wanted to I knew he couldn't quite believe yet, but didn't want to shatter the fantasy with words. Perhaps he saved those thoughts and fears for the night-times, just as I did. I would lie in my bed wondering whether it would have worked with Bob or even Lars, if I'd been different and, if so, why with Tony did I really feel I was good enough. Yet why I couldn't really believe I deserved any of them, especially Tony.

When the letter arrived I found myself excited and fearful as I recognised Bob's narrow slanted writing on the envelope. My first instinct was to rip it open but, remembering the stress and anger he'd put me through over the last few weeks, I stuffed it under my pillow and hurried off to work. At lunchtime I mentioned the letter to a couple of the girls in my office, and they couldn't believe I hadn't opened it. So, fired by their curiosity, I spent the afternoon in a state of nervous impatience, rushing out of the office as soon as the clock showed 5.30 and treating myself to a bus home.

> *Dear Nicky*
>
> *Firstly, I am quite shocked that after I tried to reach you twice you have not rung me back. I can only assume you were (are?) angry with me as, even if for any reason you didn't get my messages, you knew you could reach me through Mr Cazian. Perhaps you*

didn't want to speak to him, but it's hard to understand why *you don't like him as I've always found him very kind.*

Anyway, I thought a letter was probably best, so I can explain. It must have seemed strange, me going off so suddenly, but to be honest I was really shocked and hurt by that scene we had. Especially that you would hit out like that. I know your mother did that sort of thing but it's not something I'm used to. I guess after that I just needed time and space to think, and as my parents were still in town it seemed natural to get a lift home with them.

I do miss you, Nicky, but I realise we were going too fast and there's a lot we need to talk about. I'll be back in London next week and I'll ring you then. Hopefully this time I'll catch you in.

Bob

It felt so cold, especially the way he signed off, and such an anti-climax after all the days of waiting to hear and fearing he had gone forever. For a moment I wondered why Mr Cazian had made it seem like that, but I knew he hoped I'd just disappear from the scene. I wanted to ring Bob, now that I had a number on the headed paper, a number only two digits different to that of Sherbourne Library, but then realised I would get through to his parents' hotel. I decided the last thing our floundering relationship needed right now was me speaking to either of his parents or, horror of horrors, his brutally honest little sister.

I immediately felt guilty that I was still thinking of it as a relationship, floundering or not, and pictured how hurt Tony would be if I decided to be with Bob after all. This is all too complicated, I found myself thinking, it shouldn't have to be like this. Then I realised I didn't really need to make any decision right now, that I couldn't know how I felt until Bob was back in town and we met up. It might anyway be that he'd make the decision for me, which would actually be a lot easier.

What I did know I needed to do was apologise for shouting at him, and hitting out as I had. That wasn't a matter of the family you came from, it was just wrong. I managed to scrounge a sheet of paper and an envelope from one of the girls, faithfully promising to replace them, and wrote Bob a short letter apologising for my behaviour and agreeing that we needed to talk when he returned. I purposely kept it brief and as cool as his, signing it only 'Nicky', but I couldn't resist adding a postscript explaining that I had contacted Mr Cazian and what he had told me. I guess I didn't want to be the only one in the wrong, although I then regretted it and probably would have left it off if I'd had any paper to rewrite the letter. Oh well, I thought as I sealed the envelope, I wanted to be open and honest and I guess that's a start, even if Bob doesn't like it. Nobody had a stamp so I put it safely in the drawer of my bedside cabinet, ready to be posted when the post office was open for a stamp tomorrow.

The following morning was bright and sunny, and Kirsty shook me and Anne awake early to prepare for our Saturday in Brighton. I hadn't mentioned Bob's letter to either of them and decided not to let it spoil our fun over the weekend. Instead I tucked my letter safely in my shoulder bag, as there were no pockets in my new spotted mini dress.

"What are you wearing?" Tony laughed as I walked to his bike. "You look fantastic, but it's going to be a very draughty ride!"

"I've got my cardie," I said, laughing in response, but I appreciated what he meant as I struggled to keep my dignity while climbing onto his bike. My rather exposed legs certainly attracted a few stares as we raced along, disapproving from a coach load of pensioners but flatteringly enthusiastic from two young guys who pulled up next to us in a sports car. Usually I would have felt self-conscious, but suddenly it just felt good to be young and attractive and, for today at least, happy.

The sun on our bodies felt really good too and we three girls drew a lot of admiring glances as we paraded around town, the boys trailing behind trying to look mean and moody. The assistants in the record shops hovered nervously as we piled into the booths to listen to the latest tunes from groups such as the Rolling Stones and The Hollies. Once we'd exhausted all the stores we headed to the beach for a late fish and chip lunch, Tony obligingly devouring my fish for me. Then we girls had a quick paddle before making our painful way across the pebbles to lie down next to the guys. Tony's concession to the sun was to take off his leather jacket and roll it up for me to use as a pillow, then rest his head on my lap while I stroked the black hairs on his bare arm. For the first time in ages I felt really relaxed, drifting in and out of brief hazy dreams, the chatter of Kirsty and Anne seeming far away. Then suddenly I was wide awake, almost squashing poor Tony's head as I sat up.

"What time is it, guys? I have to catch the post office before it closes."

"You'll be cutting it fine," said Kirsty. "What's so urgent it can't wait till Monday?" She and Anne looked like mermaids when I glanced over, Steve and Rob having buried their legs in sand and pebbles, their bodies appearing to be growing out of the fish tails the boys had created.

"I just need to post a letter today," I said, jumping up and grabbing my bag. "I'll be back shortly."

"Hang on, I'll come with you," said Tony, putting his jacket on. As there was no time to argue, I just hoped he wouldn't see who the letter was addressed to. I really didn't want this day spoilt by discussions about Bob, all that could wait until next week. We raced up Queen's Road, holding

165

hands and breathless with laughter, only to discover the doors of the post office being locked as we arrived.

"Oh dear, was it really important?" He looked at me with an expression that seemed to hold warmth, concern and love and it felt very right to say no, it wasn't that important. I knew I still needed to send the letter, but I think in that moment I made my decision. That I was too young for the seriousness of the relationship with Bob and that this safe warm feeling, mixed with an exciting wildness, was what I wanted.

As we meandered back through the town it was almost as if Tony had read my thoughts, stopping by the window of a department store to point to a beautiful black snake skin effect leather dress with deep pockets and metal studs on the shoulders.

"Hey, that would look stunning on you," he said excitedly, "then you'd really look like my rocker chick. Quick, they're still open," he added, pulling me through the large front door.

"Sorry, sir, we'll be closing shortly," said a uniformed man just inside the door.

"It's alright, we won't be long," said Tony, dragging me after him as he raced up the stairs, following the signs to 'Young Ladies Department' where we saw the same leather dress on a model in the centre of the floor. I hurried to find the assistant and within moments was parading up and down in front of Tony, the dress clinging in all the right places and his admiration pretty evident.

Unfortunately, in our enthusiasm neither of us had checked the price, and I think we were both shocked when we looked at the ticket. The assistant must have noticed the expression on our faces because she came over and made flattering comments, then added that they only had the one in my size but that they could 'offer a payment plan'. When I asked what that meant she explained that if we made a down payment they would keep the dress for us, and once we'd paid it all the dress would be mine. I was hesitant, knowing that although things were a bit easier financially since I'd had a promotion there was little to spare.

"How much is the down payment?" Tony asked and she explained the minimum that would reserve it was five pounds.

"I've got about two pounds, Nicky. How about you?"

I knew it was daft, but suddenly I really, really wanted that dress. I rummaged through my bag until between us we produced four pounds, eight shillings and six pence, which Tony held out with a big optimistic smile. The assistant went off briefly to speak to her manager and returned with a smile almost equally big, to tell me the dress was now mine, as soon as we came back and paid the balance.

The other girls joined in our excitement about the dress when we got back to the beach. They wanted to pool their money to collect it until Steve pointed out there'd be no money for the evening food or drink then, and the shop would be closed anyway. So, amid excited plans of returning to claim my dress the following weekend, we went off for an evening of food, tenpin bowling and moonlit beach walks before, in their own time, each couple gradually headed back to London.

16

I struggled awake, aware of a blinding light shining in my face. It was coming from the window, and I shook Tony.

"Wake up, there's something out there." I got a whiff of stale cigarette smoke as he turned towards me, but before he could say or do anything the light came closer and a tall uniform hovered over us.

"What you two up to here then?" the policeman asked, flashing the torch between our startled faces.

"Nothing, sleeping," Tony muttered.

"Oh yeah?" said a second officer I suddenly realised was kneeling close to me where I lay on the floor. "Did you get much sleep, love?" I was confused to hear laughter in his voice, laughter and something else that made me feel uncomfortable. Tony was putting his leather jacket on. "You need to get dressed, dear?" asked the policeman as I pulled the grubby old blanket up to my chin, but before I could answer he turned back to Tony. "Hope for your sake you checked her age first, mate, looks like you've got a young one here."

"I'm sixteen and I am dressed," I blurted out. Then, feeling Tony's tension, added "We haven't been doing anything."

"Sixteen huh? Suggest you get up then and we'll check all that out at the station."

It was so scary sitting next to Tony in the back of the police car, neither of us daring to speak or even look at each other. I felt really guilty getting him into this mess, and planned in my head the apology that I owed him later when this ridiculous episode was over. I just managed a muttered "sorry" as he stood aside to let me go first through the door of the police station, but he was too scared to even look at me. We were taken off into separate rooms, where a policewoman joined me after what seemed an eternity of terrifying suspense.

"So," she said, smiling, "what have you been up to, young lady?" She scribbled in a notepad as I explained about getting locked out of the hostel, because a punctured tyre on Tony's bike had made us late back, and how the nun on late night duty had refused to open the door because this was the third time I'd been late.

"We tried going to Tony's flat," I continued, explaining that their mum and dad were on holiday and Steve hadn't heard us knocking at the door. So the empty squat was our only option. "We didn't break in really," I said, "the door was open. I think other people had stayed there and left the blanket." She looked me up and down, taking in my rumpled bleached hair, smeared mascara and crumpled mini dress.

"That was convenient," she said with a sneer. "Had you been there with him before?" I shook my head. "What about your young man, love, has he taken other girls there?"

"No." I hesitated. "I don't think so, I don't know. No, he hasn't."

"So you're the only one he's sleeping with?"

"Yes, I guess we're sort of going steady," I muttered, then the meaning of what she'd said dawned on me. "But he's not sleeping with me. I mean, he was tonight when the police turned up, but not like that. I'm not like that. Nor is he." I added as she raised one eyebrow and leaned towards me across the table.

"He's a man isn't he?" she asked in a disparaging way. "Look, dear, it's best you tell me everything he did. It's ok, you're just young, it's not your fault. And it can feel nice can't it?" she said in a low voice. I was horrified as she went on to describe several things she said she and her boyfriend 'enjoyed', repeatedly asking me if I had done this to Tony or he had done that to me. I couldn't believe what I was hearing, things I knew nothing about, and I just kept repeating "No, no." as my face grew hotter and my head felt as if it would explode. It was almost a relief when her smile turned to an angry scowl as she jumped up, pushing the formica table into my knees.

"You know what, love? Not worth me wasting my time on little liars like you. Seems you're certainly not a victim. We all know what you've been up to don't we?" It was a rhetorical question. As I started to protest she interrupted me, saying no-one was as naïve as I was making out. I was later to reflect that she had a point, somehow I had managed to remain amazingly naïve and ignorant of such things, but right then I just felt angry and hurt and frightened at how she spoke to me.

It was a long night, questioning and form-filling being interspersed with lonely frightening stretches of time isolated in a small room, unsure if the door was locked or simply closed. I wanted to check, to try to find Tony, to somehow get away from the nightmare, to turn back time just hours to when life was pretty good. I wanted to, but instead sat rigid in the chair, seeing the dawn light appear in the small window. I was terrifyingly aware that I was powerless, not knowing what was going to happen but suspecting my life was yet again going to change forever when I finally left that place.

The officer who eventually drove me back to the hostel must have phoned ahead, because the three nuns lined up by the door with sad pitying looks on their faces did not seem surprised to see him. I turned to thank him for dropping me back but he shook his head, looking surprised.

"Didn't they explain at the station?" he asked in a gentle voice. "We're just here to collect your belongings, you're going to a safe place for now, miss." Somehow I was too shocked even to argue as we followed Sister Josephine up to the dormitory, where I found my bed already stripped. The box I kept all my things in was on top of the bed, open and empty apart from my wash bag. I was about to demand where my belongings were when I noticed Kirsty, finger on her lips, pointing under her bed. I understood; she was keeping my things safe until I came back. I was about to ask her for them when Sister Agnes pushed past me.

"As you see, officer, it's just as I told them on the telephone, she didn't really have any belongings. I think she just borrowed from the others so she could spend all her money on the wild nights out that got her into this mess." I couldn't believe my ears, thinking how hard I'd struggled to buy my clothes, shoes, makeup and the few luxuries including three 45s and one treasured LP.

"My record player's in the lounge," I blurted out, as I gathered up the few items of clothing on the chair by my bed and the book and brush on top of the bedside cabinet.

"The lounge is a communal area and all items in there are shared items," said Sister Agnes. "Do you consider it would be right to deprive all the girls of their music just because of your mistake?" she asked in a deceptively soft voice. I was totally confused and snapped at her.

"I haven't made a mistake. You locked me out."

"Rules are rules, my dear, and have to be obeyed. That's right isn't it, officer?" I felt sorry for the poor young policeman, who didn't quite know what to say.

"Don't worry," I said wearily, reassured that Kirsty would look after the rest of my stuff. "I'll sort it all out when I get back. Enjoy it for now, girls." There was a hum of sympathy then Kirsty, Anne and several other girls followed me outside to give me a quick hug by the wall where I'd been so happy, before I climbed into the police car and headed off to the next stage of my life.

17

The house didn't look any different from others in the suburban street, just your average semi-detached red brick with an open porch, a small paved front garden and some roses in a half-moon shaped bed under the window. I soon learnt that they joked that the roses were there so the thorns would stop the local boys climbing in at night. The only real differences you could see were a dormer in the roof and three high narrow oblong windows in the attached garage. It was no longer a garage, but had been converted into a cold and draughty bath and utility room, which smelt strongly of bleach and carbolic soap. The prospect of chilly strip washes at one of the four small sinks, keeping socks on when no-one was supervising to ward off the iciness of the concrete floor, made mornings a daily challenge. The metal bath in the corner, which cooled the hottest water as soon as it touched the sides and provided no privacy at all from others going in and out, was a questionable weekly luxury. Yet on the days when I got permission to use one of the large Belfast sinks on the other wall, to wash my clothes, I really appreciated that room for the space it provided. Although the windows had been put above head height, to stop girls looking out at the street, they made it quite bright. It seemed to be the only place in the house where I didn't feel crushed, either by the small subdivided rooms or by the perpetual presence of others.

Considering it had to house six youngsters of varying ages and two adults, it seemed a surprisingly small building for a children's home, not at all what I'd expected on the drive there. It was probably only the discipline and structure of the days that made it possible for us all to live there in reasonable harmony.

There were two reception rooms on the ground floor. The first, to the left as you came in the big wooden front door with its flowered leaded lights and brass fixtures, was simply called the front room. It looked reasonably cosy, with big bay windows, two large settees, two- high back chairs and a large glass-topped coffee table that dominated the centre of the floor. The chintzy flowered curtains, patterned rugs and a tall bookcase full of hardback books contributed to the look of a family room. In fact, this was the most formal room in the house. This was where, each evening, we were expected to sit in silence on one of the settees. Unless one of the house mistresses in her allotted chair started a conversation, in which case we were not allowed to sit in silence but required to contribute. These discussions were usually about political events, topical news matters or the arts, and were expected to be sombre and mentally stimulating. There were also various activities on different evenings and, despite no previous experience, I gradually became quite talented at darning and at embroidering flowers onto the corner of handkerchiefs, tray cloths or antimacassars. I soon understood how I should do it but I never quite understood why. I did ask in the early days, and recall the answer involved words such as 'young ladies', 'homemaking' and 'self-discipline' but I was really none the wiser. We were also expected to write weekly letters home, and were allowed up to three each. Whilst I'd previously enjoyed writing, this experience was for me quite stultifying. I could write one to my mother but knew, from collecting the post on the front door mat, that on at least one occasion she had returned my letter unopened. My aunt just didn't reply, and I could only assume she had heard bad stuff about me. It seemed pointless to write to other family members who had never contacted me, and perhaps hadn't even been told where I was. Kwesi and Laura were now in Canada, so that only really left me Kirsty to write to. Even that weekly letter had to be superficial and emotionless enough to meet the privacy requirements, and to pass the censored reading by Miss Atkins. I had tried writing to Tony, mainly to apologise for any trouble I had caused him, but the letter was given back to

173

me and Miss Atkins told me I was not allowed to contact him. I never discovered who made that rule.

Other evenings would be for reading, either one of the hardback books or your own magazine, if you had one and if it had passed scrutiny. Saturday evening was the highlight of the week in the front room, as the record player was brought out. The atmosphere was much more relaxed as we listened to light classical music, Gilbert and Sullivan and 'approved' popular songs by well-known groups. Unfortunately, the Rolling Stones never gained approval, so we slightly overdosed on Cliff Richard or The Beatles, which wasn't to my taste at all. Nevertheless, I would join the others in singing along and laughing at our tuneless voices; opportunities for laughter were precious.

The second room on the ground floor was Miss Atkins' office and was at the back, with French doors to the garden which was strung with washing lines and planted with salad vegetables, more roses and an apple tree. The first time I was sent to hang out washing I'd found a fallen apple, which I'd munched as I pegged out the sheets. Miss Atkins must have seen me from the window, as I was called into her office to be given a lecture on stealing and to spend the rest of the afternoon cleaning the dark mahogany desk, chairs and bookcase with vinegar, before smearing with a strong smelling lavender polish and buffing energetically with old woolly socks pulled over my hands. From then on I joined the others in leaving the fallen apples to rot where they landed.

At the very back of the house, adjoining the bathroom, was the small kitchen where we were taught to cook basic food and other diverse skills such as pouring soda down sinks to unblock them and boiling the kettle with water and lemon juice to descale it. Oh, and washing the stainless steel tea spoons we used for eating boiled eggs in cold water, not hot, to avoid staining. Although we were fed quite well, for me the kitchen seemed to be more about cleaning than food, with cupboards full of various brushes, cloths, creams and liquids that we were expected to become experts in using. There was a vacuum cleaner which was kept in a small closet just inside the front door, where we hung our outdoor coats, but many of the floors were covered in lino which we washed every day then buffed to a shine by tying dusters around our feet and pretending to skate.

Housekeeping seemed to be the dominant theme of our days, at least for those like myself who didn't go out to school, actually didn't go out anywhere. So that even the onerous chore of polishing the brass on the front door became a privilege, because it allowed a brief glimpse of the outside world. Of course, being on brass duty that day also meant the rest of the morning was spent at the dining table, in the open area outside the office and close to the foot of the stairs. The table would be covered with newspaper and various brass objects, including a kettle, an assortment of animal statues, candlesticks and a warming pan, which were gathered up each week and polished until you could see your reflection. Or until Miss Atkins could see hers when she checked them; if she couldn't you did the whole lot again. As she explained, "There's little point in doing anything unless you do it properly, and keeping a filthy house is not doing it properly. You won't keep a husband that way, dear," she would add with a knowing smile. A rather wicked part of me wanted to ask what her brass polishing skills were like, given that she was ancient and still single.

It wasn't a good idea to cheek Miss Atkins, as the consequences could be severe. When Miss Leigh was alone she was slightly more flexible, perhaps because she was younger and could remember what it felt like to be a teenager. Yet she had her own style of discipline, which involved looking hurt and making you feel guilty if you bent the rules on her watch. I soon realised that she didn't have it easy, and in a way both she and Miss Atkins were as much prisoners as we were. They both had to keep to the rules as well as being on duty, watching that we also obeyed those rules and ensuring that they set us an example. Although it was true that they could go out of the house, it was always for very short periods, except for their individual 'free day' one Sunday a fortnight. Just as we were constantly with them they were constantly with us, could never relax and just be themselves. I wished they could have. As young as I was, I sensed that they were having to hide parts of themselves that were possibly much more loving and caring than we were allowed to see, parts they perhaps rarely allowed themselves to see. It never felt to me that they were bad or cruel people, just two lonely individuals trapped in the roles they had chosen and struggling to do it the best they could, albeit somewhat misguidedly at times. In a way I felt sad for them: I knew one day I would be free of all this, but I wasn't as sure that they would.

The two of them shared the attic, which had been converted into two tiny bedrooms with a sink in each and a toilet in between. It was so cramped that you couldn't actually get up there, from the narrow second staircase, if one of them forgot to close the toilet door firmly. The older ones amongst us had to take it in turns to set our alarm for 6 a.m. so that we could creep out of bed without waking the others, and make our shivering way to the kitchen. There we would uncover the tray we had laid out the night before with the silver teapot, milk jug and toast rack plus the china cups, saucers, plates and sugar bowl. All on a hand-embroidered tray cloth of course, the two matching napkins in their silver napkin rings, and the knives and teaspoons sparkling by the forget-me-not border. I had my own little routine for those mornings. I'd put the sugar lumps in the bowl and milk in the jug while the four slices of bread toasted and the kettle boiled, watching for that first sign of steam so I could take it off the ring before it whistled. In the early days I'd dropped the tray in the hall and woken up the whole household, not a mistake I planned to make again.

Apart from anything else, this was a precious time to me, when the house was silent and I could feel alone, in control and at peace. Pot duly warmed, I'd add the tea leaves and re-boiled water and place the toast, cut diagonally, in the toast rack. Finally, I'd take the dish of butter from the bowl of water, where it was left at night to keep it cool, and peel off two serrated rolls of butter onto each plate. I'd once added a little jam for each, because I knew it was Miss Leigh's birthday, but it was pointed out gently to me that jam was for Sunday tea, not weekdays.

Sunday tea was indeed a special occasion for us girls, not just because of the jam in the china dish in the middle of the dining table but also for the radio. The shared anticipation would start mid-afternoon as we all hurried to complete our chores, praying that no-one had done anything during the week to incur a ban. Eventually we would excitedly sit around the table, eyes closed as grace was said, until Miss Leigh rose from her chair and, with a little smile, turned on the radio. A buzz of warmth and excitement would fill the room, as Alan Freeman's familiar voice welcomed us with "Hi there, pop pickers." Then for the duration of the programme we were just ordinary happy youngsters, like all the others out there, sharing the music.

Once the morning tray was ready I'd climb the stairs as quietly as possible, gradually becoming expert in avoiding the creaky patches. When I reached the landing I'd almost hold my breath as I passed the two bedrooms with their young occupants, perhaps hearing a childish dreaming murmur or the creak of a bed frame as a sleeping body snuggled further into the warm bedclothes, temporarily safe from the cold hard world.

I'd see my empty bed just inside one of the rooms, the door left ajar as the clanking latch could wake one of the two youngsters who shared the room and for whom I was partly responsible. Whilst it was their job to make their beds, fold

177

their clothes and keep their drawers neat and tidy, it was my job to make sure they did those things. Quite a challenge at times, with two disoriented young girls, who could be sad, frightened and angry all at once, missing their family so much that they would cry into the small hours of the morning.

Balancing the breakfast tray up the second short, but very narrow, staircase was an art in itself, especially as one hand had to be free to tap gently on Miss Leigh's door.

"Come in, dear," she would whisper. Her response was so quick I was pretty certain that, even though it was my job to wake her, she had set her alarm to ensure she could respond immediately, sitting up with her hair already combed and her bedcover pulled up neatly over her legs.

"Good morning, Miss Leigh," I would whisper, placing the tray on the bedside table, and she always responded with a warm smile. My world so lacked mental stimulation I'd catch myself wondering whether she would pour a cup of tea and take that and a plate of toast to Miss Atkins, remove her own breakfast then take the tray in to the other room, perhaps even sit in the other room so they could breakfast together. To lose your physical freedom is terrible and humiliating, to lose your mental freedom, to the extent that such pointless puzzles as these become part of the challenges you create to preserve your sanity, is truly terrifying.

Mental stimulation and the need to be alone became the dominant ambitions in my narrow little life, and many nights I lay awake in bed not only to enjoy the silence but also racking my brains for a way to achieve these. Finally, I found what I believed was the solution, and it was with a mixture of excitement and dread that I knocked on the office door after breakfast the next morning. Miss Atkins looked up from her paperwork.

"Is it your turn to clean in here today?" she asked, pushing her chair back.

"No, no, Miss Atkins," I said quickly.

"Well then run along, young lady, I'm very busy." I took a deep breath, summoning all the courage I could find.

"I just need to speak to you briefly please, Miss Atkins," I said in my sweetest good girl voice.

"Oh dear, well make it quick then," she said, pushing her papers aside, propping her chin on her hands and studying my face with her piercing green eyes.

I knew Miss Atkins loved Shakespeare, so I started there.

"I'd like to learn some speeches from Shakespeare, Miss Atkins. I feel it's quite an important thing to develop an interest in." I could see the surprise on her face but also a warm sparkle in her eyes, so knew I was on the right track. "So I wondered if I could borrow the collected works please?" I added hastily. As I spoke I glanced up at the bookcase I'd polished so often, where the large tome in question lived.

"Well, I actually find that quite admirable, dear. It seems you are finally getting a sense of what is important in life."

"Oh yes," I responded quickly, lowering my eyes so she wouldn't see the excitement in them. Now for stage two of my plan. "I have tried to memorise things a couple of times before, Miss Atkins, but I found it very hard to concentrate with the others around. I do feel it deserves my full concentration. So," I paused for a calculated moment, "well, I wondered... As no-one is allowed upstairs in the daytime, I wondered if there was any chance I could study in the bedroom?" Miss Atkins looked completely taken aback by my outrageous suggestion, and I feared I'd pushed my luck too far. The silence hung there for a moment, then Miss Atkins pulled her papers back in front of her.

"I will certainly need to give such an idea some serious thought," she said briskly. "We don't have rules for no reason at all you know."

"No, Miss," I replied then, responding to a flick of her hand, left the room and buried myself in my chores, trying not to hope, trying not to despair.

179

She tortured me for three days, until one morning she appeared by the breakfast table with the volume of Shakespeare's collected works in her hand.

"I am prepared to give you a trial of an hour a day. We'll see how that goes." I'd mentioned nothing of my plan to the other girls so all looked up from their breakfasts with puzzled faces. "It is to be hoped you will all benefit as well," Miss Atkins added, looking down at them. It was my turn to be puzzled. How could it benefit them, apart from getting rid of me for a short while each day? Cathy was one of the braver girls there; at fourteen she'd already lived on the streets for months before being brought here.

"What's gonna benefit us, Miss?" she asked, her mouth full of toast.

"Going to, not gonna, and do not talk with your mouth full, child. How many times do you have to be told?" She walked around the table and picked up Cathy's plate, half of her breakfast still on it. "I suspect popping this in the bin will be a better reminder than my words, won't it?" She disappeared to the kitchen and shortly returned empty handed.

"Well, girls, I have told you how important William Shakespeare's writing has been in shaping the language of this country, haven't I?" Nobody responded but she didn't seem to notice. "So, as a treat for you all, I have decided that I am going to let Nicola learn some speeches from Shakespeare's plays. She will then recite them to you, as a special evening entertainment." Everyone sat dumbfounded, myself included. This hadn't been part of the plan. The Shakespeare stuff was just an excuse to get some quiet time alone in the bedroom, to think my own thoughts, develop my own ideas, dream my own dreams. I hadn't actually planned to learn the speeches. If my head was to be filled with the writings of a sixteenth century dramatist, what space would be left for me? My slightly panicky silence was interrupted by Miss Atkins' voice. "Well, I certainly expected a thank you from each of you, especially you, Nicola." There was an automatic united chant of "Thank you, Miss." and she handed me the book.

"Don't let your chores slip because of this, dear," she said with a small smile. "Obviously I'll have to test you before the performance, we'll discuss that later."

After she returned to her office Cathy turned to me with an angry look on her face.

"Was this your bright idea?" she asked and I shook my head.

"No, not at all." I was getting quite good at white lies.

"Wouldn't be surprised," she said. "Bloody posh rubbish. And I lost my breakfast, charming!" I could have pointed out that the two weren't really connected, but my head was having enough trouble adjusting to the new circumstances without getting caught up in another of Cathy's angry outbursts. On the rare occasions when she would open up to me, I got the sense that Cathy had been constantly angry since her father was replaced by a stepfather when she was nine. Although she wasn't specific, I was shocked that a man could abuse a child in that way and more shocked that her mother apparently knew what was happening. Despite being confused and angry about my mother, at least I had felt in the past that she was trying to protect me. Although now I was less sure, and could only imagine that it was the level of her anger with me that stopped her visiting. Cathy's mother hadn't intervened when a young man appeared on the scene, and gave her 14-year-old daughter the pretence of love and protection by moving her into his flat. In return she walked the streets of her home town each evening, doing with anonymous men what her stepfather had taught her, but feeling that now it was her free choice and that, in return for his protection, her boyfriend deserved the money she brought home to him. When she spoke of those months her voice was hard and she boasted of fights she'd had with older girls on the street, and how she'd earned more than most of them because she turned more tricks. As most of these

181

conversations were held in the bedroom after lights out I couldn't see her face, but in the silence that would follow her excited chatter I was sure I heard muffled sobs, whether mourning a lost freedom or a lost childhood.

Although my literary plan hadn't worked out as intended there were still positive repercussions. One was the fact that I did get my five hours of peace a week, and certainly didn't spend every moment studying the words of the Bard. The silence in the empty bedroom was magical to me, the room smelling of the lavender polish used to clean the furniture in the morning and a brightness shining in the window that never seemed to penetrate the rooms downstairs. I lay on my bed, eyes closed, the sound of children playing in a nearby garden drifting through the window. At such times I was able to find a calmness in myself which allowed me briefly to stand back from the organised preoccupation of my daily life and see the bigger picture. Whilst that brought memories and sadness, it also brought the reassurance that this would pass and I would somehow make a new, happier life for myself. I think Miss Atkins had hoped I'd learn speeches a lot more quickly than I did, but I still managed well enough to keep my privilege and bore the others with my hesitant, slightly monotone, recitals. The other positive outcome was that Miss Atkins started seeing me in a better light, possibly as more mature, and I knew her approval was essential to progress within the system. She regularly had meetings with all of our social workers and Lesley, who had been allocated to me, fed back to me some of the points discussed. It did feel they were actually talking about someone else; it seemed that being taken into care had attached to me a whole persona I didn't even recognise. Quite an exciting persona in some ways. A wild street girl who had lived it up in London, partying and playing the femme fatale. Facts like me having held down a responsible job, being sexually naïve and having lived with nuns seemed to get overlooked. As did the fact that I had actually done nothing

182

wrong, and was officially in care for my 'own protection', not as a punishment. Gradually Lesley was discovering who I was, but I knew Miss Atkins' reports were also significant in shaping my daily life and my future.

I really knew I had made progress with her when I was told I would be allowed to go out! Admittedly it was only down the road to the local shop, to buy embroidery silks, and I was to be accompanied by Miss Leigh and another girl who had earned this privilege two weeks earlier. Only someone who has themselves been under house arrest for nearly two months could understand the overwhelming feeling that news brought. Although I had very few clothes, I kept changing my mind about what I would wear on that momentous day, and trying different styles with my hair. The style had grown out and mousey brown roots had appeared, whilst the blonde had dulled. No makeup was allowed, so the glamorous image Kirsty had tried to create for me had disappeared. Perhaps that was one reason Miss Atkins felt she could risk me being seen in public.

Finally, the magical morning dawned and I walked out of the front door, past the hated brass fittings, to the gate. Stepping onto the pavement made me feel quite breathless, and as we walked the short distance to the shop my senses were bombarded with what were once ordinary sounds, sights and smells of cars and people, dogs, trees, a post-box, a baby in a pram…all so ordinary, yet all so alien in my world. I was surprised that, when we entered the haberdashery shop, I was actually too nervous to speak to the old lady behind the counter. In such a short time the outside world had become a slightly dangerous unfamiliar place. Although we were a few roads from the Home Miss Leigh chatted in quite a familiar way, and I felt the old lady's smile contained pity and judgement of me, that she knew I was one of the lost souls from 'The Home'. I felt hurt and embarrassed.

In some strange way it was a relief once we got back and closed the big green door, but very quickly the relief was replaced for me by an overwhelming sadness. In bed that night I was the little girl crying herself to sleep, as for the first time I fully acknowledged the awful sequence of events that had swept me along. I had tried to be positive all the way through and had pushed down any feelings about the mother I had left behind, the painful betrayal by the nuns, the disappointment at losing the job I had become good at, the guilt I felt at any problem I might have caused Tony and the sadness at losing him and my friends. Most of all I'd tried to suppress the terror at having the freedom I had struggled so hard for, and enjoyed so briefly, suddenly and painfully snatched away from me. My eyes were so swollen and closed the next morning, they reminded me of how I would wake up with my eyes stuck shut when I was small, and how my mother would have to bathe them with warm water each morning before I could see anything. This memory led to more tears and a blinding headache. As bad as I felt, I yet again tried to find the positive in my situation and this one was almost worth all the pain, as it gained me a visit from the doctor and three glorious quiet days in bed without even William Shakespeare to impinge on my privacy.

Those days restored my strength and helped me realise that, whilst I needed to continue to find ways to make day to day living bearable, it was even more essential that I start structuring a plan for discovering the way out of this institutional nightmare. Whilst freedom was potentially on the horizon at my eighteenth birthday, that was an eternity to me and I was far from sure I could survive it. I had heard that babies deprived of oxygen at birth develop brain damage and, feeling constantly suffocated; I was terrified at what would happen to me if I continued to be deprived of mental and emotional nourishment.

18

It was a red coat, and a chance remark by Cathy, that eventually started me on the long and challenging road to freedom. Cathy was saying one day how being shut up in this little house was driving her crazy, and she couldn't see how she would survive it until she was eighteen.

"I'm telling you, Nicky, I am so ready to make a run for it, if it wasn't that they'd catch me and put me somewhere worse."

"I know how you feel," I said. "Seems like we're trapped, with our only taste of freedom being trips to the haberdashers for those bloody embroidery silks." Cathy laughed.

"For you," she said. "I'm not even allowed that cos they know I'm a runner."

This was true; after two mad dashes through the centre of town, one ending with a fall that resulted in a sprained wrist and the other with a late night drive back in a police car, Cathy was no longer allowed out.

"Except they tell me I can have that luxury again, when I prove I can be trusted. Problem is, how I am supposed to prove it locked up here? Like you, Nicky. You said they put you here on a 'Care and Protection' order. So, you being seventeen now, they'd have to let you go if you could prove you could look after yourself and keep yourself safe. But how you gonna do that in here, I ask you?"

She went on about the system being stacked against us, but I wasn't really listening, shocked as I was by this revelation. My birthday the week before had been pretty miserable, despite the efforts of Miss Leigh and Miss Atkins, with only a card from my aunt and nothing at all from my mother. But perhaps this was the positive side of it. There *was* a way out it seemed. If I could prove what I needed to prove I could be free! Although I had no idea how I would prove it, that glimpse of a potential partly open door gave me the strength to believe I would eventually find a way to push it wide open and run for my life.

After that less of my energy went into tiny secret rebellions, or thinking of ways to earn privileges like time alone or trips out. Instead I was focussed on the conundrum set by Cathy of how to prove I could do the very thing they were stopping me from doing. I did realise it would have to be something devious, as I had been there long enough to know that anything at all dramatic or emotional would be picked up as a weakness, a sign that I could not be free. I didn't even dare raise it directly with Lesley, my social worker, but with small comments and apparently casual questions I did manage to establish that Cathy was right. This didn't surprise me, given her extensive experience of the system, but nevertheless the realisation filled me with an excitement I had never ever felt. Excitement and sadness, for what I had lost and could potentially have again. They say a runner can be spurred on or slowed down by the sight of the finishing line and that is how it felt for me, aware of the possibility of the end of this nightmare road but also of the challenge to reach it. The red coat was to give me a vital clue as to how to do so.

Although Lesley had collected my belongings from the hostel, except for my record player which had mysteriously disappeared, my wardrobe was all light stuff apart from the fake leather skirt and black plastic mac, both of which had been confiscated by Miss Atkins. As days grew cooler Lesley told me that she had funds to buy me a warm outfit and a coat, and that we were going to the main county town some distance away to buy them. Apparently there was a big store there, where the council had an account. So children from all over the county were taken there, to be suitably clothed for the weather. I wasn't too interested in the details but was excited at the prospect of a day out. We left right after breakfast, and when we got to town Lesley parked up outside a Forte bar, explaining she hadn't had time for breakfast before collecting me. I think this was her way of being kind, as she actually only had a slice of toast with her tea while she treated me to crumpets and a hot chocolate. As the sun was shining, despite the chill in the air, we left the car there and walked across town to the big bright department store. The changing scenery and the buzz of people and traffic was another treat for me after months of confinement. On the way we passed a tall building, with lots of windows and a large glass entrance to a luxurious looking foyer with maroon carpeting.

"That's where I'm based," said Lesley. "The council offices. Quick," she added with a smile, "before they call me in for something urgent!"

"Looks a really smart place to work," I said, but she shook her head.

"No, that's just the foyer. We're up on the 4th floor in tiny little offices with scuffed lino on the floor." I glanced up at those 4th floor windows, wondering how many lives had been changed forever by decisions made in those tiny offices. Then I shook off the momentary melancholy to enjoy the walk, and by the time we reached the department store we were both happy and chatty, ready for the challenge of the clothes department.

None of the clothes were really what I would have chosen to wear, and I found myself thinking back to my last shopping trip, hand in hand with a laughing Tony. I fought back the threatening tears, as I wondered if he ever thought of that day and whether my beautiful leather dress still waited for me, reserved for all eternity by a couple of notes and our handful of coins.

Lesley and I disagreed on many clothes, but we eventually reached a compromise on a dark grey woollen skirt and a cosy black polo necked jumper. I turned away in embarrassment while she paid with the tokens that proclaimed I was 'in care', before we headed off to the coat department. There we rummaged through rails of school type coats in blacks, greys and browns, and I was about to compromise yet again when I saw a red double-breasted woollen coat on a mannequin on the other side of the department.

"Look, Lesley," I said quickly, pointing to the coat and choosing my words carefully. "That coat looks really warm and smart, and I'm sure it will last me forever." Lesley laughed.

"I suspect your interest is more in the colour than the functionality, Nicky," she said. We both knew she was right of course, that I loved bright colours, but I continued to play the game of highlighting how it met all the department's specifications, apart from the one about practical colour, and I think she admired my persuasive powers. "Well," she said slowly, "if the price is alright and they have your size. And if you never, ever, wear it in the council offices and get me sacked!"

"I won't," I agreed and neither of us realised then that she'd just made a prophetic statement. Two assistants, smartly dressed in black and white, were chatting behind the counter.

"I just need to pop to the ladies, Nicky," said Lesley. "How about you?" I shook my head and smiled, appreciating her trust at leaving me alone. "Well, wait here a moment then. See if you can get those girls' attention." I was a bit too shy to actually interrupt the girls' lively conversation, but I stood close to them, hoping they might notice me. They didn't and continued to talk, loudly enough for me to be able to hear.

"Godsend," said the short plump one. "Don't know what I would have done otherwise."

"Well," said the tall one with a pimple on her chin, "you'd have had to stay with him, wouldn't you, June?"

"Suppose so," said June, "although think I'd rather have been on the streets than slapped by him again."

"That's what I was worried would happen," said the thin one. "That's why I told you about the hostel. Ok, it's only a room but at least it's yours and you're safe there till you get somewhere better." June nodded.

"As I said, godsend, working for somewhere that has a staff hostel. That's shown him for sure." She looked up with a smile and seemed to notice me for the first time. "Yes, Miss, can I help you?" she asked, her voice suddenly posh. Luckily Lesley appeared just then and organised everything about the coat, as my mind was full of the conversation I had just heard.

Although I still wasn't sure how it would be achieved, it felt that day I had gained another stepping stone on my path to freedom. My thoughts were racing as we drove back, Lesley chatting happily and me snug in my new red coat, which I had put on once we had passed the council offices on our way back to the car.

In the following weeks I began to formulate my plan, knowing I now had the ingredients and just needed to figure out how to put them together. Firstly, I needed to get out of the house. Although I now went regularly to the haberdashers with Miss Leigh, I knew from Cathy's experience that any escape attempt from there would be very short lived, and once I was caught I would be more restricted than ever. The latter applied to any attempt; if it succeeded I had so much to gain, if it failed at any stage so many hard earned privileges would be lost.

Another girl and I had also recently earned the privilege of going, one evening a week, to the youth club held in the village church hall. There we played table tennis with the local boys and girls, and I occasionally managed sneaky sips of disgusting cheap wine which a couple of the boys smuggled in. This was despite the constantly hovering vicar, who had tainted our outings on our first visit by telling everyone we were from 'The Home', and so they were to act in a kind and Christian way towards us. Needless to say, this encouraged secretive jibes and taunts from the others until they got to know us a bit. His wife supported him in his supervisory role and also in the humiliation, by initially greeting the two of us at each visit with an apple 'freshly picked by my own hands'. Given that we were quite well fed, and in fact had an apple tree in our garden, I guessed this gesture was more for her wellbeing than ours.

Escape from the youth club seemed slightly more feasible than from the haberdashers as, although we were delivered and collected, there were two hours of only the elderly vicar and his wife to elude. However, there was one very big obstacle which was Margaret, the girl who came with me. She was thirteen and had been sent to the Home for her own protection, as her mother drank very heavily and was often violent when she staggered home after a night out, having left Margaret to mind her three siblings. Despite the beatings, and a couple of scars on her arm that would remind her of them forever, Margaret worried constantly about her mother and the siblings that had been put into other homes. She attributed some blame to the alcohol, which is why she wouldn't indulge in the sneaky sips, but mostly she blamed her violent father, who had left when her youngest sibling was born. Her dreams for when she left the Home were not, like mine, of freedom, job, home, but of revenge on her father and then saving her mother and siblings. But the revenge took priority for her and, although she seemingly managed to conceal it from the staff and her social worker, she would tell me quite graphically what she would do to 'that evil monster' as soon as she got out of there.

Given that she and I were together the whole time at the youth club, and that I had in fact been told to look after her, escape from there without her noticing was impossible. Even worse, in my mind, was the fact that if she was aware I was escaping I was sure she would try to come with me or make her own getaway. I did not want to be responsible for that, as I had no doubt her first destination would be her father and that the pent up hurt and rage in that young girl would possibly

190

lead her to years in juvenile detention for assault, or even murder.

The only other time I was out in the wide world was on the rare trips with Lesley, to the doctor or dentist or just to have our regular 'little chats' in a different environment, such as a café or park. Whilst the likelihood was that attempting escape when with her would have the same outcome as when going for embroidery silks with Miss Atkins, Lesley always seemed very caring and a little part of me fantasised that she would delay raising the alarm long enough to give me a chance. However, I realised not only was that a fantasy but that, if it proved true, she would probably be risking her job by not supervising me closely enough. Given that she was the only really caring person in my life right then, even if only because it was her job, I didn't feel I could put her in that position or take that risk.

It was therefore clear that my escape had to be made from the house, despite all the strict security precautions there, with external and some internal doors being locked. It was possible to get into the back garden, either to hang laundry, collect apples (when permission stopped it being a crime) or occasionally to do weeding. I had even considered whether I might be able to climb from my bedroom window during my Shakespeare time, jump to the roof of the bathroom extension and again to the garden. However, apart from the risk to life and limb, once in the garden we were surrounded by a very high solid fence with no footholds. My memories of ritual navy-knickered humiliation in the school gym, when expected to miraculously climb up a rope or jump over a horizontal pole way higher than myself, assured me that all the positive thinking in the world would not get me over that fence.

The solution to this part of my challenge came unexpectedly some time later, when I was told to vacuum the front room. As I was lifting the vacuum cleaner it caught in the piles of coats hung in the closet where it was kept, and a few of them fell down, revealing a smallish frosted glass window behind them. I had never seen this before and suspected it had been forgotten about by everyone, as it was covered in dust with a cobweb across the latch. Nervously, I stood on tiptoe and could just press my fingertips against the bottom of the glass. The window didn't budge, but my fingertips left incriminating clean marks on the pane. I quickly pulled the closet door almost closed, dragged the vacuum cleaner under the window and balanced myself on it, to firstly try more pressure on the window to no avail and to then smudge the evidence.

"Nicola, what is taking so long?" came Miss Atkins' voice, and I could hear her on the bottom squeaky stair.

"Coming, Miss," I responded quickly, grabbing the fallen coats and covering up the forgotten window just as she opened the closet door.

"Goodness, girl, what a mess," she said, and I almost turned to look at the window, thinking she could see it. "Did you brush your hair at all today, Nicola? It certainly doesn't look like it." She must have been confused by my nervous laugh, as I was told not to be cheeky and lost my pudding that day in punishment.

The idea of the secret window, just big enough for a slim teenager to slide through, occupied my thoughts constantly. I wondered why I hadn't seen it from the front of the house and then realised I had, without even noticing it, because it was on the side wall in the part set back slightly to accommodate the dustbins. I took rubbish out there regularly, lifting aside the small wicker screen that hid the bin from the road.

My next breakthrough came about a week later, when I was polishing the shelves in Miss Atkins' office and one of the smaller children fell down the stairs. Miss Atkins rushed into the hall to respond to the scream, and I was about to follow her when I saw the bunch of keys on her desk. I pictured myself hastily sorting through the keys and, within seconds, finding and removing the little one that would fit the small lock hole I'd seen on the closet window. Such plans worked in books but I knew immediately they wouldn't in real life, with so many keys and possibly only seconds to spare. Especially as I didn't even know what the key looked like. So I went for option two, grabbing the whole bunch and stuffing them in my pants, while watching the door breathlessly.

"Miss Leigh, I'm taking Maureen up to bed," I heard Miss Atkins call. "She's alright, but rather shaken. Could you bring up some warm milk for her please?" I realised this meant they would both be upstairs, and my opportunity had come. As soon as I saw Miss Leigh pass the office door towards the stairs I came out into the hall and, as she reached the landing carrying the hot drink carefully in front of her, I slipped into the closet, shutting the door behind me in case any of the other children became curious. It seemed to take forever to get the vacuum cleaner in place, wriggle myself behind the hanging coats and start trying out the keys. I almost thought I had imagined it when I heard a click as one finally turned in the lock, and in fact turned it several times before I could believe and breathe properly again. Trying not to cry with the overwhelming sense of relief, I left the window closed but unlocked, put everything back as it had been and hurried back to the office, the keys in my hand. To my horror Miss Atkins was already sitting at her desk, peering into a drawer. I hesitated only a second before I held out the keys, saying,

"You dropped these, Miss. I was going to take them up to you," quickly adding, "is Maureen alright?" I thought I saw a flicker of uncertainty on her face, then she smiled and took the bunch.

"Thank you, Nicola. Yes, she's just a bit shocked. You can pop up and check on her in a while." I did so soon after and, finding her sleeping, took the opportunity to bury my face in my own pillow and release some of the tension by taking several deep gasping breaths.

Finally, I was almost ready to put my grand plan into action. The next time I took rubbish out I checked the position of the window, and was glad to see I was right in thinking I could climb out onto the top of the metal dustbin, rather than having to drop all the way to the ground. The big question in my head had now become when, as I knew that timing could be crucial. The bin aspect narrowed options a little. I already knew my plan wouldn't work at a weekend, and now Wednesday was eliminated as the bin was put out by the gate on Tuesday night for collection. So if, as I planned, I was to make an early morning escape, I initially thought that gave me the choice of Monday, Tuesday, Thursday or Friday. However, the following Thursday it was narrowed down further when I realised that with very little rubbish in it the bin was quite unstable, and there was a good chance that me climbing onto it from the window could easily knock it over. If that happened, not only could I end up injured but the whole house could be woken up by the crash of the metal bin and lid on the concrete, I remembered reading once that Napoleon had said nothing is more difficult, and therefore more precious, than being able to decide. In this case I was glad my choices had been limited as, crazily, it felt that if all went wrong I somehow wouldn't be as much to blame. Of course if the plan somehow failed because of the day, the consequences of the choice wouldn't actually be about self-blame but about despair and loss of hope.

Sunday was a busy day in the house with everyone home, trips to church, Sunday tea and then preparations for the return to school the next day. I therefore settled on Tuesday as my escape day, Monday being quieter to make any last minute preparations. I also decided I needed to wait a couple of weeks, in case the unlocked window was discovered, a nervous wreck every time someone opened the closet door for the vacuum cleaner or their coat. So, by a process of elimination D-day was finally chosen.

Although it was autumn and pretty chilly, I decided I would have to wear one of my light summery outfits and wrap up the warm clothes Lesley had bought me to keep them clean, including the bright red coat. It wasn't as if I could take a suitcase, so I mentally narrowed it down to as few things as possible that would squash into one of the larger brown paper bags the groceries came in. The priority once I was out would be to keep myself looking clean and respectable, so I could blend in with everyone else. I had my own brush and flannel of course, but as the time drew closer I fearfully dreaded the discovery of the toothpaste and bar of soap missing from the store cupboard and secreted under my mattress, wrapped in toilet paper in the hope of smothering the strong carbolic smell.

The other thing I knew I would need was some money. Not necessarily a lot but, as in the Home we were given none at all, even finding a little was a challenge. After racking my brains, I realised that, apart from the staff and my social worker, the only people I met who had any money were the kids at the youth club. I would see them exchanging it for a cigarette or some of the cheap wine, and I wondered how I could get some myself. Again a chance remark, this time by one of the younger children, gave me an idea. Two of them were talking about another child at their school, who had told them he had six 45rpm records.

"I don't believe him," mumbled Sally. "How could he get all those?"

"Guess his parents bought them. He told me his dad works in a shop and gets them half price," said Maureen.

"Lucky devil," Sally exclaimed. "Wonder if his dad would get me that new Beatles one that we heard on Sunday?" They both laughed and agreed everybody would want that one. So my plan was hatched, and the next time I was at the youth club I mentioned to one of the boys that I had a friend who could get the new Beatles 45 really cheap.

"She can't get many and she needs the money up front," I added. He looked a bit doubtful, but when he heard just how cheap he rummaged in his pocket and found enough to order his copy. As I expected, he then told others and by the end of the evening I had a lot of coins in my socks and a firm order for eight copies. I did feel bad, but I'd charged them as little as possible and knew they got pocket money every week. I felt worse about Margaret, who I ended up promising a free copy if she didn't say a word to anyone at the Home. I cringed slightly as she gave me a warm hug and thanked me, feeling sure I'd just added to her already extensive trust issues. It now felt D-day was set in stone, as if I changed my mind I would have to go back to the youth club next week, return the money and bluff the reason why there were no records.

The next few days were frightening and exhilarating. They also held some sadness, filled as they were with 'last times'. I'd become very close to Cathy and to Margaret to a lesser extent, but I was fond of all the children in the Home and it was weird not to be able to tell them, to say my goodbyes. Miss Leigh and even Miss Atkins had also become pretty central figures in my life, and I would have liked to be able to explain to them why I was doing this, how it was the right, the only, course for me. I just hoped they would eventually understand and, despite the fact that they themselves could be in trouble over my escape, might also eventually forgive me.

The last Friday was pretty uneventful, apart from Sally being off school with a sore throat and headache. Luckily she shared the other bedroom with Margaret and Maureen, so I still had my room to myself for the study time which I used to go over and over my plan, searching desperately for weaknesses and flaws. That evening I stitched as quickly as possible, hoping I could finish the bouquet of lilies in the last corner of the tray cloth I had been working on, and had hoped to give to Miss Leigh for Christmas. I thought she could add it to the collection of household linens I had once seen in the trunk in her room, which I assumed was in anticipation of eventually finding a prince charming to whisk her away from all of this.

The last Saturday morning Cathy and I spent in the washroom, pummelling her school uniform and those of the three younger girls. Even the smell of the carbolic soap brought on a sense of nostalgia, as I vigorously rubbed the white socks and the grimy line around the inside of the white blouse collars. Hanging them out in the garden I remembered my first time out there, when I had eaten the apple, and the lecture I had later received. Now the tree was bare and the grass frosty despite the autumn sunshine, reminding me of walking in St. James park with Bob early in the year.

Saturday evening was no different from usual Saturday evenings, the record player being brought out for the after dinner hour. I wondered if either of the housemistresses were aware of the irony of playing us the Beatles' *Ticket to Ride* and *Yesterday*. On this Saturday they were particularly poignant for me, *Ticket to Ride* because that was about my hope and *Yesterday* because, ever since I first heard it, the words had summed up my despair at the suddenness with which everything can change. A punctured tyre, a locked hostel door, a torch shining in the night and the world was altered forever. However, I managed to hide how much I was affected by the music and laughed along with everyone else, as the youngest three did dramatic impressions of a policeman whose lot was not a happy one. A glow of love reminded me how I would miss these poor little girls, who could be stuck here for their whole childhood.

It was hard to sleep that night, my plans racing through my head as I lay there listening to the deep breathing of Cathy and young Barbara, who shared the room. Although I had thought it all through, I kept examining every aspect, looking for the weaknesses where I could be tripped up. Of course it

197

was all dependent on things going as planned and the whole thing was like a giant domino effect where one slip up would ruin it all, but there was nothing I could do except mentally rehearse the bits within my control as carefully as possible. I recalled the feeling as I'd left the Billy Graham meeting so long before, of how I vowed then I never wanted to be controlled by others and thought how I'd ended up being controlled constantly, my only freedom within my own head and my own spirit. The silence was broken by someone from the other bedroom going across the landing to the bathroom, their shadow projected through the open door onto the ceiling of my room by the tiny night light in the hall. Barbara seemed to be responding with a fit of coughing and I saw her sit up momentarily in her bed under the window, then rub her eyes with both hands and snuggle back down. I found myself becoming quite breathless with anxiety, thinking how easily everything could be ruined if tomorrow night someone went to the bathroom at the wrong moment or Barbara's cough got worse and Miss Leigh came down to see her or...the possibilities seemed endless, and rushed round and round in my head until I exhausted myself and slept fitfully for the last couple of hours before dawn.

I struggled awake as the alarm clock by my bed beeped, reaching out to switch it off before it woke others yet hearing a mumbled "Morning," from Cathy.

"Go back to sleep," I whispered. "I'm on tea duty."

"Poor you. Night then," came the muffled response and in the dim light I saw her burrow back down under the blankets to escape the early morning chill. As I carefully made my way downstairs, avoiding the squeaky floorboards and wondering yet again why we couldn't even be trusted to have closed bedroom doors, I prayed I wouldn't need the alarm on Tuesday.

That Sunday passed in a bit of a blur, as I felt myself an observer to the usual rituals of the house rather than part of it anymore. I considered going to church, just to spend a little more time with the young ones, but decided it would look suspicious if I changed my pattern. Instead I guarded the closet by carefully passing down their coats and hanging them back up when they returned, then briefly played in the chilly garden with them before the usual Sunday tea and radio. As I looked around at their smiling faces I wondered where I'd be when I next heard Alan Freeman's cheery greeting.

Monday passed quickly, the usual chores done automatically as I mentally rehearsed my plans over and over. I spent my Shakespeare hour packing my new clothes, and the mysterious black dress my mother had sent me, into the grocery bag I had smuggled from the kitchen. I looked for somewhere to hide it, but eventually simply slid it far under my bed. When, as usual, I returned the Collected Works to the office I felt a momentary pang of sadness alongside the relief.

19

Any worries I had about not waking in time on Tuesday were easily dispelled by the fact that, try as I might, I just couldn't get to sleep. Every noise in the house, from the ticking of the grandfather clock downstairs to Cathy's gentle snore, seemed magnified and intense. Despite reminding myself that these were usual, and wouldn't wake the adults, I still lay there holding my breath for fear my plan would be uncovered. Every movement I made in the bed seemed to cause creaks of the frame and rustling of the sheets, so that I found myself lying stiffly in one position for ages. Eventually aches in my muscles forced me to move each limb slowly and gently, before settling into another position that shortly became equally uncomfortable.

Mostly I wanted to talk, to tell somebody of my plans before I burst with the pressure of them going round and round in my head, presenting me with endless possibilities of failure. It felt so long since I had had anyone to talk to, really talk to, in a way that emptied me out enough to be able to sense the fullness of the feelings I was left with. I wondered if this was how my mother had felt when she bombarded me with her words. I wanted to cry, if only to relieve the tension, but was scared of the noise that might make. Instead I found myself reflecting on other sleepless nights and all the different pillows I had sobbed into over the years, from the little girl in boarding school and hospital to all the teenage angst I had gone through with Nazir, Lars and Bob.

Eventually a very dull glow of light appeared outside the window, and I knew that finally it was time for perhaps the most important adventure of my life. I climbed out of bed as quietly as I could and carefully lifted the edge of the mattress to retrieve the wash things tucked away days ago, then knelt and reached under to pull out the brown paper grocery bag I'd yesterday filled with its precious contents. The rustle as I tucked the bag under my arm was really loud in the quiet room, and I froze like a statue as I heard Cathy grunt and turn over in her bed. Then her gentle snores reassured me, and I gathered my shoes and ordinary clothes from the chair and tiptoed to the bathroom. Once dressed and ready to leave, there was a temporary moment of panic deciding whether to flush the toilet, to justify my presence if anyone had heard me go there, or whether doing so risked waking them. You're being ridiculous now I told myself and, leaving the toilet alone, I crept onto the landing and down the stairs, grateful for all the early morning practices of avoiding creaky steps. Once in the hall I took a last look around, struck by how it could be any family home, then eased open the closet door and slipped inside. The door safely pulled to, I took what felt like the first real breath since the night before, and wrapped my arms around myself for a moment to try and stop the nervous trembling.

The escape went just as planned, the window propped open and the brown bag and my red coat dropped out of the window before I pulled myself up, and eased myself over the sill onto the dustbin. I had a brief panic that I couldn't push the window fully closed from outside, but then realised it really didn't matter as they would know I was gone as soon as the house awoke, whether they saw the window or not.

The dawn air was bitterly cold, the top of the bin slightly icy as I climbed down. It was tempting to put my jumper or coat on but I knew I had to keep them clean so, as planned, I folded the coat inside out and put it over my arm. I heard crunching beneath my feet as I tiptoed to the gate, seeing the track of shiny flattened grass patches as I glanced back. The street was empty and silent, the curtains on the identical houses all closed and dark. I jumped as a dog suddenly started barking but then realised it was in one of the houses, the sound carrying in the emptiness of the night. I looked back at the place that had been my home for so long now, and was

201

shocked to see a faint light in the attic window of Miss Leigh's bedroom. As I watched, her shadow crossed the window and my whole body shook with fear of discovery, then suddenly the light went out and I was left with the cold air that smelt like long gone bonfire nights, and the dull circles of light from the streetlamps.

Although I wanted to run I made my way to the end of the road quietly on tiptoe, imagining the twitching of curtains as I passed. When I turned into the next road I was shocked to see bright light shining onto the pavement, then realised I had forgotten about the newsagent, how early they get up to number the papers and sort them into bundles. Ready for the youngsters to arrive and load them into their bags, before riding around the streets on bicycles delivering them. "You idiot," I muttered under my breath. I had been one of those youngsters in my long ago past, sleepily riding around on frosty mornings like this, so I should have thought.

I hurriedly crossed the road, praying the old man in the shop wouldn't look out of the window, then quickly turned into an alley that I hoped would cut through to the main road. The blackness of the alley was really scary, my imagination running riot as I pictured rapists and murderers hiding in the shadows. I hugged my bag and coat to me as I ran to the other end, almost screaming aloud as my hair caught on something protruding from one of the walls. As I shot out of the darkness, into the unexpected glare of passing cars on the main road, I heard my breath rasping and felt tears stinging my eyes. My body gave me no choice but to stand there for what seemed like ages, breathing heavily and fighting nausea, until I was sure I caught the eye of a passing motorist. Instinctively I rushed between the roadside trees and stumbled down the bank, gratefully sinking onto the cold damp ground by the edge of the fields, where no light penetrated, apart from the moon.

Once I'd rested briefly I set off towards town, picking my way through the brambles and trying to spot the muddy patches in the dim light before I trod in them. As the light increased I could just make out the cars on the raised road beyond the trees, panicking slightly as a double-decker bus passed but reassuring myself that even if there was anyone on the top deck this early they wouldn't see me down here. The siren of a passing police car was different and I instinctively dived into a nearby bush, temporarily convinced they had already discovered my escape. It was probably ten minutes before I found the courage to emerge, my arms scratched and spotted with blood, relieved that they hadn't seen me. "You know they're still all sleeping, you numbskull," I whispered, and was shocked to hear myself laugh out loud, a nervous relief of tension as I rubbed my sore arms with a dock leaf.

It was daylight by the time I reached the roundabout just before town, where the fields and trees ended. I smoothed my hair and skirt before climbing back up the bank, hoping I wouldn't look as weird and wild as I felt when I mingled with the early morning shoppers. I had mixed feelings about how the Social Services tried to place children near to home, perhaps in the hope that family would visit. It hadn't brought me any visitors, but now I was glad I knew the layout of the town although really nervous that someone would recognise me.

Despite being hungry I couldn't risk spending too much of the little money I had, so settled for a cup of tea in the Wimpy bar where I'd once gone with school friends, huddling in a corner to avoid being seen from the road. I saw the assistant staring at the scratches on my arms, so put my coat on to cover them and was grateful for the warmth of that and the tea. I couldn't quite believe I was out in the world, all alone, doing something as ordinary as sitting in a coffee bar. It felt alien and grown up, until I reminded myself how long I had lived in London and realised the Home had almost reduced me to a child again.

When the clock on the wall showed half past nine I knew it was time for the next scary step in my plan, so I walked to the centre of town where there was a telephone box. After flicking through the directory, I piled my coins by the phone and dialled the department store where we'd bought my coat, asking for the personnel department and watching my coin pile shrink as I hung on. When they eventually answered I was reassured to hear that yes, they did have vacancies, but panicked slightly when they offered me an interview late the following morning.

"Um, thank you," I said hesitantly. "I don't suppose it would be possible to have an interview today by any chance?"

"Goodness, you are keen," said the friendly voice on the other end of the line, "but I'm sorry to say we can't see you today. Do you want tomorrow's interview time?"

"Oh yes please," I almost shouted down the phone, hesitating again when she asked my name but realising I had no choice but to tell her and just hope news of my disappearance didn't reach there before I did.

That day felt so long and hard, probably made worse by my tiredness and hunger as I cleaned myself with cold water in the public toilets and tried to keep away from busy areas. I briefly played with the idea of visiting my mother and her new husband, but was pretty sure she would just contact Social Services. When I'd been taken to the children's court I'd seen her sitting across the room but she hadn't acknowledged me in any way and. in that strange environment, with a social worker next to me, I wasn't even sure if I was allowed to speak. I could hardly concentrate on what was said by the three people sitting behind a long table at the front, who I assumed were judges, but Lesley later told me they had asked mummy if she was willing to have me home and she had said no. Which was how I had ended up under a supervision order, in the children's home.

I had a crazy moment when I pictured turning up at Nazir's house, sitting at that big table in the warm kitchen and waiting for his mother to bring delicious food. Or would his wife be doing the cooking, now that their baby would be a toddler?

I bought crisps and a drink, making them last through the afternoon as I sat in a small quiet park, remembering the early hungry days at the hostel when I didn't even have the money to buy that much. Once it started to get dark I felt a bit safer walking around, but also pretty daunted by the realisation that I was somehow going to have to get through the night before my interview tomorrow. I considered catching an evening bus to the larger town where the store was, but decided I was probably safer here, where I knew my way around and where there were people I could go to in a real emergency.

I knew there was nowhere near the town centre where I could remain invisible for the night, so decided to head for the common, remembering playing happily there with school friends years ago, creating our own excitement and dramas as we hid from each other among the ferns, enjoying the temporary relief from the dramas of home. As I walked there I saw the church where I had gone to Sunday school and, shortly after, another church where I had briefly attended their youth club. There were a few people standing outside and a big sign proclaiming 'Charity Soup Dinner'.

Wow, I thought, perhaps He does work in mysterious ways. Suddenly a thin wiry man with thick white hair appeared by my side.

"Are you interested in joining us, young lady?" he asked. I figured I must still be looking pretty needy despite my newish coat and nodded, thinking soup would definitely be better than nothing.

"Is it alright?" I asked nervously and he smiled warmly, taking my arm and guiding me through the doorway.

"Of course, everyone is welcome, my dear," he said, showing me hooks just inside the door where I could leave my coat. However, the church hall was only dimly lit and felt quite chilly, so I decided to keep it on. I nervously sat on one of the folding chairs at a long trestle table which had baskets full of chunky slices of bread strategically placed along the middle, so everyone could reach them. I put the paper bag with my few precious belongs on the floor, squeezing it securely between my feet. Most of the chairs were taken and I was surprised how many middle-aged and elderly people there were, but before I could give it much thought two young girls placed big bowls of hot thin vegetable soup before each of us and the lights were suddenly dimmed. A large square of light was projected onto the end wall and all heads turned towards it, as a woman silhouetted there thanked us for coming and told us the film we were about to see would make us all reflect on the riches of our lives. I was a bit confused as to why she would say that to people qualifying for charity meals, but thought she was probably right, that however bad our lives were it helped to focus on what we did have rather than just see ourselves as victims.

The room fell almost silent as the film started and, amid the clink of spoons and the slurp of soup, we were shown images of thin black women with even thinner babies, sitting on the ground outside huts in what appeared to be a village. Tiny toddlers with old faces, prominent ribs and rounded naked bellies tottered across the screen to stand before women I assumed to be their mothers. There was almost a question in some of their eyes but generally their expressions were passive, seemingly resigned, as their mother moved the skinny baby attached to her breast and looked away from the child. Gradually the little ones toddled away, the whole scene being enacted in virtual silence as the camera moved to some elderly women sifting through a small pile of grain, then some emaciated men coming into the edge of the picture holding what looked like small dead birds. The whole film was unexpected and temporarily took away my hunger, and I was reminded of being lectured about starving children in Africa as I had sat in front of a plate of congealed gravy in boarding school. I probably would have left the soup if I hadn't known there was little chance of food in the near future, but that knowledge made me guiltily reach for several slices of bread as the film ran, one even being tucked surreptitiously in my coat pocket in the hope that nobody would notice in the dim light.

A series of clicking noises brought the film to an end, and the screen was briefly full of flashing dots of light before the projector was switched off. The main lights flooded the hall to reveal dozens of empty bowls and bread baskets, and upturned faces showing a mixture of emotions.

"So, ladies and gentlemen," boomed the voice we had heard earlier, "I think the images of those hungry black babies shows only too clearly how important these regular charity dinners are, in raising money to help the poor of that dark primitive continent. So, as always, I ask you to dig deep and, in return for the bread and soup, contribute what you would have paid for a full meal out at a restaurant. The pot will be passed down the tables shortly, after which we will sing 'All Things Bright and Beautiful' before ending the evening with a prayer of gratitude."

For a moment I was paralysed with shock, as I watched people at the far end of the table passing along a large multi-coloured ceramic pot into which they were stuffing pound notes. Fortunately, my survival instincts kicked in while the pot was still some distance away, and I pushed my chair back quickly, asking the lady next to me where the toilets were.

"Just over there, dear," she said, pointing to a door at the back of the hall, "but the pot will be here shortly."

207

"I'll be really quick," I whispered, forcing a smile. "I certainly don't want to miss the hymn."

She nodded, smiling in response as I grasped my brown bag and headed through the door she'd indicated.

Perhaps someone was looking down on me after all, as when I went through I was hit by a cold draft and saw that in front of me there was an open door to what looked like an alleyway. I ignored the door to my right marked 'Toilet' and ran through the open door, to what turned out to be the side of the church. Within moments I was back on the road, running so fast I could hardly breathe and not stopping until the church was just a distant building.

Imagine them leaving that door open, I thought as I balanced on the edge of a wall to catch my breath. Then I realised that was a pretty crazy thought, as they had no reason to think charitable church people were going to steal soup and race out through the back door, cheating the 'poor black babies'. "You have seriously been locked up too long girl," I told myself, laughing, then felt a thrill of excitement as I remembered that tomorrow that could all become history.

My memories of the common were of childhood friends, laughter and fun, sun shining on the ferns in which we hid, bringing out their golden tint. After our games in the ferns we would make our way to the plateau and once there would climb to the top, in order to roll wildly to the bottom before starting the process again. Oh to be young again, I thought, as I followed that old route, scratching my legs slightly as I pushed through the bracken and wondering if anyone else would be there in the fading light.

The common was very different after dark and the further in I went the darker and lonelier it felt, the trees huge shadows looming above me. The plateau was empty, apart from one woman sitting on a bench watching her spaniel racing around in frantic circles. We exchanged greetings and I almost joined her on the bench, but then realised I needed to find somewhere safer and more sheltered before it got much later. So I headed over to the wooded area and, once two men walking their dogs had passed, I started to gather leaves and pile them in the space behind one of the larger oaks, which I hoped would hide me from the path. As I squashed them down I remembered primary school, where we had made whole houses out of leaves. Now I just needed to make a reasonable bed to get me through the night.

The pile of leaves was quite soft and although I had to take my coat off for fear of it getting dirty I turned it inside out and put it over my shoulders, while pushing my chilly feet into yet more leaves. I knew there was no way I would sleep, terrified as I was by the rustle of the wind in the trees, the flapping of what I hoped were birds and not bats, and a myriad of strange unidentifiable noises. I held my hands in each other, pretending it was someone keeping me safe, and reassured myself that given everything I had survived so far this night was nothing.

I felt a warm glow on my face and opened my eyes to bright sunlight. A little boy was weeing against a tree close by and I thought he glanced at me lying there, but suddenly a shrill voice from the path called "Bobby!" and he dragged up his grey trousers and ran off. As I sat up I saw him take hold of his mother's hand, where it rested on the handle of a pushchair, and they disappeared along the path.

Despite being bitterly cold I felt surprisingly refreshed, and realised that, although I hadn't expected to sleep, I must have been totally exhausted. I wished I didn't have to go back to town, as I was certain the police were now looking for me and they could well have circulated my description to local shops and cafes. However, the bus I needed went from near the town centre so I plucked up my courage and made my way there through back streets, risking buying a small bottle of orange juice in a corner shop as my lips were cracked and my tongue was sticking to the roof of my mouth.

A police car approached, sirens blaring, as I stood at the bus stop. With a gasp I quickly jumped behind a large woman in a brown tweed coat and a cream polyester headscarf. She studied me curiously when I re-emerged and I felt my cheeks start to burn. I was relieved when she got on the next bus, still staring at me through the window. My bus followed soon afterwards and I rushed upstairs to a more private seat, disconcerted at how few coins were left as I handed the conductor the fare. It was the same bus I used to take to school each morning, often spending the journey thinking up convincing lies to cover the less believable truths of my home life. I thought perhaps I was sitting in the same seat I'd sat in the first time I saw Nazir, when he smiled at me across the aisle and I'd started to believe life was going to be wonderful. I saw the empty playground of my old school and wondered if Sally and Janet were still there, if they ever thought of me. Then the bus continued out of the area full of my memories before eventually pulling into the centre of the larger town.

I knew I had to be really careful, as Lesley and other social workers were based here and would definitely be on the lookout for me by now. Although I also suspected thy would think I had gone back to London, rather than further out. Having seen my reflection in the bus window I realised the reason the plump lady had stared at me was probably more to do with my muddy face and the leaves in my hair, than my panicky behaviour. So my first priority was finding the public toilets, where I wet screwed up bundles of hard shiny toilet paper, rubbed them on my stolen soap, and scrubbed all the visible parts of my body until I glowed red. My shoes and socks were muddy too so I took them off, wiped the shoes clean and put the white socks back on inside out. I was glad of the toothpaste, which I rubbed on my teeth with a finger as I'd stupidly forgotten my toothbrush. But I did have my hairbrush, so I dampened my hair down and brushed it neatly behind my ears. Finally, I went into a cramped cubicle and changed into my smarter clothes, remembering the cubicle in the hotel where I tried to cool down while Bob's sister stood outside the door, ready with revelations about family wedding plans.

The nerves set in as I entered the department store, asking directions at the perfume counter then taking the back stairs up to the offices so as not to risk passing the children's department where social workers shopped. Upstairs I was taken to a little room with a desk and chair and given a form to complete. I put my mother's address and gave the name of the department store in Brighton, where perhaps my leather dress still awaited me, as my previous employment, hoping it was far enough away for them to not bother checking. Every time someone passed the open office door I jumped slightly, fearful that the store had contacted the police, and when a young woman came and asked me to follow her I fully expected to follow her into a room full of police officers. Instead there was one smiling man behind a large cluttered desk, who reached out to shake my hand and take my form before indicating the chair where I should sit. He glanced over the grammar and maths tests on the back of my form, and I was pleased to see he looked satisfied with my answers.

"Well this seems very satisfactory," he said, smoothing his hair with his hand. "We certainly need bright young girls, with Christmas on the horizon, and I see you have the right experience. I assume they can supply references?"

"Oh yes, I'm sure they can," I responded with a smile, hoping he didn't hear the shakiness in my voice.

"Good. So, perhaps you could tell me why you want to work for us. Especially in view of the distance we are from your home; quite a daily excursion!"

My moment had come; he had given me the perfect opening and I knew everything rested on my reply, which I had rehearsed constantly over the last week. I moved my hand under the desk and crossed my fingers to cancel the lie.

"Well, I used to live and work in Brighton, but I gave up that job to come home and help my mother because she was injured in a car accident. Now she's completely recovered and, with all my sisters and brothers, there isn't really room for me. So when I heard you were not only a great employer, but also had a staff hostel, it seemed exactly what I needed."

He had listened in silence, his eyebrows rising slightly when I mentioned the car accident, and a look of concern crossing his face when I said there was no room for me.

"Goodness, that's quite a story," he said, and I almost protested that it wasn't a story. Luckily I kept quiet, as he went on to say he could see it was difficult for me, meanwhile rummaging in a pile on his desk and finally producing a file that he flicked through.

"Well, you seem to be in luck, young lady. It's not often rooms in the hostel come free, but it seems another young lady left last weekend."

The following hour was a complete blur, with more form-filling and waiting around while phone calls were made. Then, finally, not only was I offered the job, which I eagerly accepted, but I was also being handed a form that would entitle me to a precious key and my own room at the hostel.

Closing the door to the little room that was almost filled by the single bed, a chest of drawers and a wardrobe, I felt as if I was in a palace. For the first time in so, so long here was a space that was mine, just mine, and I didn't have to share it with anyone, apart from the speedy cockroach that had disappeared into the skirting board as the housekeeper unlocked the door for me.

"Sorry, love, we are trying to get rid of them but they're persistent buggers," she said as she crossed the room and opened the bottom of the sash window, to let in cool refreshing air.

"Haven't you got a suitcase or anything?" she continued, glancing briefly at the crumpled brown paper grocery bag I'd placed on the bed.

"All that will be sorted shortly," I answered with a smile, unsure whether this was true but desperately hoping that it somehow would be, once I found the courage to take that final step.

"Well, I'll leave you to it," said the motherly housekeeper. "I think all the girls are working today, so you'll get some peace and quiet before they descend on us!"

"Oh, I've got to go out anyway," I replied, clutching the door keys she had given me, but she'd already closed the door behind her. No, not 'the' door, 'my' door! I unpacked my few belongings and laid the black and white dress out on the bed. How ironic I thought, that mummy should have sent me a dress I had never seen before which was now perfect for my required work outfit. A big part of me just wanted to curl up on that bed next to the dress and stay there forever, safe in my own little space. Yet I knew that despite having yet again found myself a job and home in one day, as I had once before, this time one more very grown-up step had to be taken.

As I entered the smart lobby of the Social Services building I remembered Lesley saying I should never wear my red coat in these offices, and desperately hoped her light-hearted comment about me getting her sacked didn't prove right. On the way up in the lift, escorted by a young man who'd been behind the reception desk, I realised these moments could be the beginning of my new life or the last remnants of my freedom.

"What's she like, the head woman?" I asked the man, and he glanced at me briefly then shrugged his shoulders silently. He'd shown some excitement when he had rung through to the offices after I nervously gave him my name. I could only imagine the reaction he'd heard when they realised their prey had walked right into their den. Quite a lot of excitement I

213

guessed, from the way faces turned towards me as we left the lift and walked past several desks and down a short corridor, to a small office where he left me.

Mrs Thompson, as she introduced herself, tried to not show her shock as I shook her hand and started my well-rehearsed speech, but I could tell she was unsure quite how to respond to me. I had anticipated there might be anger, reproaches, dramas. Instead she actually listened in silence as I told her of the job and hostel, of my understanding of how I had created the situation that brought me to the Home, of how I had learned from the experience and how I no longer felt that being there was in my best interest. I didn't really know the legal ins and outs of what I was saying but I knew from various conversations with Cathy and Lesley that these last words were the significant ones, and I was scared to look at her as I spoke them. However, I glanced up at her in the silence that followed and was shocked to see a smile on her face.

"It must have taken a lot of courage to come here," was all she said, before picking up some papers from her desk and leaving the room. I gripped the sides of the hard chair as I waited for her to return, trying to stop the shaking that had set in as I reached the end of my scripted role in this scenario.

The following hours were filled with both hope and fear. Lesley turned up quite quickly. When I apologised to her she simply gave me a quick hug then took me to another small room, where we were joined by various people who asked a stream of questions. I didn't know what answers were wanted or needed, only that the glances Lesley gave me as each left were quite encouraging. She herself was called out several times, returning to bring me biscuits and glasses of squash and to reassure me before the next person joined us. Eventually she told me to come with her and we returned to Mrs Thompson's room. It was there that the magic words were uttered: "It has been decided that you can take the job and hostel place."

214

There was lots more about conditions and checks, and returning to the Home to collect belongings, and even that I would still be under a supervision order with Lesley as my supervisor, but it all washed over me as a giant wave of sound and all I could really hear was a little voice inside that kept repeating, over and over, "I'm free!"

Lesley drove me back to the Home and I was grateful to have the chance to say goodbye to everyone and to give Miss Leigh the tray cloth I'd been embroidering for her. I was even glad to have a last brief lecture from Miss Atkins, on how a young lady does not shout in the street, as I called a final farewell to Cathy, who sobbed just inside the front door as I left. As we drove back to the hostel I said it all seemed too easy, and that I should have done it long ago, but Lesley shook her head. "No, you couldn't have, Nicky. You thought you were grown-up back then but you were still a little girl inside. You could only do this now, and we were only able to agree to this now, because you really have grown up in your time with us. The way you went about this, especially turning up at the office, showed us that."

I was never sure whether she was right, or whether I had just learnt to rebel within the rules of the system. I didn't really feel much more grown-up than I had in the hostel in London. Except I no longer felt the need to get my sense of self from others as I had with Sally and later with Kirsty, Bob, Lars and all the guys, including dear Tony. I still didn't know who I really was, but over the following months of working and living in my own little room the stronger my sense of myself became. Deep inside I knew that, in time, I would become strong enough to have a relationship with my crazy mother without feeling squashed.

"Perhaps I'll even look for my father," I told Lesley, when she took me out for a goodbye lunch the day before my eighteenth birthday, and she smiled and squeezed my hand.

"I'm sure you can achieve anything you put your mind to," she said warmly, and handed me a small parcel.

"Can I open it?" I asked excitedly.

"Well, it's for your birthday really, but go on then," she said, looking excited herself as I ripped off the paper. Inside was a beautiful umbrella, the exact same shade of red as my coat.

I laughed as I pulled it out.

"I thought it might protect you," said Lesley, smiling.

"Protect me, Lesley?" I asked playfully. "Then I definitely could have done with it over the years, but I'm not sure I need it anymore."

Long ago, someone told me that pride comes before a fall......

Thank you for buying and reading my novel, I really do hope you enjoyed it!

If you belong to a book club, below are some suggested questions that will hopefully provoke lively discussion. I would love to hear feedback on any of the questions or on how you felt about the novel. This can be left on http://www.anitaheavens.co.uk.

BOOK CLUB DISCUSSION POINTS

1. Do you feel Nicola was selfish in abandoning her mother as she did?
2. Why do you think Mr Cazian was so hostile towards Nicky?
3. Could Nicola have handled Lars' controlling behaviour differently?
4. How real did the characters seem? Did you feel strongly about any of them?
5. Did you think Laura made the right choice, given her circumstances?
6. How do you feel the central character developed during the novel?
7. Would the prejudice met by some of the characters in 1960s London be any different now?
8. Do you feel Nicola was a victim?
9. Do you think the English class system was relevant in the story?
10. How did you feel about the way the book ended?
11. Did you consider the book conveyed any important messages?
12. Should Nicky have eaten the sausages for an easier life?